A RUSH ON THE ULTIMATE

A group of friends gather for a friendly croquet tournament, but before it is finished, Humphrey Boddershaw, an amiable headmaster, is murdered. He is killed by the very instrument used to play the game – a croquet mallet.

Bert Rogers, the haughty hostess' jailed handyman has escaped from Broadmoor and is now in hiding under their very noses. Everyone is under suspicion, and each and every person seems to have a sufficient motive for murder.

A RUSH ON THE ULTIMATE

H. R. F. Keating

·BLACK·
·DAGGER·
·CRIME·

First published 1961
by
Victor Gollancz

This edition 2000 by Chivers Press
published by arrangement with
the author

ISBN 0 7540 8570 8

British Library Cataloguing in Publication Data available

Printed and bound in Great Britain by
Redwood Books, Trowbridge, Wiltshire

'In croquet "to have a rush on" an objective means that you are in a position to make your own ball hit another towards it. If, or in so far as, the stroke is successful you will, by following this with a stroke made after placing the two balls in contact (a croquet stroke, as it is called) have a good chance of continuing your turn. Thus to "have a rush on the penultimate" means that you are so placed that the resulting croquet stroke should find you in a position to hit your ball through the last hoop but one.' – Maurice B. Reckitt, Men's Singles Croquet Champion in 1935 and 1946.

Author's Note

Had I not been dissuaded from equipping
this work with a proper critical apparatus it
would have been cast in the following
form:

1 Reckitt, Maurice, *Croquet Today*, Macdonald
   and Co., London, 1954.
2 *Op. cit. passim.*
3 Reckitt, Maurice, in a personal
   communication.

Failing this I must simply record my
thanks to Mr Reckitt for a great deal
of patience and kindness.

Chapter One

The bright orange helicopter nosed its way inquisitively along the coastline. A cumbersome dragonfly. Its single passenger prowled from side to side, crouching slightly because of his height. From time to time he glared out of the wide windows and shook his big head in a pantomime of doubt as he looked down on the countryside robbed of its familiarity by the unusualness of his viewpoint.

He turned to the impassive pilot and said something. But the thunderous drone of the engine made his words inaudible.

The pilot put his hand to his ear and smiled.

The big man in the black jacket and striped trousers started to shout his remark out, but suddenly abandoned the attempt after only a couple of words. He shook his head wearily and flung his arms wide as if to say 'What does it matter anyway?'

Below them the coast wound along in the full September sunlight. The green sea flecked with crisp white wavecaps by the strong wind, the narrow stretches of beach half dark brown sand half dark grey pebbles, the geometrical neatness of the front, the rows of houses and plots of garden behind them. And clearly visible from their moderate height the violent scutter of human activity – figures running up and down on the beach in short sharp, bursts, groups jostling, meeting, mingling and breaking apart on the promenade, and behind them in the town cars on almost every road stopping and starting in jerky multicoloured snakes of movement.

The pilot flicked open a map and held it on his knee to study. He beckoned to the passenger who had slumped angrily in one of the seats. Jumping up, the passenger threaded his way impatiently through piles of glossy luggage and peered down at the map. He jabbed a blunt forefinger – cherished by the manicurist – down on the pilot's knee. The pilot bent forward and looked carefully at the spot indicated on the map. He nodded his head up and down with puppet-like explicitness.

He smiled and pointed downwards about a mile ahead of them.

The confidently extended arm.

X marks the spot.

The young man crouched listening, his unshaven face taut with anxiety. Only the distant roar of traffic. Slowly he raised himself and looked over the wall. The short length of quiet residential road was empty. He scrambled wearily across to the other side of the wall straightening himself up as his feet touched the pinkish stone of the pavement. Two more quick glances up and down the road, an impatient flick of the hand at a strand of dried grass clinging to his ancient pair of denim trousers and he set off at a rapid pace.

As he neared the corner he heard footsteps coming along the road crossing his path. In an instant he flattened himself against the low wall and neat ornamental hedge of the house he was passing. His right hand clutched the top of the wall till the knuckles were white under the grime.

With a visible effort he forced himself to move away from the hedge and walk slowly forward. For a moment he succeeded in straightening out his shoulders and achieving a semblance of casualness, but the fatigue which showed plainly in the deep shadows under his eyes and the strained line of his mouth was too much for him. His shoulders drooped again and he went slowly onwards with a furtive shamble.

The footsteps came to the corner and a spruce nursemaid pushing a smart grey pram crossed over without looking along towards the shambling young man approaching her. As soon as she had disappeared past the opposite corner he stopped and wiped his forehead with the tattered sleeve of his jacket. His scarecrow jacket.

When he had regained his courage – an innocent nursemaid not a ravening prehistoric swamp creature – he half walked and half ran on to the end of the road. With visible desperation he peered round the corner hedge, a flourishing holly clustered with unripe green berries, and looked up and down the road running at right angles. No one was in sight. The nursemaid had evidently turned the next corner.

The young man turned and looked at the trim road-name notice behind him at the level of his knees.

NELSON AVENUE.

A faint smile lifted the corners of his mouth and he crossed the deserted road with a new purpose.

With a wild throbbing noise the bright orange helicopter settled down towards the ground. The pilot leant out intently, watching his landing place as it slowly rocked up towards them. He seemed satisfied that the smooth area of short grass was suitable and with a casual movement of his wrist allowed the machine to drop down towards it more rapidly. His passenger went quickly from the window to his scattered piles of luggage and back again. He had raised his hand in non-committal greeting when he first saw that his arrival was being watched from near the house, and had then gone back to check over his cases. Now he went back to the window again and glanced at the two men standing on the broad veranda. He gave a quick impatient frown as if something was unexpectedly, and disconcertingly, wrong.

The helicopter touched down, its wheels sinking slightly into the soft turf. The passenger fumbled at the door, wrenched it open and jumped out.

His faultlessly polished black shoes made two slight indentations in the ground and a flick of mud from the damp grass spoilt their shine.

'Hello,' he said, 'I didn't expect it would be soft like this. What a piece of luck.'

*

The furtive man knelt and fumbled with his shoe lace – the cracked and broken shoes – as the solitary car swished its way to the end of the road. As soon as it began to turn the corner he heaved himself to his feet, gave a hurried, almost reckless, glance over his shoulder and pushed open the narrow gate marked 'Tradesmen'. With the sureness of familiarity he ran up the asphalt path beside the house, ducked down just an instant before he came to the only window which looked out on these back regions, and darted on till he came to the door of a small lean-to shed.

He put his hand over the top of the door, which was three or four inches shorter than the opening, felt about for two seconds, found the latch inside, swung the door wide, and flung himself down on a pile of sacks of potatoes.

The door of the shed flopped back closed again. The latch clicked.

Ned Farran, bouncing on his toes impatiently, followed the wallowing form of Humphrey Boddershaw over to the bright orange helicopter, looking more than ever like a giant exotic insect in the tame surroundings of Ambrose House Preparatory School for Boys (boarders 87 gns. a term).

'You're surprised about the softness of the ground,' Humphrey said to the new arrival. 'I thought you wouldn't expect that. But until the wind blew from the south-west today we've had a week of the haar.'

The newcomer looked up at him.

'What the devil's the haar?' he said.

'The haar? It's the word they use in the north-east for a sea mist.'

'Then why not call it a sea mist?'

The aggressive tone.

'You haven't met Mr Farran, Leonard, have you?' Humphrey replied.

He swept his enormous hands over the shining surface of his bald head.

'He's Ned Farran who joined my staff last term,' he went on. 'I think he's going to be a bit of a surprise for you. Farran, this is Leonard Driver, of Driver Products. You've heard me speak of him. No doubt you've read about him in the papers, if it comes to that.'

Ned stepped forward and thrust out his hand. The wide palm, the toughened skin. Leonard Driver gave him an unabashed glance.

'Did you know what a haar was?' he asked.

'I know now all right,' Ned said, 'but I didn't a week ago. Not until Humphrey gave me the drum.'

'The drum?'

Leonard Driver's aggressive look was replaced by a moment of bewilderment. A teased four-year-old on the edge of tears. A moment only.

'Jees, I'm sorry,' said Ned. 'I never know what's Australian and what's English. I meant the facts. The gen. Can you call it the gen over here? Is that right? Is that it?'

'Oh yes,' said Humphrey Boddershaw, 'the gen means "the general information". The term originated in the R.A.F. in the war. From what I gather from the boys it's a bit dated now, but it's English English all right.'

'Australian are you?' said Leonard Driver. 'Are you staying on at the school then? Humphrey's generally pretty keen to pack his staff off at the end of term.'

'Aha,' said Humphrey, 'that's where my little secret comes in.'

The helicopter pilot jumped down beside them. Leonard turned to him.

'You'll be wanting to get away I dare say. If you'll just dump my kit out, Mr Boddershaw will have a man to take it up to the house.'

'Mr Boddershaw will not,' Humphrey Boddershaw said. 'Mr Boddershaw's been without a handyman since his last one was hauled off to Broadmore. Mr Boddershaw's reduced to a single girl by way of domestic staff. And Mrs Boddershaw is in a state of chronic anxiety.'

'Irene?' said Leonard. 'And how is Irene?'

'Much as ever, much as ever. I don't know what I'd do without her. She's wonderful, you know.'

Ned Farran hurried over to the helicopter.

'I'll give you a hand with this stuff,' he said to the pilot. 'I hate standing about.'

He stationed himself at the door of the machine while the pilot scrambled in and began handing him the mass of cases and packages strewn about inside.

Leonard stood looking on. Humphrey moved forward once or twice but each time found nothing to do. He gave up and started

13

prowling round the little piles of glossy luggage on the damp grass of the playing-field.

'Careful with that,' said Leonard sharply as the pilot handed Ned a long thin brown canvas bag.

'That your oboe?' said Ned.

'It's my mallets as a matter of fact.'

'Here, what's this?' said Humphrey. 'Bottles?'

'It's a crate of champagne,' said Leonard 'A little present. I thought we might drink it on finals night. It's good stuff.'

'Good stuff?'

Humphrey laughed. A snorting performance.

'What do you know about wine, for heaven's sake?' he said.

Leonard's fleeting expression of chagrin.

'I may not know about wine,' he said 'But I do know how to buy champagne.'

'Oh, and how's that? Let's hear this piece of wisdom.'

'It's perfectly simple and it's a thing you'd never think of in a million years.'

'Listen, Farran,' said Humphrey. 'Listen to this. Leonard can't tell a Benedictine from a Beaujolais, and he's about to instruct us in the gentle art of choosing a champagne.'

'What's a Beaujolais?' said Ned. 'No, don't answer that one. Don't answer.'

'I know perfectly well what a Beaujolais is,' said Leonard. 'And I bet I could buy a better one than you any day, Humphrey.'

'Oh, come on, come on,' said Humphrey. 'I can't wait any longer to hear this. It's going to be so good.'

More snorts. Both hands smacked down on the shining bald head.

'It's quite simple, 'said Leonard. 'You go into this shop wherever it is.'

'A shop,' said Humphrey. 'A shop. Just like an ironmonger's, I suppose.'

'Do you want to hear?'

The aggressive voice. The fleeting hurt expression in the eyes.

'Oh, my dear fellow,' Humphrey said. 'I want nothing more in the world.'

'Very well then, stop these tomfool interruptions. You go into the shop, or the wine-cellar, or whatever, and you ask to see the list. And when you get it, you run your eye up the contents – but you don't look at the names, you look at the prices. And when you get to the biggest figure of all, you say "I'll have that one". And you get the best. Perfectly simple.'

Humphrey clapped his enormous hams of hands together in a frenzy of delight.

'Well, what's so funny?' Leonard said. 'Don't try to tell me I wouldn't end up with a better bottle than you would.'

'My dear chap,' said Humphrey, 'I've no doubt you would. You can afford it. But don't think you'd get the best there is: they keep special stuff at a special price for people like you.'

Leonard turned sharply to the helicopter pilot who had just jumped down from the machine holding the last case.

'Watch out, you fool,' he shouted. 'That's a tape recorder. You could damage it. Now if that's the lot, you'd better push off. I'll ring the works if I want you in the next week, but it's unlikely.'

The pilot gave a casual salute and climbed back into the helicopter. A moment later the engine started and the others walked away in the deafening noise. They stood watching in silence as the rotor blades gathered speed. The pilot looked round and up into the sky where only a few high clouds were to be seen. The machine tilted slightly forwards awkwardly and left the ground. It rose steadily and soon the watchers on the ground were able to hear themselves speak.

Leonard Driver shook himself slightly.

The cares of the world.

He looked round.

'A haven of peace,' he said.

The noisy helicopter began to move away over their heads.

'What was that?' Humphrey asked.

'Well,' said Leonard, 'have the others come? When are we going to begin?'

'You're the first,' Humphrey answered. 'And remember the rules. No practising until the whole party's assembled.'

At the mention of rules Ned Farran put his hands through his wiry hair and gritted his teeth. Humphrey turned to him.

'It's no use trying to run a show like this without some rules, you see,' he said. 'If you've got a bit of organization everything goes smoothly. If you haven't, sooner or later you get some awkwardness and then there's a row. And after all, you see, this is meant to be a week of perfect quiet.'

They watched the helicopter as it faded into the distance, a rapidly diminishing spot of brilliant orange.

'Why on earth did you choose that colour?' Humphrey said.

'That's a special paint they've just brought out,' said Leonard. 'It's been scientifically tested to give the maximum possible visibility. It gives you the optimum protection against collision.'

The gleam of schoolboy pride.

'It's nevertheless a very ugly colour,' said Humphrey. 'Don't you think so, Farran?'

'You can see it all right,' Ned said.

'But you could see almost any other bright paint almost equally well,' said Humphrey. 'Look at your vans, Leonard, they're painted pretty brightly. You ought to have the helicopter in the same colours. The aesthetic effect would be at least tolerable then.'

'But the machine wouldn't be seen from as great a distance,' Leonard said.

Tetchiness.

'Listen,' he went on, 'this paint has been proved, scientifically proved, to give the greatest possible protection against air collision.'

'That's typical of you,' Humphrey said. 'Always at the mercy of a bit of scientificating. That's my word for it. A mixture of science and pontificating, you see.'

'But it's a simple sci— A simple fact '

'I'm not denying it. But what you don't see is that it doesn't matter a bit whether your helicopter is visible from a few extra yards more or less. Your firm's colours are quite bright enough, you see, to save you from collisions anyhow.'

He gave three resounding claps and stamped about the field in a transport of pleasure. The September sun glinted and glanced off his shiny bald head.

Ned walked quickly back to the heaps of Leonard's luggage.

'I'll give you a hand with these,' he said. 'Come on. '

He stooped and picked up a tiny miniature suitcase small enough to fit the palm of his broad hand.

16

'Here you are, Humph,' he said. 'Here's your share.'

Humphrey slapped his spreading paunch and honked with laughter.

'Do you hear the chap?' he said. 'These antipodeans. Did you ever meet an assistant master who called his head Humph before? Mr Farran's going to be a big surprise in more ways than one.'

He caught up two of the biggest cases and started to stagger towards the house with them swaying clumsily from side to side. The minature case slipped from his grasp.

'Sorry,' he said, 'I've dropped your little thing. I don't know what it is. It seems too small to be yours: you generally go in for the outsize.'

'I don't go in for the outsize, thank you very much,' Leonard said. 'I simply go in for the best. And that's the very best, that you've been so careless with. It's the latest from Driver Products, a transistor radio – all waves, v.h.f. everything – and three inches by two by one. Not bad, eh? I think it's going to do us a lot of good if I can get it launched properly.'

Humphrey dropped one of the cases he was carrying with a deep thwack. He swung the other round, clasped it to his wide chest, and staggered on.

'I thought you went in for gramophone insides,' he said.

'We do, only the bottom's falling out of the record market,' Leonard said. 'We're having to diversify. And – '

He stooped and retrieved the transistor set.

' – this is going to be the thing to save our bacon.'

'Save your bacon, eh?' said Humphrey. 'Don't tell me the invincible Driver Products are in the soup?'

'Nonsense,' said Leonard.

He stopped on the veranda and lowered the crate of champagne with a sharp bang.

'The firm's perfectly healthy financially.' he said. 'What do you mean by implying anything else? Let me tell you – '

'Jeeze,' said Ned, 'a haven of peace.'

Leonard Driver looked at him. Then he smiled.

'You're quite right,' he said. 'This is a time to forget business cares. A week of complete change.'

He stretched.

'There will be just one thing I have to talk to you about, Humphrey,' he said. 'Some shares your sister has. But it needn't bother us. Any time will do.'

He broke off and cocked his ear in a listening attitude.

'Do you hear what I hear?' he said.

They listened.

'There's a hell of a noisy car in the road outside.' Ned. said. 'That's all I hear. Is that it?'

'But that's no ordinary noisy car,' said Leonard. 'There's only one in all the world that makes just that particular sort of row.'

'You're quite right,' said Humphrey. 'It's the unique combination of engine noise and rattle, you see.'

'All right,' said Ned. 'I'll buy it. I'll buy it. Whose car is it, for heaven's sake?'

'Cicely Ravell's,' said Humphrey.

His ham hands smacked together in one tremendous clap.

'So who's Cicely Ravell?'

'You must have heard me speak of her,' Humphrey said. 'She's a very old friend, Mrs Ravell. A dear creature '

'A dear creature when she behaves,' said Leonard.

'Oh, but that's nonsense,' Humphrey said. 'She gets a bit nervy at times, you see. But it's nothing. Here in the peace and quiet she'll forget all that.'

'Well,' said Leonard, 'I'm not going to risk anything. You know what she's like after a trip in that car. It excites her. I'm going to concentrate on getting my stuff up to my room. Am I in what's it, in Passchendaele again? What a name for a room, Passchendaele.'

'It serves to remind the boys of their country's glorious past,' Humphrey said. 'They all do – Passchendaele, Ypres, Somme, Mons, Aisne, Vimy.'

'Only you should hear what they call Passchendaele,' said Ned. 'You know I nearly chucked the job when I saw that name over the door?'

He turned to Leonard.

'Can I help you up with the bags?' he said. 'It won't take a minute.'

'No, no,' said Humphrey, 'I want you to come and meet Cicely. You'll like her. She's vivacious, full of life.'

He set off briskly round the side of the big house, Ned walking beside him darting glances all round. The racket from the car in the front reached a climax and abruptly ceased.

'Come on,' said Humphrey, 'she's here. And besides, the sight of a stranger may help to calm her down.'

Ned followed him as he lumbered round the house and out on to the short orange-gravelled drive in the front. Cicely Ravell's car stood askew in the centre of it. Faint steam was rising from the bonnet.

The car was not very old. It had nothing of the romantic vintage aura. It must have started as an ordinary black saloon and been subjected for ten years or so to simultaneous subtraction and addition. It had lost various small pieces from the edges of the bodywork, it had lost all its shine, and one of its headlamps had at some time been neatly shorn off at the base. It had gained to replace this a rakish looking foglamp, and to counteract any loss of attractiveness it had acquired a thin pink line rather wavily painted from nose to tail on either side. The interior decoration was flowered chintz.

Cicely Ravell herself was sitting at the steering wheel looking intently in front of her at a large rhododendron bush. She was aged about sixty, a slight figure with fluffy hair in various shades of grey. Her arms resting on the steering wheel were thin and dark brown. The flesh on her hands seemed to have been used up long ago leaving a tracery of large knotted veins. She wore a flowery much-washed cotton dress which had something of the same appearance as herself: of having struggled with circumstances to the point of exhaustion.

'Cicely, how nice,' Humphrey called.

She looked up from the rhododendron bush and blinked.

'Oh, Humphrey,' she said. 'I didn't notice you. I was thinking about the journey down. I had a perfectly foul time. There are some pigs, some absolute pigs, on the roads today. It didn't use to be like this. In the old days drivers had some sense of courtesy, but nowadays everybody, simply everybody, is perfectly ghastly. I don't know what's become of them.'

As she spoke she became increasingly animated. The veined hands gripped the steering wheel in front of her and gave it a convulsive shake.

'Never mind,' said Humphrey, 'at least you got here.'

'But, Humphrey, I do mind,' she said. 'It's no thanks to the people on the roads that I got here. If I hadn't been a simply superb driver – and people have always said that I am a superb driver – I would have had I don't know how many crashes. It's simply not good enough. People have got to be taught. I made one of them pull up. I drove right across him. Of course, I knew what I was doing. And when he got out, I told him just what I thought of the sort of swine he was. But with some people you might as well talk to a deaf wall. All he did was to accuse me of dangerous driving. Me. So I told him just exactly how well I can drive. Still, I felt better for that. There's nothing like a good row.'

She gazed ahead of her. The reminiscent light of battle.

'I want you to meet, Ned Farran,' Humphrey said. 'Ned's an Australian. He joined my staff last term and I asked him to stop on with us for the week. I think he'll provide a bit of a surprise for some people. He's by way of a replacement for your John. It's sad he couldn't come.'

Cicely Ravell got out of her car, leaving the door swinging crazily, and came quickly across to Ned. She shook him vigorously by the hand.

'Delighted to meet you,' she said. 'I nearly went to Australia once, only I thought I couldn't possibly bear that dreadful accent twanging away in my ears all day.'

'Too right,' said Ned.

She looked at him sharply and turned to Humphrey.

'Don't waste any sympathy on John,' she said. 'He's only too delighted not to have to come. He never really liked it, and after all he has his fortnight off in Scotland for the salmon.'

She swept round to Ned again.

'John's my husband,' she said. 'I had to leave him at home. We have pekinese, you know. And the two girls are on heat, so of course it was simply impossible to bring them, and someone had to look after them. I wasn't going to send them to a kennels. I don't trust them. I simply don't trust them. So I arranged it all. John is staying at home and getting his meals out. I saw the hotel and made them promise to look after him, and Peke Dame and Peke Indarien are staying with him. But, of course, I

20

brought Peke Abou with me. My poor darling, I must get him out. He'll be simply longing to do his wee-wees on the grass.'

She dashed back to the car, dived half over the front seats and emerged a minute later clasping a scornful looking pekinese.

She lowered him tenderly to the ground.

'There, my darling,' she said.

She looked at Humphrey and Ned.

'He's such a good boy, this one,' she said. 'He never, never, never disgraces himself. He's what I call a perfect gentleman.'

The perfect gentleman stood unmoving, emanating a strong impression of sulkiness.

'What's the matter, my darling one?' said Cicely.

She dropped to her knees beside the dog.

The tribute went unacknowledged.

Cicely darted up again and went to the car.

'Abou, you perfectly damnable fiend. If I've told you once I've told you a thousand times: you're to ask if you want to do that on a journey.'

She scrambled out of the car again, bent down to Peke Abou and thrust her face into his.

'Ask, ask, ask,' she shouted.

Peke Abou walked sedately forward, climbed the three steps to the panelled oak front door with the words 'Ambrose House School' painted above it, and stood waiting.

'Well, there's something to be said for that,' Humphrey said. 'Come along in, Cicely, and I'll find you a drink. We'll see to your kit later on.'

Ned went with them into the house.

'We're in the school dining-room as usual,' Humphrey said. 'Come along. We've really managed to make it most comfortable. Cicely, of course, you know what we do. This year the same as ever. We bring in the chairs from our own sitting-room and the school television set, you see, and we eat there as well as one of the long tables originally in the room. Farran, you know all this naturally as you were good enough to help with the work. It really is the devil being without a handyman. Sometimes I've half a mind to put on the uniform myself and get the work done.'

He rumbled with laughter as he ushered them into the dining-room.

The contrast between the ineffaceably spartan atmosphere of its normal use and the imported comforts from the Boddershaws' private sitting-room. Its walls, which were painted brown at the bottom and white at the top, were bare except at one end of the long room where there were two large varnished wooden panels bearing the names of successive head boys on the left and of scholarship winners on the right. Also from the school side was the bare light wood narrow dining-table put across the other end of the room near the serving hatch. Between the two rolls of honour the utilitarian television set.

The Boddershaws' contributions were two large dark brown leather covered armchairs and a similar large sofa, three smaller easy chairs, a large vase of dahlias, and heavy blue curtains at the big windows overlooking the playing-field.

Humphrey went to the built-in cupboard underneath the serving hatch and produced a bottle of sherry and some glasses.

'Well, Cicely,' he said, 'a little Uncle Peter, as we incurable Englishmen say, or would you prefer something less dry?'

'No, no,' said Cicely, 'Tio Pepe, if you please. I must, always must, have my sherry as dry as dry. I can't possibly drink it otherwise.'

Humphrey poured the drinks and brought them across to the circle of armchairs grouped round the ugly all-night stove.

'Well,' he said as he handed Cicely her glass, 'and how's all the family? What about those grandsons? When are we to see them at school here?'

Cicely jerked herself upright on the big brown sofa.

'Never,' she said.

A drop of sherry splashed over the rim of her glass with the violence of her movement. Peke Abou darted from underneath the sofa and greedily lapped it up.

Humphrey flopped down into one of the heavy armchairs.

'Do you hear that, Farran?' he said. 'To tell you the truth Mrs Ravell doesn't always quite agree with our teaching methods here.'

'It's not your teaching methods I disagree with,' Cicely said,

22

'as you know perfectly well. It's simply that I consider that you as a person are totally unfitted to be in charge of growing children.'

'Oh come now, that's going a bit far,' said Humphrey.

He flopped his arms about on the sides of the chair thwacking away at the leather.

'My dear Humphrey, you know perfectly well that those are my feelings on the subject,' said Cicely. 'You've heard them time and time again. You are, quite simply, absolutely incompetent for the profession you have chosen. I'm perfectly frank with you because you're an old friend – or at least Irene is – and I feel I can speak my mind.'

She jumped up and stood looking down at Humphrey.

'Let me make myself perfectly clear,' she said.

'Excuse me a minute,' Ned said, 'could I be making a start on getting your bags in? I hate all this hanging about.'

'No, you could not, my dear fellow,' said Humphrey. 'Mrs Ravell is about to make an entirely unwarranted attack on me, and I want you to hear it. You'll be able to judge between us for yourself.'

'Thanks, but all the same I think I'd better get the bags,' Ned said.

He started towards the door. Peke Abou was sitting in front of it.

'Move over, doggie,' said Ned.

For an instant a flick of pink tongue appeared. Otherwise Peke Abou remained motionless.

'I could always kick you,' said Ned.

'Very well then,' said Humphrey, 'if you want a row, Cicely, you shall have one. Let me tell you a few home truths. For years you've been presuming on my good wife's friendship to utter the most atrocious scandals about me in a professional capacity. Well, it's got to stop.'

He lumbered to his feet dwarfing the small figure of Cicely Ravell. But not intimidating her.

'I've told you nothing that wasn't for your own good,' she said. 'I've told you and told you thousands of times : you are not fit to be in charge of children. What's the point of talking about libel or slander, whichever it is, when all I've been saying is the simple truth? Why can't you just face up to it? You ought to give up this school at once – at once – and find something else to do. It's your simple duty.'

Humphrey sank down on the arm of his chair, his linked hands smoothed his bald head perplexedly.

'Give up the school,' he said. 'But – but it's my life.'

'Then it oughtn't to be your life. You must find some other life.'

'Hey, wait a minute,' said Ned. 'If I'm supposed to be listening in on this I might as well know what it's all about. Just why is he supposed to be so unfit, Mrs Ravell? I hadn't noticed anything.'

Cicely wheeled round and faced him

'There's one very simple reason,' she said 'I suppose you think I'm a silly old woman who doesn't know what she's talking about. But I'm not. I've thought a great deal about this, and I know that I'm doing nothing but my simple duty. And no one has ever said that when I see my duty clear I don't do it. That's what they've always said about me. Even the people who disagree with me admit that.'

'I'm sure they do,' said Ned. 'But just why is it your duty to persuade Humph to give up the school? You're wasting your time anyway, I can tell you that.'

Cicely Ravell trembled with conviction.

'Humphrey's a violent man, Mr. Farran,' she said. 'A violent and wicked man.'

Ned laughed.

'Humph a violent character?'

'Yes, violent. And you can't pretend to me he isn't. He may have got round you: but I know. I tell you I've seen him with my own eyes in an ungovernable rage. And with a child. I said to myself then "That man isn't fit to be in charge of un-formed minds". And the more I've thought about it since – I don't sleep very well in the early part of the night, you know, and I have time for a great deal of thinking – the more I've been convinced of it. Humphrey, you must give up the school before next term, or I shall make you.'

'Look,' said Ned. 'Humph gets into a paddy with the kids. Everybody knows that. But it doesn't mean anything. The kids laugh at it. They know it's all on the surface.'

'They laugh, do they?' said Humphrey.

He stood up and looked round.

Smith Minor not to be found.

He sat down again.

'Oh, so you're in this conspiracy, too,' said Cicely. 'Let me warn you, Mr Farran, don't let Humphrey lead you by the nose as he leads other people. You may think he's a happy-go-lucky sort but that's because he knows he can get his own way best if he gives that impression. But it's not true. Underneath he's fiendishly obstinate, fiendishly obstinate, and boiling with violence. I know: I've studied him for years. Humphrey Boddershaw is a violent and wicked man.'

Ned flung himself down in one of the armchairs and laughed. He laughed till the tears came into his eyes.

There was a sudden noise like a sharp motor jerked abruptly into life.

Peke Abou advanced growling towards Ned. Step by step. His fangs bared.

Ned sat up.

'Jeez,' he said.

Behind the advancing pekinese the door opened. A tiny little maid in the chocolate brown uniform of the Ambrose House School domestic staff came into the room.

'Please, Mr Boddershaw,' she said. 'Please, sir, there's someone at the door. A policeman, sir.'

Chapter Two

'A policeman?' said Humphrey.

'Yes, sir, he said he wanted to see you, sir, personal.'

'Well, show him in then.'

The little maid – four foot eight if an inch – left, and Humphrey got to his feet and walked up and down the length of the room.

He hummed a few bars of music.

'A policeman's lot is not a happy one, pom, pom.'

'As a matter of fact,' said Cicely Ravell, 'I haven't mentioned a word to the police about you. I know it wouldn't be any good. All the police ever do these days is to persecute, absolutely persecute, motorists. However good a driver one is, one simply isn't safe from them. I think I'll leave you to see this man on your own. I suppose I'm in Ypres as usual?'

She scooped Peke Abou up and left.

'Don't you go, Ned,' said Humphrey. 'Just – er stay here. That's it, stay here.'

The maid put her head round the door and said:

'Superintendent Pinn to see you, sir.'

She sniffed loudly.

'Come in, come in, superintendent,' said Humphrey.

The man who appeared in the doorway was enormous. At least six foot six and with shoulders so wide they looked as if they might jam between the doorposts. His face was proportionately big and of a uniform deep pink colour. His sandy hair almost invisible against the pinkness, and a pair of light-coloured eyes did nothing to take away from the vast area of flesh. Two large ears of the same shade with long pendulous lobes stood out from the side of his head like rubber flaps.

He came across to Humphrey in three long strides and shook

hands. Humphrey's ham-like palm was for once matched in size.

'I regret to have to trouble you, sir,' he said. 'But it's concerning Bert Rogers. I dare say you've already been informed.'

'Rogers?' said Humphrey. 'Bert Rogers, what about him? Not more trouble come to light, I hope.'

'You haven't heard then,' said the superintendent. 'He's escaped. Got clear away this morning early. They've been issuing broadcast warnings all day.'

'Got away,' said Humphrey.

He spoke slowly. Information to be absorbed.

'No,' he said, 'I haven't had the wireless on all day. I've been very busy. It's the start of our ... But I won't bother you with all that. Tell me about Bert.'

'There's very little information to hand,' the superintendent said. 'He had some sort of altercation with one of the other prisoners and they put him in a cell by himself. Apparently he succeeded in forcing back one of the bars in the window aperture – he's exceptionally strong, you know – and then he made his way along a narrow ledge, dropped about twenty feet and effected his escape. A pretty daring piece of work in its way.'

'Who is this Bert Rogers, for heaven's sake?' said Ned.

Humphrey started.

'Oh, Farran,' he said, 'I'd forgotten all about you sitting there. Superintendent, this is Mr Farran, one of my staff.'

'Pleased to meet you, sir,' the superintendent said. 'This Bert Rogers is a pretty dangerous man. He used to be employed here in the capacity of handyman, and one day he lost his temper and committed a serious assault on a person in the town. They put him into Broadmoor – he's pretty simple in his outlook – and today he got out.'

'And you think he may come this way?' Humphrey said.

'It's a reasonable assumption,' Superintendent Pinn said. 'After all he's got nowhere else to go. He's a local product, but his parents are deceased.'

'Yes, yes,' said Humphrey. 'It's a sad case That's why I took him on, you see. And it seemed to be being a success. He was an awfully likeable fellow.'

'Likeable?' Ned said. 'He doesn't sound all that likeable to me.'

'But he was,' said Humphrey. 'Provided he didn't lose his temper he was always a thoroughly nice chap – though, of course, by no means bright.'

'Oh yes,' said Superintendent Pinn, 'he was doing well here. Got himself a female friend and was settling down nicely.'

'Girl friend?' said Humphrey. 'I didn't know anything about that.'

'A young person called Rosalynn Peters. One of your domestic staff.'

'Rosalynn Peters. But she's still here. I didn't know about this at all. Why, she was the little creature who let you in.'

A frown of annoyance creased the superintendent's broad pink brow.

'That's not too good,' he said. 'If he did come here by any chance she may have had an opportunity to dispatch him.'

'Jeez,' said Ned, 'he's hardly the sort of visitor we were expecting. Is he really likely to have got here? Tell me that.'

'I've got men posted all round the house,' said the superintendent.

Rosalynn Peters lay prone on the table on the other side of the serving hatch with her ear pressed as close to the thin wooden panel as she could get it. Although the table was small only her feet projected beyond it. For all the shortness there was nothing deformed about her. On the contrary.

Carefully she wriggled down from her perch and tiptoed across the big kitchen to the back door. She opened it, stepped out, and cautiously shut the door behind her.

The narrow asphalt yard outside had a row of outhouses running along it parallel to the wall of the house. Rosalynn darted across to them and one by one jerked open the doors, reaching her arm through the gap on top of them and twisting the latches from the inside.

In the potato store she saw Bert.

'Come on out of that at once,' she said.

The nanny.

Bert heaved himself off the potato sack where he had been crouching and came to the shed door.

'You may have a head like a spud,' Rosalynn said, 'but you

didn't think the rozzers would mistake you for one, I should hope.'

'Oh, Rosy, don't be so irritatious,' Bert said. 'I couldn't think of nowhere else.'

'You're enough to make a cat sick, Bert Rogers I don't know what you were thinking of coming here in the first place.'

'I wanted to see you, Rosy.'

Rosalynn Peters lost her severity.

'Okay,' she said, 'but we've got to hide you quick. The coppers are all round the house and the super's coming poking round himself straight away.'

Bert looked from side to side. The trapped beast.

'I'll get out over the back and head for the shore,' he said.

'Don't be more of a fool than you have to be. You wouldn't last five minutes.'

'No, I must. It's the only way. I can't wait for them to come and find me here. I can't do it.'

A wildness in the whites of his eyes.

Rosalynn Peters reached up high, caught hold of his left ear and gave it a violent tweak.

'You'll do what you're told,' she said.

'Yes, Rosy, yes.'

The burly young man looked down at her. Waiting for orders.

She stood for a moment thinking. Darting glances up and down. Then a gleam came into her eyes.

'All right,' she said. 'Follow me, and for pete's sake be quiet, you great big oaf.'

The old hand from *The World* pushed open the door of the saloon bar.

'Hello, chum,' said the up-and-comer from *The Daily Post*, 'you're slipping, we've been here for hours.'

'Then it's time you bought me a drink,' said the old hand.

He rested a hand on the girl's shoulder.

'So *The Clarion* think this is a nice little women's story, do they?' he said.

She widened her lips in a mock smile.

'Not now, not now,' she said. 'Couldn't we have some new line just for once?'

29

'All the same,' said the young man from *The Examiner*, 'this chappie sounds quite a brute. Did you get the story that came into our office about his escape?'

He smoothed the nap of his bowler and rested it gently on the bar counter.

'No,' said the old hand, 'what story was that?'

The elaborate casualness.

'Oh go on,' said *The Examiner* man. 'I may not have been in Fleet Street since before Northcliffe, but that story was on P.A. There's no secret in it.'

'My, my, *The Examiner* takes P.A. does it?' said the old hand. 'I thought you made it all up.'

'Just for that you can buy me a drink.'

The old hand signalled to the barmaid.

'Four, please,' he said.

He lifted his glass.

'Expenses, bless 'em.'

They drank.

'Still, it sounds as if there may be a story in it,' said *The Clarion* girl. 'Has anybody ever had a look at him? You should see the efforts our art department dished up. He may be as violent as they say, but he just looked a blur.'

'Oh, he's violent all right,' said the old hand. 'Our stringer in Brighton dished out a powerful piece when he was found guilty of assault down here. We didn't use it, of course. But if half what he said was true this bloke's going to mess up a lot of good policemen before they put him back.'

'Excuse me.'

The pale youth at the other end of the bar came across to them.

He blushed.

'Excuse me, but are you talking about Bert Rogers?'

The others glanced at each other. The old hand nodded to the girl.

'Yes,' she said. 'We were as a matter of fact. He comes from these parts, doesn't he? Did you know him by any chance?'

'Oh, no, no.'

The utter disclaimer.

The three men buried themselves in their drinks again.

'You don't happen to know anybody who did know him, do you?' the girl asked.

'Oh, we've got several stories in the office,' the pale youth said.

'In the office? Are you from a paper, for heaven's sake?'

'Yes, I'm on *The South Sussex Trumpet and Messenger*,' the youth said. 'I'm the Selham district man actually.'

'Very good, very good,' said the girl. 'Let me introduce you around. I'm *The Clarion*. This aged gent is *The World*. The smart bowler belongs to *The Examiner*, and this is *The Daily Post*.'

'Pleased to meet you,' said the youth.

'He tells me he's got some good background stuff,' the girl said.

She hitched herself back on the barstool.

'Let's hear it,' she said.

'I'm – I'm awfully sorry, but our chief reporter told me not to tell anybody what we'd got.'

The old hand put his fatherly arm round the youth's shoulders.

'That's what all chief reporters always have told everybody,' he said. 'Now, what are you drinking?'

'Bitter. But – '

'Bitter? You don't want to drink that stuff: it swells you up. Hey, miss, another double Scotch, please.'

He gave the youth a pat.

'Bitter's all right if you have to pay for it,' he said, 'but when you're on a job the expenses pay for something better.'

'Not my expenses,' the youth said. 'Our chief reporter's a terror. Why, do you know, he even wants to see your bus ticket.'

'Bus ticket? What's a bus ticket, chum?' said the up-and-comer.

'Never mind all that,' *The Examiner* man said. 'As my old tutor at college used to say *C'est le premier pas qui coute.* What sort of stuff have you got in these background pieces?'

'I'm awfully sorry,' the Selham district man said, 'but my chief reporter – '

'All right, all right,' said *The Examiner*, 'I'm beginning to get just a trifle blasé about your chief reporter, old man.'

'Well, I'm sorry, but I have to work with him. I can tell you one thing though. I heard you all saying just now about Bert Rogers being so violent. Well, it's not true.'

'Not true?' said the up-and-comer from *The Daily Post*. 'Listen, chum, I wouldn't have been sent to this dead-and-alive hole if Bert Rogers was own brother to a lamb, now would I?'

'But – '

'Hey,' said the girl.

She dug *The Examiner* man in the ribs.

'As your dear old tutor would say, old boy, it's your round.'

'So if it's agreeable to you, I'll inspect the premises,' Superintendent Pinn said.

Humphrey flopped to his feet from the deep leather armchair.

'Of course, of course. I'll show you over.'

He slapped himself on the belly and chuckled.

'I suppose I'll have to let you see all our secrets,' he said. 'All the dark corners we don't show prospective parents.'

'I'll have to be pretty thorough, sir,' said the enormous superintendent.

'And what happens if you find him?' said Ned.

'I'll take him into custody.'

The plain statement. The towering figure.

'Jeez, but has he got a gun or anything?'

'I've no reason to believe he's armed,' the superintendent said. 'Though he may well have possessed himself of some sort of means of attack.'

'I'll come along too,' Ned said. 'If there's going to be a bit of a blue, I'd like to be in on it.'

He bounced up and down on the balls of his feet.

'If there is any trouble,' Superintendent Pinn said, 'I'd be obliged if you'd allow me to handle it, sir. We have our methods.'

'I dare say in any case I could persuade him to "go quietly" as you policemen put it,' said Humphrey. 'He always seemed comparatively well disposed towards me. And. of course, he almost worshipped my dear wife.'

He lumbered to the door and opened it wide. The other two followed him into the high echoing school corridor, their feet noisy on the well-worn dark lino. Humphrey opened every door they came to and they trooped into the dank empty class-rooms with their neat rows of battered desks and the smell of chalk still in the air. The superintendent glanced quickly round each one, and where there was anywhere invisible from the door went straight across and inspected it. He opened all the cupboards and peered quickly into them.

They went methodically from room to room : the classrooms first, then the Boddershaws' private sitting-room, partly de-nuded to improve the dining-room, and Humphrey's study – a dark blue-tipped oar hanging over the mantlepiece in the place of honour – and on to the kitchen, larder and pantry, all empty. They inspected the serried lockers of the boys' changing room, bare and echoing, and the black fastness of what Humphrey called the boothole with its rows of empty pigeon-holes each labelled with a bleak surname.

When they had dealt with the ground floor they went up-stairs and visited one by one the dormitories – Somme, Mons, Aisne, Vimy. When Humphrey knocked on the door of Ypres Cicely's voice said sharply :

'Come in.'

They entered. Some attempts had been made to soften the bare dormitory into a guest room. Only one black iron-framed bed had been left, although the positions of seven more could be made out from the shapes of dark finger-marks on the yellow distempered walls. A small table mat had been put on top of the battered chest of drawers and Cicely had been busy arrang-ing her belongings on it – on one side a silver-framed photo-graph of her husband and children, and on the other two silver-framed photographs of dogs, Peke Dame and Peke Indarien indistinguishably remote at the far end of an enormous slightly sloping lawn.

'This is Superintendent Pinn, Cicely,' said Humphrey. 'He is conducting a search of the school because it's just possible a man who escaped from Broadmoor is here.'

Cicely scooped Peke Abou off the floor and clutched him glowering to her breast.

'I'm extremely sorry to have to disturb you, madam,' the superintendent said.

He looked implacably round the room.

'May I see behind that curtain?' he said.

'Certainly,' said Cicely.

Protocol. The correct treatment of the enemy.

The superintendent crossed to the far end of the room where a curtain had been hung across a corner to provide somewhere to hang clothes. He paused in front of it for a moment.

He flicked it back.

Half a dozen summer frocks swayed slightly in the sudden movement.

'Thank you, madam. I am sorry to have inconvenienced you,' said Superintendent Pinn.

They went out.

As Humphrey shut the door Cicely said:

'Broadmoor. They don't need to look far to find someone to send there.'

The superintendent appeared not to hear. He went rapidly along the corridor, opened the window at the far end of it and leant out.

Humphrey and Ned stood back watching him.

Humphrey pawed at the floor with his left foot.

'I'm awfully sorry about – er that,' he said.

'Oh, you get them like that,' said Ned. 'Mad as a two-bob watch. There's nothing to apologize about.'

Humphrey patted his bald head sharply three or four times. In the gloom behind the window blocked by the superintendent's vast body it shone.

'Anything like that upsets me,' he said. 'All these rows and unpleasantnesses.'

'You can't go for long without getting into some sort of shindy,' Ned said. 'Forget it, forget it.'

'You don't believe what she said is true, do you? It was awfully decent of you to stick up for me, and I appreciate your loyalty. But between ourselves, she isn't right, is she?'

'That you're some sort of a sadist unfit to be a schoolmaster? Listen, sport, you're not even a beginner.'

'It's very decent of you to say so,' said Humphrey.

A hasty mutter as Superintendent Pinn swiftly drew his wide shoulders in at the window.

'I was looking to see if there was any hiding place on the roof,' he said.

'Don't talk to me about the roof,' said Humphrey. 'It causes no end of trouble. You can't get out on to it at all from anywhere inside and every time a tile gets loose we have to have a squad of workmen in with ladders.'

'That's one eventuality the less,' said the superintendent. 'I was having a look at that house next door too where the demolition work is going on. I haven't been by this way lately and I hadn't realized it had commenced. It sets certain problems.'

'Oh, The Towers,' said Humphrey. 'They only began pulling the old place down a few days ago. It's extremely annoying. It's going to ruin the peace of the place just at the time when we need it most.'

'Your guests, of course.'

'Yes, they look on Ambrose House as a haven of quiet for this week, and now we're going to have those blessed drills going all the time and heaven knows what else.'

'Very unfortunate, sir.'

Humphrey knocked on the door of Passchendaele.

'Come in,' said Leonard.

Once again they trooped in and Humphrey repeated his set piece about the escape. Leonard was finishing changing from his black coat and striped trousers into tweeds. The richly subdued cloth.

'No one in here,' he said. 'I've poked into every nook and cranny to find places to stow my gear.'

'I think all the same, sir, if you'll excuse me,' said the superintendent.

'I assure you there's no need.'

But the superintendent had crossed to the big cupboard. He opened the doors.

From top to bottom it was filled with the paraphernalia of Leonard's existence – tape recorder, transistor radio, typewriter, dressing case, picnic basket, travelling tantalus.

The superintendent stooped to lift the counterpane and look under the bed.

'Seems all clear, sir. Thank you very much.'

Humphrey led the superintendent up a narrow flight of stairs to the floor above. Ned followed.

'This leads to the attic, you see,' said Humphrey. 'Where we keep our store of Attic wit, and our domestic staff. Reduced at present owing to the holidays to Rosalynn Peters.'

'I shall be glad of a word with her, sir,' said the superintendent.

They looked into five of the six servants' rooms, tiny with sloping ceilings and small awkwardly shaped windows. Each was empty and too small for concealment.

'Any lofts?' said the superintendent.

Humphrey pointed to a trapdoor in the ceiling of the small landing. It was edged with a thick tracery of cobwebs.

The superintendent looked at it carefully.

'That dispenses with the necessity of a messy job at any rate,' he said. 'And now there's only this room here left, am I right?'

'Yes, it's Rosalynn's room,' said Humphrey. 'I left it till you'd finished elsewhere.'

He knocked at the door.

'Who ever's that?' called a voice.

'It's me, Rosalynn, Mr Boddershaw. I've brought the superintendent. May we come in?'

A giggle through the thin door.

'Half a mo'. I must just put away –'

The superintendent briskly opened the door.

Rosalynn was standing in the middle of the room holding a brightly coloured nylon garment.

'Ooh,' she said.

'Hm,' said the superintendent.

They looked at each other. Rosalynn Peters, four foot eight. Superintendent Pinn, six foot six.

'I want to talk to you about Bert Rogers,' said the superintendent.

'Bert? I've done with him since they put him inside.'

'Oh, have you? Do you know that he isn't inside any longer?'

'Did he get out? It won't do him no good.'

'Have you seen him?'

'Seen him? 'Course I haven't.'

'Are you hiding him anywhere?'

'In here, you mean? You can look under the bed if you like.'

A giggle.

The bed was very low, but the superintendent knelt down, grim-faced, and peered under it well.

'Now,' he said, 'what's behind that curtain?'

'Only a girl's dresses.'

The superintendent drew the curtains aside. Some bright cotton skirts, a pair of jeans, a frou-frou petticoat.

Suddenly the superintendent whirled round.

'Something moved over by the window,' he said.

Slowly Rosalynn turned her head.

Chapter Three

'It's only my bikini,' said Rosalynn. 'I expect the wind moved it. I had a swim this afternoon in my time off, and I put it on the window ledge to dry.'

'It doesn't look very wet,' said the superintendent.

'It dries very quick. There's not much of it.'

A smirk.

'Care to look?'

'No thank you,' said Superintendent Pinn.

He marched out of the room.

Humphrey followed him, flinging out an arm in a gesture which conveyed fatherly protection mixed with a certain disapproval. A subtlety that appeared lost on Rosalynn.

As Ned closed the door he gave her a wink.

An immediate response.

Ned followed the others down the narrow stairs.

Rosalynn ran to the door and pushed the single chair in the room under the knob.

She ran over to the window, flung aside her bikini, and said:

'Are you okay? When you moved your hand like that I thought we'd had it.'

From outside the window Bert said:

'Give us a lift, I can't hang on much longer.'

Rosy braced her legs against the wall under the window, leant out and caught hold of Bert. With a heavy grunt he heaved himself up, knelt for a moment on the window ledge, and then half-scrambled half-fell into the room. He sat on the floor leaning against the low truckle bed and slowly massaging his right arm.

'I'm proper exhaustiped,' he said. 'I've done too much of that just lately. Did you hear how I had to swing myself along a ledge to get out of that place?'

'No. I didn't hear a thing. I've been run off my feet this last day or two with all the visitors coming and no other staff kept. Was it awful?'

'I thought I was a goner more than once. But anything to get away from there.'

Rosy said nothing.

Bert looked up at her sharply.

'Well, aren't you pleased I got away?' he said

Rosy knelt beside him and put her arms round his neck.

'Oh, Bert,' she said, 'I don't know what's for the best. Really I don't.'

'For the best?'

He sat up straighter.

'It's for the best for me to be out of there.'

Again she was silent. Then she said slowly.

'I hope it is. But what if they're right about you, all them specialists and that? What if you're not safe to be out? What if one day you went and did something terrible?'

When Ned returned with Humphrey to the dining-room after they had seen the superintendent off, Leonard was there, legs apart in front of the ugly all-night stove looking down at Irene Boddershaw, who was sitting in one of the big leather arm-chairs.

She was a short dumpy woman with a square determined face without make-up and with straight iron-grey hair. She wore a tweed skirt and a purple pullover which although large was stretched out tightly in front of her like the sails of an enormous purple ship straining before a half-gale.

She looked up at them as they came in.

'I was just telling Leonard about the hoar,' she said. 'Only he's got the wrong word for it into his head.'

'It's haar as a matter of fact, bobbit,' said Humphrey.

He lolloped into the room and crumpled down on to the sofa.

'No, no, you've got it quite wrong,' Irene said.

She emphasized each word with a sharp toss of her head and

a corresponding jerk in the purple sails in front of her.

'It's the hoar,' she said. 'It's the same word as hoar frost. It's perfectly plain.'

'But the haar is something quite different from hoar frost,' Humphrey said.

'Nonsense. They're both to do with the weather.'

A violent affirmation.

'But, my bobbity, they're different words. "Hoar" comes from the Old High German "her" and "haar" comes from the Middle Dutch "hare".'

'Double-dutch, more like,' said Irene. 'The fact is you've entirely muddled yourself up with your dictionaries and what not. It's perfectly plain the word is "hoar" for frost as well as for the mist.'

She looked up at Leonard. Squarely.

'Hoar, the hoar,' she said. 'You can take it from me.'

'I shall call it a sea mist in any case,' said Leonard. 'And the main thing is it suits me admirably. I always find – '

There was a knock at the door.

Rosalynn Peters appeared. Her head not much higher than the door-knob.

'Please, Mr Boddershaw,' she said 'It's Miss Penny, Miss Driver, sir.'

'Penny.'

Leonard hurried towards the door. A teenage girl came rushing past Rosalynn into the room. Litheness and freshness. The slim figure a whirl of movement, a little leggy under the short bright blue cotton skirt. The pink and white complexion. Almost edible. Coconut icing.

'Oh, Daddy, Daddy. I wanted to get here before you.'

She threw herself into Leonard's arms. He patted her warmly and lowered her to her feet.

'You'd have been hard put to do that,' he said. 'I came in a helicopter.'

'A helicopter? Have you got a helicopter now?'

'The firm has.'

'Same thing, isn't it?'

She smiled up at him. The pretty pink lipstick, the bobbing pony tail.

'Well, Penny,' said Irene. 'You're looking very grown up.'

Penny looked round the room at last.

'*Buenos dias*, everybody,' she said. 'And I am grown up, Aunt Irene.'

She came up to Irene and gave her a peck on the cheek and in return was clasped for an instant to the enormous bosom.

'Grown up and not fifteen yet,' said Irene.

'Oh well, it's not your actual age. It's what you feel like.'

'That puts us about equal then,' said Humphrey.

He snorted with laughter and slapped himself vigorously on the thigh.

'Hello, Uncle Humphrey, you old darling,' said Penny.

'And we've got a surprise for you,' Humphrey said. 'Company of your own age for once – assuming you don't count me, that is.'

Penny looked at Ned and smiled.

'The name's Farran, Ned Farran,' he said. 'I work here. I'm what they call a schoolmaster, for heaven's sake.'

'Yes,' said Humphrey, 'and you should see the difference he made to the standard of cricket. We won every match except against St Christopher's.'

'What,' said Penny, 'you let old Michael's boys beat you?'

'It was a draw,' said Humphrey. 'I'll explain just what happened. We went into bat first, and – '

'Just a moment,' said Leonard. 'You keep on presenting Mr Farran here as a surprise. I meant to ask you about it. Just why is he going to be such a great surprise?'

'Aha.'

Humphrey flung himself back on the sofa and honked with laughter.

'Aha, what a surprise he'll be.'

'Well,' said Leonard, 'what surprise will he be?'

Humphrey clapped his huge hands together over his glinting head.

'As a player, my dear Leonard,' he said. 'As a player of croquet.'

'A croquet player?'

Leonard looked at Ned. A look of violent appraisal.

'So you're going to take part in our little tournament?' he

said. 'You've played in Australia, I take it. I know there's a lot of croquet played there.'

Ned shook his head.

'Mostly by old women,' he said. 'Old women of both sexes.'

'Then you aren't very experienced?'

Leonard leant back again against the mantelpiece.

'I never picked up a mallet in anger till just the other day,' Ned said. 'Then I had a crack, and Humph here enrolled me for this party on the spot.'

Humphrey Boddershaw slapped the top of his shining bald head.

'Leonard,' he said, 'meet the finest natural stroke player I've set eyes on in forty years of croquet.'

Leonard glanced at him sharply, and then turned to look speculatively at Ned.

'That's splendid, Mr Farran,' he said. 'If what Humphrey tells us is true you could become a croquet player really quite quickly. In a couple of years even. It's tactics, you know, that are more than half the battle.'

'Jeez, yes,' said Ned. 'Humph has tried to explain the lay-out to me, but I can't even grasp the basic terms. He keeps saying things like "When you're for one-back you ought to be thinking about laying a rush on three-back" and they mean nothing to me. Nothing. I haven't time for them all.'

Leonard laughed.

'You'll learn,' he said.

'And think of the doubles,' said Humphrey. 'Farran and I have entered into partnership.'

Leonard jerked round.

'If he's replacing John then he ought to be Cicely's partner,' he said.

'I didn't think it would be fair to saddle her with a novice,' said Humphrey. 'Irene and she will get on famously as a team, and I'll be glad to teach Farran his tactics as we play.'

'Uncle Humphrey's a wonderful tactician,' Penny said.

The light shining in her eyes.

'If only I could improve my wretched standard of stroke play I really believe I'd be a very low bisquer indeed,' said Humphrey.

'A low bisquer.'

Ned moaned.

'It just means a low handicap,' Penny said.

'All the same,' said Leonard, 'I don't think the established partnerships ought to be broken up.'

'Nonsense, nonsense,' Humphrey said. 'I know what's worrying you. You think we'll stop you pulling off the doubles as well as the singles.'

Leonard walked briskly away from the mantelpiece and went to stare out of the window at the dusk falling across the trim playing field and the smooth croquet court in front of it.

'It's not that at all,' he said. 'I don't particularly care who wins.'

'Oh, but Daddy,' Penny said, 'you must pull off both championships. No one ever has before, and now I'm coming on for the doubles I think you're bound to do it.'

She ran over and put her arm round Leonard's shoulders. He continued to look out into the gathering darkness. In silence.

'But tell me about the helicopter,' Penny said

'There's nothing much to tell. I got it to speed deliveries. Humphrey says it's painted the wrong colour.'

The sulky schoolboy.

'The wrong colour?'

'It's got special luminous orange anti-collision paint, and that apparently offends Humphrey's eye.'

A note of savagery.

'It sounds wizard. I wish I'd seen it. I came down from London to Brighton and took a taxi specially to be here to welcome you. But I hadn't reckoned on a helicopter.'

'You took a taxi?' said Irene.

'Yes, to be quick.'

'But it must have cost the earth. A taxi all the way from London.'

'Don't be so appallingly mean,' Leonard said. 'The money's there. Why not use it? it may not be there so much longer.'

'In any case, bobbity,' Humphrey said, 'she only took the taxi from Brighton. That's far enough, but it's nothing like as far as from London.'

'What's this about taking the taxi from Brighton?' Irene said.

'The child distinctly told us she came from London and took a taxi, and I feel bound to say that I think it was frightfully extravagant.'

'But, Aunt Irene, I didn't –'

'Now, it's no use trying to wriggle out of it. You took a taxi from London; it was thoughtless and silly but it's done now and let's hear no more about it.'

'But, honestly – '

The injured schoolgirl breaking through the deb exterior.

'Not another word. We won't spoil the week with recriminations. I know there'll be no more taxis from London: you're a sensible girl at heart.'

Penny raised her eyebrows and shook her head behind Irene's back.

'How's Helen, Daddy darling?' she said

Irene jumped up. Her purple prow swung round on Leonard.

'Really,' she said, 'your private life's your own concern, but I do think you oughtn't to let the girl know about it.'

'But, Aunt Irene, this isn't the Victorian age. Everybody knows all about that sort of thing nowadays. Besides they may get married soon. I know Helen wants to.'

'No.'

Leonard wheeled round from the window. His heavily flushed face.

'There's no need to mention Helen's crazy notions,' he said.

Penny looked hurt.

'Oh, but, Daddy, everybody knows· all about her here.'

Leonard put an arm on her shoulders.

'Yes, yes,' he said, 'I suppose they do. It's just that Helen has been going on – But never mind all that.'

'Never mind all that,' said Rosy. 'You're here now anyway.'

'And I'm staying,' Bert said. 'I'm a fizzture, just remember that.'

'We'll see about it. But not just yet. We'll hide you here for a day or two anyhow. Then perhaps you'll feel different.'

'I won't.'

'We'll see. Now it's no use keeping you up here: they might

notice me going up and down all the time. You'd best come down and – I know – hide in the boothole.'

'But people are always going in there '

'Not out of term-time, silly. In the holidays nobody ever goes in there at all. It's so out of the way, and I could nip in easy from the kitchen.'

'All right.'

'Okay then, we'd better go at once Mr B. always locks the glass door leading to the changing room at night so we've got to get there first.'

'But that'll mean I'll be locked in.'

'No, it won't, silly. You can always nip out by the door on to the playing-field.'

'Suppose that got locked too.'

'No lock on it, stupid. That's why Mr B. locks the other door.'

Bert looked at her.

'You aren't trying to fool me, are you?'

Rosy put her arms round his neck, reached up and kissed him.

'Oh, all right,' he said. 'You make me feel sort of confident.'

An amiable grin.

He lowered her to the ground and turned to remove the chair from under the door-knob.

Rosy looked at him speculatively.

The pale young man from *The Trumpet and Messenger* came into the pub dining-room to find the others still having breakfast.

'Well, have you caught Bert Rogers all on your jack?' said the old hand.

'He wouldn't be looking so pretty if he had, chum,' said the up-and-comer. 'That bloke's strictly a job for half a dozen great big coppers.'

'So you haven't got anything either?' said the youth.

'Nothing to get, laddie,' the girl from *The Clarion* said. 'If you ask me Bert Rogers was never nearer here than Victoria station.'

'There's what my old tutor would have called a substratum of truth in that,' *The Examiner* man said.

'So you'll be going?' the youth said.

Sadly.

'Going?' the old hand said.

He choked with laughter over his tea.

'Laddie,' said the girl, 'we've been sent down here by news editors with money to throw away. We can throw away an awful lot in a few days by the briny.'

'Well,' said Leonard as the breakfast things were cleared away, 'when are the other two going to come? Since Humphrey's tinpot rules have prevented us from practising we might as well start serious play right away.'

'It's all very well for you,' Cicely Ravell said. 'You get plenty of tournament play. You don't need practice. I get my one week in the local competition and this year I had a perfectly lousy time. I think I wasn't keeping my head down properly – that's my greatest fault, you know. I simply can't control it.'

Peke Abou jumped off her lap and looked up at her disgustedly. It was not clear whether this was because the jerky violence of her speech had disturbed his slumbers or because he too despaired of her touch with the croquet mallet.

'They should be along any minute now,' Humphrey said. 'Sebastian is driving down and picking up Michael on the way.'

'That's Commander Goodhart, isn't it?' said Ned. 'All these names.'

'Oh yes,' said Penny. 'He's awfully sweet *Tout à fait adorable.* In a way it was terrible when he left here to set up on his own.'

'It was terrible for the cricket, if the style his team showed against ours is anything to go by,' Ned said. 'And is this Sebastian Mr – Whatsit? – Skuce?'

'Who is anything but sweet,' Irene said.

Her commanding bosom, covered in bottle green today, shook in affirmation.

'He's a cripple, you know, Mr Farran,' she went on. 'Got a short left leg and a weak left arm. He and Humphrey were at school and college together. Actually, Humphrey was in some way responsible for the accident which maimed Sebastian. And Sebastian has never forgiven him. One day, I'm certain he'll – '

'Bobbity,' said Humphrey,' 'I really cannot – '

He turned as there came a sharp tap on the door.

Rosalynn came in

'Please, sir. It's Mr Skuce. And Commander Goodhart, sir.'

The two men coming in together. A striking contrast. Sebastian Skuce, the cripple, short, slightly twisted to the left by the lack of strength in his leg, and slight in stature. Michael Goodhart, the sailor, tall and upstanding with fair hair brushed neatly back and piercing blue eyes. His pink and white complexion. Skuce's sallow skin and crop of vigorous coarse reddish hair and bristly reddish moustache.

Michael Goodhart stepped smartly across to Irene and shook her by the hand.

'It's perfectly splendid to be back on board,' he said. 'I'm going to enjoy this thoroughly. A week of delightful peace.'

Sebastian Skuce standing behind him laughed. A sharp bark.

'Delightful peace, provided there's no croquet,' he said. 'And no week's stay unless we play croquet.'

'Now, Sebastian,' said Irene, 'you're not going to be cynical. I hope we're all capable of playing a pleasant game together without quarrelling.'

'Hope is a charming virtue,' Sebastian said.

'Hope springs eternal in the human breast,' said Humphrey.

He lumbered up to Sebastian and gave him a hearty clap on the shoulder.

Sebastian winced.

'You doubtless remember the rest of the quotation,' he said. ' "Man never is but always to be blest".'

Humphrey looked abashed.

'You and he would make a pretty pair,' he said.

'Sebastian and who? What is this?' said Leonard.

'Sebastian and the poet we were quoting,' Humphrey said.

Elephantine malice in the circumlocution.

'What poet in heaven's name?'

Leonard glowered. Child in the grown-ups' world.

'I refuse to tell you,' said Humphrey. 'When my boys ask me a question like that I always refuse to tell them. I say to them "Boy, go and look it up, then you'll remember".'

'What's it matter anyway,' Leonard said. 'Stupid pedanticism.'

'Pedantry, I think you mean,' said Humphrey.

He slapped his large belly in rolling delight.

'Never mind what I mean. Now we're all here let's get out on the lawn and play.'

'What, without making the draw?'

Humphrey snorted and rocked with more laughter.

'I've no doubt Leonard considers the draw an unncesssary formality, a mere delay in his majestic sweep to victory,' Sebastian said.

'Oh, come on,' said Penny. 'Let's have the draw. I love the excitement.'

Leonard who had been glaring at Sebastian subsided into silence.

'All right,' said Humphrey.

He went to the mantelpiece above the ugly all-night stove and lifted down a large silver cup.

'We always use this, you see,' he said to Ned. 'It actually was presented to the school years and years ago as a trophy for the three-mile walk, but as we cut that out of the sports about a quarter of a century ago we've appropriated this as a croquet cup.'

'It's never been won so far,' Penny said. 'We decided that as there's only one cup it only goes to whoever wins the singles and the doubles, and nobody ever has.'

'Leonard got near it last year,' Humphrey said. 'And I suspect he thinks he's going to pull it off this time.'

'If he does and he claims the cup,' Sebastian said, 'I shall institute proceedings against Humphrey for betrayal of trust over the three-mile walk.'

'Oh, do let's get on with it,' Cicely said. 'I know I shall have the most appalling luck in the draw. I always do. I've been knocked out in the first round for the last ten years.'

Humphrey took a thin bundle of visiting cards from his pocket.

'We draw for the singles and play a knock-out,' he said to Ned. 'And then for the doubles, you see, we have an American tournament. You know what that is, I take it.'

'Sure, sure. Come on then.'

'Well, it means that each of the four doubles teams plays each of the other three, and whoever wins most matches is the total winner.'

'Yes, yes, I know.'

'And, of course, you see, if any two teams have an equal number of victories, then we count up the points scored in the games they lost.'

'I get it. I get it.'

'You know, of course, that in croquet the winners always score the maximum of 26 points, and so you have to – '

'Humphrey, for heaven's sake get on.'

Cicely's frustration bursting out. She jumped up, took a couple of nervous paces, and sat down again.

'Oh, very well, I was just explaining to Farran, who – '

'Humphrey,' said Irene

'Straight away, bobbit.'

Humphrey dropped the cards into the cup.

'Each one has the name of a competitor on it,' he said. 'Now, Penny, come and draw them out.'

Penny stepped forward, dipped her hand into the cup that Humphrey held out to her and pulled out a card

'E. Farran Esquire,' she read.

'Must be me,' said Ned.

Penny pulled out the next card.

'Humphrey Boddershaw Esquire.'

'That means I meet you in the first round, you see,' said Humphrey.

'I see.'

'Mrs John Ravell.'

'Now wait a minute,' said Cicely. 'If I get up and walk three times round my chair, perhaps I shall draw someone I stand a chance against. Not that I haven't already missed two of the weakest players.'

Penny waited until Cicely had darted three times round her chair. Peke Abou set off in the same circuit, in the opposite direction.

'Sebastian Skuce Esquire,' Penny read.

'It's happened again, damn and blast it', said Cicely. 'Sebastian's certainly the number two.'

'I'd rate myself rather higher,' said Sebastian. 'I'll give myself the pleasure of beating you 26–nil for that, Cicely.'

'It's perfectly beastly,' Cicely said. 'Abou, I think it was all your doing, you little fiend. I distinctly saw you unwalking my spell.'

Peke Abou wagged a feathery tail.

'Mrs. Humphrey Boddershaw,' Penny read.

'So we meet in the first round, Sebastian,' Irene said. 'I hope I shall give you a good game.'

'No, bobbity,' said Humphrey, 'you're the top half of the next draw, and Sebastian's the bottom of the last.'

'Nonsense, nonsense. You've completely missed count.'

The emphatic shaking of the bottle-green prow.

'Penny, how many cards are left in?' Humphrey said.

'Three.'

'Then you're bound to be waiting for a partner, bobbit.'

'Partner? But surely Cicely's to be my partner? I thought that at least we'd got all that settled after Leonard's objections.'

'Draw the next card, Penny,' said Leonard.

The pursed lips of impatience.

'It's you, Daddy. Er – Leonard Driver Esquire.'

'Well, Irene, you've never beaten me yet,' said Leonard.

'We'll see about that if I survive against Sebastian,' said Irene.

'No, bobbity – '

'Miss Penelope Driver. And that means I play you, Michael.'

'Youth and beauty versus the other things,' Michael said.

Leonard looked at the slim gold watch on his wrist. The slots showing the hour, day and month.

'Let's make a start, straight away,' he said. 'Let's get on with it, for heaven's sake.'

'Anxious to meet your fate?' Sebastian said.

'My fate? If you think I won't beat Irene . . .'

'Are we meeting in the first round?' Irene said. 'Penny distinctly announced that I was to play Sebastian. But I expect she got it all wrong.'

They trooped out towards the croquet lawn. Humphrey unlocked the door of the changing room and they clattered through it, past the closed door of the boothole and out on to the concrete veranda.

An incongruous sight greeted them.

Rosalynn Peters, looking almost like a dwarf in the neat chocolate brown uniform of the school domestic staff, was standing holding a long croquet mallet and looking anxiously round her.

'Whatever are you doing, girl?' said Humphrey. 'That's one of my spare mallets. Put it on those clips by the dining-room windows.'

'Yes, sir. I'm sorry, sir. I was just giving it a bit of a dust like, Mr Boddershaw, sir.'

'A dust?'

Humphrey roared with laughter and stamped up and down for fully ten seconds.

'Dusting the croquet mallets. Jove, what a service we provide.'

His snorts subsided at last

'Come on, Farran,' he said. 'You take that mallet. It should suit your style. Come and watch this everybody: he plays side style. I haven't seen anyone do that for thirty years, but it suits a cricketer, and this boy will be hard to beat one day.'

They stepped down on to the smooth croquet lawn with its close-cropped grass, six neat rectangular hoops and gaily topped long peg in the middle.

'How are you on the rules of all this, pretty ship-shape?' Michael Goodhart asked Ned.

'I've got the main idea,' Ned said, 'but I'm not too good on the fal-lals. All this rover hoop and penult and ultimate and what-not.'

'No, no,' said Humphrey. 'Not the ultimate. That's the rover. The only way you reach the ultimate is when you are about to peg out.'

He honked with laugher.

'The less you know about the game the better,' Sebastian Skuce said. 'Then you'll have no inhibitions about cheating your way out of trouble.'

'But one thing you really ought to know,' said Humphrey. 'And that's the story of what the timid man heard outside the croquet club.'

He flourished his mallet in anticipation.

'All right, I'll take it,' said Ned.

'Well, there was this chap, as I say, rather timid, and he happened to overhear what the first old dear said to the second old dear. And this was it. Now listen carefully, "It was just a question of which of us would peg out first; I hit her again and again; she was black and blue and when she thought she'd got me tied up in a corner I saw red, got my shot in, and rushed towards her, first with a cut and then a split, and it was soon all over".'

'Good on you,' Ned said.

'You see what it was all about?' said Humphrey. 'Pegging out is ending the game by hitting the peg; all the colours are just the balls; a cut and a split are types of shot; and rushing is simply progressing towards a hoop – we talk about having a rush on the rover, not, of course, on the ultimate. There's no such thing as a rush on the ultimate.'

Chapter Four

'Now I know why you invited Mr Farran to join the party,' said Sebastian Skuce. 'All the classic croquet stories and a fresh audience.'

'I'd rather get cracking,' Ned Farran said. 'If I'm going to play croquet the sooner I start the better. Otherwise I might get cold feet.'

The golden sunlight, the carpet of fine grass, the four brightly coloured balls – the blue, the black, the red, the yellow – running smoothly at the touch of the mallets. The white hoops each casting a thin rectangular shadow, except at the corner of the lawn next to The Towers, the partly demolished house, where a giant mulberry tree with splashes of deep red fruit in its dark green foliage gave a patch of shade.

The calm rhythm of the game. The tap of mallet on ball, the click as ball hit ball, the occasional quiet remark. Ned and Humphrey played steadily on, the others watching came and went. Leisure.

The game went surprisingly evenly. Ned seldom missed any shot he attempted but often attempted the wrong shot. Humphrey's elephantine swings missed their cunningly chosen target as often as not. From time to time each succeeded in running a hoop or two with one or other of their balls. The game progressed wanderingly towards a conclusion.

'You know,' said Michael Goodhart, who had come back to watch, 'you've got a nice position there, Mr Farran.'

'Call me Ned, call me Ned. Do you mean I could win on this turn?'

'May I answer that, Humphrey?'

'Certainly, certainly. We must allow a novice some latitude. If he's not helped he'll never learn to think as I say "croquetically". And that's the secret.'

'All right then. You've got your first ball right round and now you've got an excellent rush on that hoop in front of you, four-back. So as long as you think about where the balls you hit are going and use the right strength of stroke you should be able to use both Humphrey's balls for a simple three-ball break which will take you out with your second ball to win.'

'Okay then,' said Ned. 'Here goes.'

He took his stance.

His ball, the blue, neatly tapped Humphrey's red and sent it rolling near to the four-back hoop. Ned picked up the blue ball and placed it in contact with the red. A simple stroke sent his blue through the hoop. With the stroke he had won by doing this he hit Humphrey's other ball, the yellow, and with the stroke this gained him he was able to send his own ball through the next hoop.

With clockwork simplicity he repeated the manoeuvre, running the remaining hoops without a fault. At last only four feet of green turf lay between his ball and the peg.

He faced the ball, swung his mallet smoothly back, swung it equally smoothly forward through, hitting the ball with a solid flat stroke.

The ball ran easily over the clipped grass without the least deflection.

With a conclusive tock it hit the peg fair and square.

Humphrey strode across to Ned with outstretched hand.

'A splendid win,' he said. 'I'm proud to have lost. Proud indeed.'

He dipped and swung his shining bald head high and low and gave Ned a tremendous swipe on the shoulders with his ham hand.

The only window in the boothole was a small square of frosted-glass louvres high in the wall. By putting a foot in each of two pigeon-holes and holding on to the shelves of two others Bert Rogers could look out of the gap between two of the louvres.

The narrow strip in his vision showed him the front half of the croquet court. He had nothing else to do and peered eagerly at such activity as he could see. When Humphrey slapped Ned on the shoulder and appeared so pleased with him Bert's unshaven bovine face darkened.

A tiny insistent tapping on the frosted-glass panel of the door.

He jumped quickly down and pulled away the discarded gymshoe jamming the foot of the door.

Rosy slipped in and Bert replaced the gymshoe.

'Here's your dinner,' Rosy said.

She spoke just above a whisper.

Bert took the bulky paper bag she held out to him. He put it in Johnson Minor's pigeon-hole.

'What's the time?' he said.

'It's early. About a quarter to twelve. I had to bring it now: there's the lunch to get.'

'Don't be late with that. Don't start them pondering.'

'Getting jumpy, aren't you? Even if lunch was a bit late, they'd have nothing to complain of. I'm all on my own and I get no help from Mrs B. when they're playing that silly game.'

'I been watching. Mr B. was playing a young chap, wasn't he? Who's he?'

'That's Mr Farran. He's a new master here. Aussie. He's nice is Ned.'

'Ned?'

A growl.

Rosy giggled.

'Hark at him,' she said. 'I've only to mention another chap and he looks like a bear.'

'Well?'

'Well what?'

'What about you and him?'

'Don't be silly. He's one of the masters, haven't I told you? I've got more sense than to get friendly with one of them. I like this job. I want to keep it.

'All right then.'

Bert slumped down on the narrow bench that ran along the wall opposite the window.

'Not that he doesn't notice a girl,' Rosy said.

Bert jumped up again.

'What do you mean notice?' he said. 'I thought you told me you wasn't friendly.'

'So I ain't. But he gives me a wink if we pass in the corridor.'

'And what else?'

He moved towards her. Towering.

She looked up at him. A sparrow.

'And nothing else,' she said.

He hesitated.

'Now, don't you be silly,' Rosy said. 'I told you already, didn't I? I wouldn't let any of the masters get fresh. It's you that goes, not them. And to give Mr Farran credit, I don't think he would get fresh, not when he knows it'd get me into trouble. He's just not stand-offish, that's all.'

Bert sat down again.

'As long as he keeps away from me,' he said.

'Keeps away from you. Why should he keep away from you? What's he done to you that he hasn't the right to come near you? You're getting a bit big for your boots, you are.'

Bert looked at her in silence.

'Oh, all right,' he said after a little, 'it's just that cooped up in here I got thinking.'

Rosy came up and sat down beside him. She put her arm round his broad shoulders.

'Old silly,' she said.

They sat for two minutes in silence. Close together.

'I'll have to be going in a tick,' said Rosy.

'Don't just yet.'

'All right. I'll stay a moment, but I mustn't be long or they'll come looking for me.'

'Let 'em come.'

'Who was it who wanted me to go in case I was missed only just now?'

Bert slipped out of her hug.

'I don't know if I want them to find me or not,' he said.

'Want them to find you? Don't be daft.'

He stood up.

'If they did I'd show 'em,' he said.

Rosy jumped up quickly.

'Now then,' she said, 'I want none of that, Bert Rogers.'

'I'd smash 'em.'

'Bert.'

The sharp note.

He turned to her.

'You're not to get excited like that,' she said. 'You were learning not to before it all happened. You seem to have only got worse.'

'What do you think I'd do in a place like that? A lot of raving nuts all round you and the screws a nasty pack of – '

'Bert.'

'Oh, all right. But that's why I had to get out. If I'd been in there much longer I really would have been barmy.'

'They weren't right not to have sent you to the ordinary nick,' Rosy said. 'I knew it all along. But what could I do? If all those doctors said you ought to be in Broadmoor nobody wasn't going to listen to me.'

She sat down again on the narrow bench. Bert sat silently beside her. The narrow board creaked under his weight.

'And they may have been right for all I know,' said Rosy quietly. 'After all, they're supposed to understand about all that.'

'I'm not going back.'

Dull stubbornness.

Rosy jumped up again.

'Well, what are you going to do, then?' she said. 'I can't hide you here for ever. Term begins again before long. As it is I'm getting late over lunch and I'll have to wriggle out of it somehow. I can't go on doing it day after day.'

'I'll think of something.'

'You think of something. That's pretty likely I must say. What did you think of when you got out? Only coming straight here when all the rozzers were watching for you. You'd have been back inside this moment if it wasn't for me, and sometimes I think it would be a good thing if you were.'

'A good thing? In there? What do you mean?'

'I mean what I say. I can't see no way out of this. And all the time I'm afraid. What if they are right? What if you really are dangerous? That's what they said on the wireless last night. "The police have issued a warning that this man may be dangerous".'

'I'll give 'em dangerous.'

'That's it. That just it. How can I know that you won't? That you won't go for someone in a temper, and – and kill them. That's what I'm really scared about: that you'll go and kill someone.'

They stood looking at each other without speaking. Looking at each other without seeing what was in front of them, each busy with their thoughts.

Bert was facing the dim square of light from the frosted-glass panel of the door. He stood with his clumsy head lowered, his unshaven face dark and brooding, his muscular arms hanging loosely in the coarse grey prison shirt. Rosy faced him, not looking up at him. By contrast with the heavy figure in front of her she looked smaller than ever – like a doll, a miniature human figure with all the shape and form of the original a little overemphasized.

The dejected slope of the shoulders. The doll had lost some stuffing, had had it knocked out.

At last Bert moved. He turned stiffly and sat down again on the narrow bench beside the rolled-up jacket he had stolen from a scarecrow in his flight.

'I don't think I'll kill anyone,' he said.

A scarcely audible mutter.

'Oh, Bert.'

Rosy ran across to him, flung herself on her knees and buried her head in his lap. Her neat curls.

He patted her back slowly.

'I wouldn't want to do it,' he said. 'I can say that truly. I wouldn't want to do it.'

Rosy looked up at him.

'I believe you wouldn't,' she said.

An act of faith.

She got to her feet and sat beside him.

'I wish I could just walk out of here,' Bert said, 'and go upstairs and put on my uniform and carry on just the way it was before.'

'The uniform's there. It's in your old chest of drawers. I saw it the other day.'

'Did you?'

'Yes. I went into your room. I was thinking of you and everything. And I went in there. I started pulling open the drawers, and I saw your uniform. That was all there was.'

She stopped.

They sat in silence.

'That was all there was left of you,' she said.

'We used to have some good times, didn't we?' said Bert.

'Yes.'

'I was happier here than I'd ever been anywhere.'

Rosy began looking round. She listened. The sound of conversation came floating into the little dark cubby-hole from outside on the croquet lawn.

'They don't seem to be in a hurry for their lunch,' she said.

'Old Mr and Mrs B. were the first decent people I ever came across,' Bert said. 'Do you remember what he used to call me? Gaius Sempronius Gracchus. I thought he was taking the mickey the first time he said it, but it was just his way of going on.'

'It's Latin,' said Rosy.

'I couldn't remember it at first. But he called me it so often that I learnt it in the end.'

'He always carries on with a thing once he starts it off.'

'Yes.'

They sat in silence again.

'Gaius Sempronius Gracchus,' said Bert.

He jumped to his feet, strode across to the louvred window, heaved himself up and peered out.

'I can still see him,' he said.

Rosy got up.

'Can you see the others?'

'Yes. Old Ma B. is there talking to that new chap. Did you say he was an Aussie?'

'Yes. Well, I suppose if she's still out there I needn't hurry all that much.'

Bert came down from the window.

'He doesn't look much,' he said.

'Who doesn't look much?'

'The Aussie. What's his name?'

'Mr Farran. Ned Farran. I told you.'

'Which do you call him? Mr Farran or Ned? Which of 'em?'

Rosy sat down again, and patted the bench beside her.

'Now don't you start all that again,' she said.

Bert continued to stand.

'What do you call him?' he said.

'Come on, sit down, do, while we can.'

'I asked you what you call that chap.'

'And I'm not going to tell you.'

'You're not, eh? I suppose it's because you daren't. I suppose it's because you call him Ned. Or Neddy? Or my own darling Neddy?'

'Stop it.'

Bert stepped forward and bent down over her. His menacing face.

'I won't stop it,' he said. 'You answer up, and answer true. What's between you and that chap? What have you been doing while I was locked up? You told me you'd wait. What have you been doing?'

She looked up at him.

'I call him Mr Farran,' she said. 'I've told you all about him. He's friendly, that's all. He says hello if he meets you anywhere.'

She smiled up at him and patted the seat again.

Too late.

His face had darkened with rage. He put his hands on her shoulders and yanked her to her feet.

'Tell me the truth,' he said.

'Be quiet. Bert, be quiet. If you yell like that someone will hear, and then it'll be all up.'

'Who'll hear? They're all out there, aren't they? And there's no one else in the house. I've got you all to myself.'

A glint of fear in the corner of her eyes.

He threw her back on the bench.

'Now then,' he said. 'Just what is there between you and this Farran?'

She sat limply, her arms hanging beside her.

'I've told you. Nothing at all. Nothing.'

'And I've told you. I don't believe you. And I'm going to get the truth out of you if I have to squeeze it out.'

'Bert.'

Pleading.

He pulled her up again by the shoulders.

'Go on,' he said, 'tell me. He's had you, hasn't he? You filthy little tart.'

Crack.

Rosy swung her open palm straight on to Bert's cheek.

He let go of her and she dropped to her feet. Her eyes blazing.

'You dare talk to me like that,' she said. 'I've always kept myself decent and you know it. If it hadn't been for me, you wouldn't even know there was such a thing. Get back into that corner and stay there till I come for you again.'

The burly figure standing close up to her trembled violently.

He drew in a breath. Noisily. Fighting for air.

His arm lifted.

And fell.

He shook his head.

He turned and shambled away.

'I should hope so,' said Rosy.

She bounced round and out leaving him in the gloom.

In the afternoon the party all assembled round the croquet court in the warm golden sunlight to watch the second match of the tournament, Cicely Ravell playing Sebastian Skuce. The light fell evenly on the close-cropped grass, sending long shadows from the hoops and the tall peg in the middle of the lawn. Only in the corner near the mulberry tree was there a sprawling patch of shade with a few berries which had fallen from the tree glowing in it like jewels.

It was peaceful at the back of the house in spite of the streaming traffic on the main road leading into the town and every now and again a burst of sound as one of the men on the demolition work at The Towers next door used a pneumatic drill.

Sebastian took a half-crown from his pocket and said to Cicely:

'Shall we toss and make a start?'

'I don't know why I bother with the toss,' Cicely said. 'My luck is aways perfectly foul. I don't think I've won a toss for ten years at least.'

Sebastian slipped the coin away.

'You concede the toss then?'

'Certainly not. It would be most irregular. Toss at once, Sebastian. If you don't I shall refuse to play. I can't tolerate people who don't stick to the rules of a game. There's a proper way of doing things and that's the way they ought to be done. People nowadays simply don't seem to understand that.'

Sebastian spun the half-crown. It glinted silver in the golden sun and fell on the lawn a few feet away from them.

'Heads,' Cicely called.

They walked over to inspect the coin.

Peke Abou, who had been standing absolutely motionless, apparently the victim of a profound dejection, waddled quickly in front of them, smelt briefly at the coin and sat on it.

'Abou, get up this instant,' said Cicely.

The hectic note of command.

Abou sat.

'Abou, you little fiend, I order you to get off that coin.'

Cicely pointed a finger at him, trembling with the violence of her feelings.

'Abou.'

'Pick him up, my dear,' said Sebastian. 'We mustn't keep everybody waiting.'

Cicely rounded on him.

'Then why didn't you pick him up in the first place?' she said.

'I suspect he would bite if I tried to.'

'Peke Abou bite? What absolute nonsense. The dog is the soul of gentleness. His particular strain has always been noted for that – even the girls are gentle. Peke Indarien has never so much as offered to bite anybody.'

'But the other beast – what's her name, Peke Dame – I've no doubt she's drawn blood in her time. You ought really to have her put down.'

Sebastian smiled, twisting the corners of his foxy red moustache.

'What do you mean? Where did you hear that? It was only the merest nip,' Cicely said. 'Besides, the boy was a fool, he was teasing her and deserved all he got. It's quite absurd. There's no question of putting a valuable dog down just because she showed an impertinent brat her teeth.'

Sebastian waved a deprecating hand in the air. The sunlight caught the fine reddish hair on the back of it.

'I'm awfully sorry,' he said. 'I'd no idea I'd hit on the truth. And now I've upset you and probably put you off your game.'

'Nonsense. I'm not in the least upset. Abou, get off that coin or I'll whip you, sir.'

Cicely turned towards the dog, her face red with fury.

Peke Abou was nowhere to be seen. The coin lay solitary on the deep green grass. Cicely had lost the toss.

'Now then let me see,' said Sebastian.

He rubbed his hands together cheerfully.

'Yes,' he said, 'I think I'll leave you to play first and I'll take choice of balls. I'll have – um . . . . Let's think . . .'

A pause.

'Yes, red and yellow.'

'Sebastian, you utter fiend. You know I can't play with blue and black. I never have the least luck unless I have red and yellow, you must have heard me say that thousands of times.'

'My dear, I'm terribly sorry. Of course I remember you telling people you had to have one pair rather than the other. But I thought it was the blue and the black you liked. How foolish of me. I'd offer to change only I know what a stickler you are for the conventions.'

'Very well,' said Cicely. 'I shall play blue and black. But I don't see why you insisted on choice of colours unless you wanted to upset me.'

'What cynicism,' said Sebastian. 'Now, start, my dear, do, or we'll never finish today.'

Cicely's first shot was a poor one.

For half an hour little went right for her, and Sebastian steadily ran hoops piling up the points. But after this Cicely appeared to have exhausted her store of pessimism and her play began to improve. She contrived a good break and began to climb towards Sebastian's total as he sat on a deck chair on the edge of the veranda watching her play. As the break built up Cicely's confidence and calm increased. She was able to hit shots she would have completely missed twenty minutes before. It began to look possible that she would even get both her balls round and go out before Sebastian could get another stroke in.

He heaved himself awkwardly out of his chair and hobbled to the edge of the court.

His shadow, slightly twisted, fell on the smooth turf at Cicely's feet. She looked up at him briefly.

She swung her mallet for the next stroke which was intended to send one of Sebastian's balls on up to the next but one hoop at the same time as her own ball made the hoop immediately in front of her. She did this neatly although Sebastian's ball ran a little short.

'Hard luck,' said Sebastian. 'You could have done with a bit more length to that one.'

Cicely glanced at the ball as she looked in the direction of her next stroke.

'It'll do,' she said.

'I thought you were lifting your head a tiny bit,' said Sebastian. 'That was probably what happened.'

Cicely said nothing, but she paused for an instant before making her next stroke.

As she played she ducked her head sharply towards the ground. The rhythm of her swing faltered.

She hit her target ball, but only at its very edge. It scarcely moved, and left her with a long approach to her next hoop.

'Oh, bad luck,' said Sebastian.

Cicely looked round the court.

'It looks as though I'd better finish off this break,' she said. 'A perfectly damnable pity when I'd just run into form. It's about the first time I've played at all decently this year. Damn and blast it, I can't think why I messed up that last one.'

'Oh, come,' said Sebastian, 'you don't mean to tell me you're going to give up here. You've got a nice little shot. '

'A nice little shot? I'd call that damn long.'

Sebastian laughed. A foxy bark.

'Leave it if you like then,' he said. 'Though if everyone neglected forward play like that it would be the end of the game.'

Cicely stood up straighter.

'No one has ever rebuked me for lack of forward play,' she said. 'It's a perfect fetish with me, as you ought to know. I've said it time and time again. The newer players are much too conservative: they're always laying up perfectly good breaks just because there is the slightest doubt about one shot. If I'd done that sort of thing twenty years ago when I really could play croquet I would never have won all the tournaments I did. I used to say then and I still say it now "Forward play is the key to success at croquet".'

'Hear, hear,' said Sebastian.

He began to walk along the edge of the court away from her. His good shoulder rising and falling as the weight left and came back to his weak leg.

'It's the sporting spirit that's so lacking in croquet today,' Cicely said.

She turned to address her ball.

Sebastian humped back towards the veranda. Behind him came the click of mallet on ball, sounding not quite as cleanly as it ought to have done.

'Damn. Damn. Damn.'

Sebastian turned.

'Oh, my dear, you missed it. I'll just fetch my mallet: I wasn't expecting to get in just yet. And you seem to have left me a very easy lie. How kind.'

He limped back to the veranda, took his mallet from beside his chair, and returned to the court.

He picked up a break in confident style, leaving Cicely only one long shot.

Cicely watched from the edge of the court standing in the shade of the enormous mulberry. There were tears in her eyes as Sebastian's second ball tocked against the peg.

She strode up to him.

'If it hadn't been for you daring me to go for that long shot at the end of my big break,' she said, 'I would have got out. The scores would have been absolutely reversed.'

Sebastian spread his hands wide.

'My dear, it wasn't a question of daring anybody,' he said. 'A short shot like that, I can't think how you missed it.'

'It wasn't short. Nobody would ever call a shot of that dis-tance short. It was a long shot.'

'Oh come, it wasn't much over four yards in any case and to a player of any class that's easy.'

'It was six yards at least, if you'll excuse me. Even seven. No gentleman would ever have dreamt of it. You're a pig, an abso-lutely unutterable pig.'

The last word spat out with all the violence Cicely could muster.

Sebastian laughed.

From the deep shade at the bole of the big mulberry Peke Abou launched himself. Straight as an arrow towards Sebastian's ankle. His sharp white teeth penetrated the cloth of the trousers.

Chapter Five

Irene picked up the little handbell that stood beside her place and rang it violently.

'Sorry to make such a din,' she said, 'but that girl's always missing the bell and then telling me I never rang it.'

'We ought to have had you at sea,' said Michael Goodhart. 'You'd have been a dab hand with a ship's bell.'

'She's a good kid all the same, that Rosy,' Ned said.

'I never said she wasn't. You've got it all wrong, quite wrong,' said Irene. 'The girl is excellent, a thoroughly good worker and reliable. I can't think whoever suggested she wasn't.'

She looked accusingly round the table. The prow bosom, back in the purple pullover tonight, pointing at each of them in turn.

'However excellent she is,' Sebastian said, 'she seems to be a little tardy in answering the bell this time.'

'She probably didn't hear,' said Humphrey. 'Ring again, bobbity.'

Irene shook the bell with redoubled violence.

'Shall I go and see what's up?' Penny said.

'No, no. Sit still. She'll come in a moment,' said Irene. 'She can't not have heard now.'

'We make an excellent klaxon at the factory,' said Leonard.

Humphrey groaned like an elephant.

'My dear chap, a klaxon at the dining table.'

'It couldn't make much more noise than Aunt Irene and her bell,' said Penny.

'The modern servant is simply appalling,' Cicely said. 'I don't know what they think they're paid for. And you have to give them a fortune, an absolute fortune. And even then they don't stay but go off and work in some perfectly ghastly factory.'

'They probably go to make klaxons for Leonard,' said Sebastian.

'I don't know why everybody keeps saying this girl is so bad,' Irene said. 'She's the best we've ever had. I only hope she'll stay for years.'

'If only our former handyman and she had united themselves in holy matrimony,' said Humphrey, 'We would have been made for life. Oh, why did the silly fellow get into trouble?'

'That was the famous Bert Rogers, was it?' said Michael.

'Yes, yes. Poor fellow. Nobody's heard any news about him, have they?'

'I listened to a bulletin on my transistor set before coming down to dinner,' Leonard said. 'There wasn't even a mention of him then.'

'So they've found him,' said Irene. 'I hadn't heard, but nobody tells me these things.'

'No, bobbity, they haven't found him.'

'Nonsense. Of course they have. They would still be mentioning him in the broadcasts if he was still free.'

'Oh no, I don't think so necessarily, my bobbit,' said Humphrey. 'If he's not been heard of they just wouldn't refer to the matter.'

'Quite wrong,' said Irene. 'He's been recaptured and I suppose that's the last we shall hear about it. I wonder if Rosalynn has been told. Perhaps she's sitting in the kitchen crying her eyes out. I'd better go and see.'

'But she can't have heard anything,' said Leonard. 'There's been nothing to hear. They said this morning that he was still at large and it was only a two-minute bulletin I listened to just now: they wouldn't refer to him unless he'd been found.'

'No, no,' said Irene.

The purple prow shook in violent disagreement.

'No, no. He's been found. There's no more to be said about it. And that poor girl in the kitchen in floods of tears, and all you can do is to stop me going to her.'

She stood up abruptly and marched out.

The moment the door had closed behind her the serving hatch shot up and Rosalynn could be seen thrusting a loaded tray to where she could reach it from the dining-room side.

Penny jumped up and ran after Irene. She left the door open and Rosalynn came in a moment later and began taking the dishes from the tray and setting them on the table. There was a big bowl of stewed mulberries and another of custard, glass dishes to eat out of, cream and sugar.

They could hear Penny's voice through the open door.

'But I've seen her, Aunt Irene. She passed me as I came after you. She's in there now.'

'Nonsense, child.'

'But honestly – '

'I tell you she must be out here somewhere. I can't think what can have happened to her.'

'But – '

'For all we know it may be Bert. He always seemed perfectly all right to me, but the police say he's violent and he may have come in here and attacked – '

Rosalynn set down the big bowl of mulberries with a sharp bang. Some of the deep red juice splashed up and marked the white tablecloth.

Rosalynn ran out of the room.

'These girls,' said Cicely.

They heard Irene's voice again.

'So there you are, my dear. Come along now we've all been waiting for you in the dining-room.'

Irene came in again, followed by Penny and Rosalynn. Irene began to serve the mulberries.

Rosalynn looked to see if she had put everything on the table and then went back to the kitchen.

'I can't make out what's wrong with that girl,' Irene said. 'She looked quite put out when I saw her just now.'

'It was probably only because she'd got late with the mulberries, my pet,' said Humphrey.

'Yes, yes, I suppose so. I can't imagine what she was doing.'

'It's nice to see the mulberries anyhow,' Michael said. 'Mulberries and croquet are inextricably mingled together in my mind because of the weeks here.'

'I take it we are to have the pleasure of seeing them every. night as usual,' said Sebastian.

'Don't you like mulberries?' said Irene. 'I thought everybody liked mulberries.'

'Aha,' said Humphrey, 'you shouldn't fuss about your food in a croquet week. Let me quote to you from my favourite work of literature. "During the week of play do not indulge your own or anyone else's fads as to the best diet to play croquet on." *The Isthmian Book of Croquet*, 1890 or thereabouts. A delightful work, delightful.'

He leant back in his chair and gave his glistening bald head three resounding slaps with the palm of his hand.

'I seem to have heard of it,' said Michael.

Humphrey roared with laughter.

'I dare say I've quoted it before,' he said. 'More than once, I dare say. You know who gave me the book, don't you, Leonard? It was my sister Frances.'

'Was it?' said Leonard.

Coldly.

'Yes, it was years and years ago. It must have been shortly after you married her, you see. Before Penny came into the picture at all.'

'You make it sound as if it was the latest best-seller when Mummy gave it to you,' said Penny.

Humphrey snorted with laughter and slapped his head again.

'In actual fact,' he said, 'the book was already well forgotten when Frances unearthed it for me. She's always been a wonder for digging up interesting finds like that. She even sends me things from America, you know.'

'I know,' said Leonard.

A grit of anger.

Humphrey spooned himself a sloppy mouthful of mulberries.

'Have you heard from dear Frances recently?' he said.

'She's not dear Frances to me,' said Leonard.

Humphrey waved his spoon in the air. A little trail of mixed mulberry juice and custard ran across the white cloth.

'Oh, I know you're divorced and all that,' he said. 'But nowadays no one bothers about a thing like that.'

'What do you mean no one bothers?' said Irene.

A thrust of the purple prow.

'I meant – I meant people who are divorced are still – friends – often can still be friends,' Humphrey said.

'You know nothing about it,' said Irene. 'You shouldn't try to be mondain, dear. It doesn't suit you.'

'Hear, hear,' said Leonard.

'He has heard from Mummy recently as a matter of fact,' said Penny. 'About some shares. She's being a perfect bitch over them.'

'Penny,' said Irene.

Genuine shock.

'Oh, I'm sorry, Aunt Irene. But it is true.'

'You mentioned something about some shares when you arrived, Leonard,' said Humphrey. 'What's all this about?'

'I don't think we need discuss it just now,' said Leonard.

'Please do,' Sebastian said. 'A humble don like myself loves to hear the inside story of how these big concerns rig the market.'

'Driver Products does not happen to be a particularly big concern,' said Leonard. 'And this is nothing to do with rigging the market. It's a purely personal transaction of limited import-ance.'

'You notice,' said Sebastian, 'that he doesn't deny that on occasion he's perfectly willing to rig the market.'

'It's nothing to do with anything like rigging the market,' Penny said. 'Daddy isn't a slick share operator. He's a manu-facturer. And a jolly good one, too. That's what makes what Mummy's doing so beastly unfair.'

'Nonsense, child,' Irene said. 'Frances is incapable of being unfair, just like Humphrey is. They're both of them the same. It's the way they were brought up. Your grandfather was not only a clergyman but a clergyman of the highest principles. He brought them up with an absolute passion for justice.'

'Well then, Mummy's lost it, that's all.'

'Now then,' said Irene. 'You don't know what you're talking about. Frances is a beautiful, cultivated and charming woman and whatever she did would always be the right thing to do.'

'But you don't know what it is that she is doing,' Penny said.

The exasperation of youth.

'I don't need to know, dear. And now if everyone's finished let's move over to the comfortable chairs for coffee.'

Irene stood up and gave the little handbell another vigorous shaking.

This time Rosalynn was quick to answer. She came in with the coffee tray which she put on a low table in front of the all-night stove. Then she started to clear away the mulberry bowls.

'You'd better put that cloth to be washed,' said Irene.

They went over and settled themselves down for coffee.

'How many years is it that you've all been coming here for this week?' said Ned.

'That's right,' said Sebastian. 'A good neutral topic, and we were so near to having a flaming family row.'

Humphrey ignored him. He clasped his hands together behind his billiard-ball head and leant back in his deep leather armchair.

'It's a very difficult question to answer,' he said. 'You see the war interfered with everything. The school was evacuated, you know. So it wouldn't really be fair to count that period, although we actually started these parties several years before hostilities began.'

'It must have been very different in those days,' said Michael. 'That was long before I sailed in.'

'Oh yes,' said Humphrey. 'We haven't always had the same people. To begin with that was before Frances married again and went off to America. She was a splendid player. I say "was" because she tells me she can't get any play over in America. She wrote only last week and told me how she envied us all.'

'She wrote last week, did she?'

Leonard Driver sat bolt upright and looked across at Humphrey.

'Just as I suspected,' he said. 'You and Frances have been in correspondence.'

Sebastian grinned and sat farther forward.

Humphrey dropped his hands from behind his head and waved them ineffectually in the air.

'But of course Frances and I write to each other,' he said. 'Why on earth shouldn't we? I'm very fond of her and she's very fond of me.'

'Exactly.'

Penny pounced.

'You were quite right, Daddy,' she said. 'He must have been putting her up to it. I wouldn't believe it of him, but this proves it. Oh, Uncle Humphrey, how could you be so beastly?'

'Beastly?' said Humphrey. 'My dear child, whatever is all this?'

'Making Mummy hang on to her Driver Products shares when she knows it means everything to Daddy to have them and be able to exercise full control. It's a filthy thing to do.'

'But I haven't done it,' Humphrey said.

'Of course he hasn't done it,' Irene said. 'And even if he had done it, it wouldn't be a filthy thing to do. Apologize at once, Penny. You should never have dreamt of saying a thing like that to your uncle.'

'I can't see the least need for her to apologize,' Leonard said.

He got up very red in the face.

'From what you have just said, Irene,' he went on, 'it seems obvious to me that Humphrey has been doing exactly what I thought. Whether it's filthy behaviour or not I leave others to judge.'

'And we shall be delighted to officiate,' said Sebastian.

Humphrey jumped to his feet. A rearing bull.

. 'I deny it absolutely,' he said. 'I don't even know what Leonard's talking about.'

'Oh no, of course you don't,' said Leonard. 'Of course you've not the least idea. Of course when I wrote to Frances and told· her I needed more voting power on the board to push through the change-over she never consulted you about whether she should sell me her shares. Of course she didn't.'

'She never even mentioned it,' said Humphrey.

'I don't believe you,' said Leonard.

'What do you mean?' Irene said. 'Humphrey's the soul of probity. How dare you say you don't believe him.'

'I do say it. Don't tell me Frances wouldn't have done what I asked if it had been left to her. It was the merest coincidence she happened to keep the shares she had when we married. Why shouldn't she let me have them?'

'Perhaps that ghastly man, Peter, her American husband, advised her,' said Cicely.

She had been perched on the very edge of the big sofa leaning forward and jerking up and down waiting to get her word in.

'I never liked him,' she went on. 'Personally I could never, never understand why Frances wanted to marry him. I remember him perfectly well. She brought him to see us once and he laughed at croquet. Well, you can tell at once about a person by their attitude to croquet. If they go on about it being a game for dodderers and making all those silly jokes, you know at once that they're no good. And I know that about this Peter.'

'The one fact about Peter,' said Leonard, 'is that he never attempts to advise Frances about her financial affairs. He's an artist and he doesn't pretend to know about money. It's the one thing in his favour.'

'So that proves Uncle Humphrey told Mummy not to sell,' said Penny.

She was standing now. Facing Humphrey, eyes blazing.

'It proves nothing – ' Humphrey began.

'And once Mummy's got an idea into her head nothing anybody can say will move it. She won't sell to Daddy now if it was her last penny on earth. You've ruined him, ruined him. I could kill you for this.'

She swung round and ran out of the room. Dishevelled. Tearful.

They sat looking at each other.

'What an extraordinary outburst,' Irene said. 'Is the girl well, Leonard?'

'She's very het up over all this,' Leonard said.

He looked down at his well-polished shoes.

'Don't pay too much attention to what she said,' he went on. 'She's got rather the wrong end of the stick. I would like those shares, of course, but it's scarcely a matter of life and death.'

'I thought the firm was doing so well,' Irene said.

Leonard looked offended.

'Of course the firm's doing perfectly well. You seem to have misunderstood the situation with your genius for looking through the wrong end of the telescope. There's nothing wrong with Driver Products, I can tell you.'

He glared at Irene as if she was the Official Receiver himself.

'Ought I to go and try to put things right with Penny?' Irene said.

'No, no, leave her, bobbity,' Humphrey said. 'One forgets she's so young because she acts in such a grown-up way most of the

74

time. But, when you come to think of it, she's scarcely older than some of the boys we have here.'

'I may say, Leonard, that I think you're utterly wrong to encourage her,' Cicely said. 'No wonder the child gets hysterical. She is only a child and you let her act as if she's adult. I'm sure I never did that with my children and they've grown up to be a credit to me. Of course I always had a great deal of sympathy with them: I knew instinctively what was the right thing to do.'

She gathered up Peke Abou on to her lap.

'That's what makes it all the more damnable of them to thwart my least wishes nowadays,' she said.

'Hey,' said the old hand from *The World*.

He lowered his copy of *The Weekend Post*. Belligerence.

'Have you seen the bit in the gossip page of this filthy rag?' he said.

'Ah, they used it, did they?' said the up-and-comer.

'Used what?' *The Examiner* man said. 'I never get round to anything but the qualities on a Sunday now they're so fat.'

'Bright boy here had a piece about that school we're meant to be watching,' said the girl from *The Clarion*.

'He got some copy out of this situation? He's what my old tutor used to call "a rising talent". What was it?'

'You want to grub about a bit, chum,' said the up-and-comer. 'Do you know who turned out to be staying at that dead-and-alive school? Leonard Driver no less.'

'Not exactly an *Examiner* figure, thank goodness. What was he doing there? Having a secret orgy with that model creature you're always linking him up with? Helen Whatsername?'

'Just Helen, laddie,' said the girl. 'That's her gimmick: let her stick to it.'

'I beg her pardon. But is she here?'

'Don't think so,' said the up-and-comer. 'Anyhow none of the tradesmen had seen any signs of her. Only the tycoon himself.'

'Tradesmen. Hobnobbing with tradesmen. There are times when I'm thankful for the lofty tone of *The Examiner*, I really am.'

'Pay days for instance, chum?'

'Well no, not pay days. They have very, very distinguished looking cheques, but somehow very, very tiny figures get on to them.'

'Too bad.'

'There's not much to this bit anyhow,' said the old hand. 'Not when you start looking at it. Precious few facts. Not what I call meaty.'

'It was enough, chum. *The Weekend Post* are always very pleased to get bits like that. They pay.'

'Did you get anything more?' said the girl.

'Not really. Only what it says there. That the head is an old friend and that the pushful Master Leonard goes there almost every year to play croquet.'

'The croquet angle's nothing new,' the old hand said. 'We've had stories about Leonard Driver dropping in on croquet tournaments for years.'

'Okay, okay, chum. But this particular party has never been touched before.'

'Have you had many dealings with the fellow?' asked *The Examiner.*

'Watch it,' said the girl. 'He's working up for one of their off-beat profiles.'

'And why not?'

'I interviewed him a couple of times,' said the up-and-comer. 'He's a go-getter, chum, there's no doubt about that. He built that firm up from damn-all, you know.'

'And by pretty violent methods, wasn't it?'

'Yes. If you want to put it that way. He didn't bother too much about how he got hold of the people he wanted, chum. Double salary offers flew around.'

'That sort of business never lasts,' said the old hand.

'You could be right,' the girl said. 'I was chatting to one of our City page boys the other day and he said they were sharpening the knives for our friend.'

'I do believe you're presenting me with a genuine high quality news peg for my little profile,' *The Examiner* said.

'You better get your stuff into type then, chum,' the up-and-comer said. 'Things might happen any day now.'

'Really?'

'Surely. I wish I could be certain Helen wasn't hidden up in that school somewhere. He arrived by helicopter, you know, and the pair of them might leave that way, but quick.'

'The tired provincialism of South America and a respectable marriage, eh? I hear the voice of my ancient tutor muttering *"l'ironie de la vie"* in his execrable French accent.'

'I can't make out why Driver didn't marry her at any time in the last five years,' said the old hand. 'He's been divorced longer than that. But we're dead certain there's been no marriage. And it's about time she got hooked up: she's no chicken.'

'It'd be a bit of a beat to get on to that, chum,' said the up-and-comer.

The romantic light in his eyes.

'I think she'd be willing enough from what I hear,' said the girl. 'The reluctance must be on his side.'

'Exceedingly odd,' said *The Examiner*. 'After all, I must admit the lady's got class. She'd make him a very good wife.'

'Maybe you'll see the full story in *The World* one of these days,' said the old hand.

He looked at the up-and-comer with contempt.

Penny Driver keeping her eye implacably on the ball swung her mallet. The ball rolled easily across the short grass and hit the peg fair and square in its middle.

'Oh, I won, I won,' she said. 'I was sure I'd never do it. Oh golly, *le suspense hitchcockien*.'

Michael Goodhart rounded up his two balls with the side of his mallet and picked them up.

'26–18,' he said. 'A very nice win. The first time I've had the pleasure of succumbing to you, I think.'

Ned, who was the only spectator at this Sunday morning match, joined them.

'Nice work, kid,' he said.

'Thank you,' said Penny. 'I was terrified I'd be completely off my game after that awful business last night.'

'Does no harm to let off a bit of steam once in a way,' said Michael. 'So long as you don't make a habit of it.'

'But it was awful of me. Uncle Humphrey's so decent about

most things it just seemed terrible that he was being so foul about this.'

'But is he?' Michael said.

'Oh, I'm sure he is. Daddy's quite right, you know. Mummy would never refuse to sell those shares without some backing. And who else is there?'

'I can't suggest anyone certainly, but – '

'Oh no,' said Penny, 'there's no doubt what's been happening. Only I oughtn't to have let it get me on the raw like that. Nobody's perfect. If Uncle Humphrey chooses to behave so badly over this it's no reason to lose one's temper.'

'You don't want to be too worried about losing your temper,' Ned said. 'That's a very English attitude. Back in Australia everybody bawls hell out of everybody else and no one thinks any the worse of them for it. As Mike here just said, it lets off steam.'

He pointed over beyond the half-demolished house next door to where the Sunday traffic roared and hooted on the main road to the coast.

'Mind you,' he said, 'even you Pommies break down sometimes. I bet there's enough bad temper on that road over there to sink a battleship.'

'Only bad temper isn't very effective for that particular job,' Michael said.

Penny's eyes shone.

'Do you know he actually did sink a battleship in the war?' she said.

'Only a little one,' said Michael.

'And I think Michael's quite right too,' said Penny. 'Bad temper isn't the best way of getting things done.'

'Correct weight,' said Ned. 'But we weren't talking about getting things done: we were talking about letting off steam. A lot of people over here seem to be scared of doing that. Look at these croquet games we've been playing. Somebody misses an easy shot, and what happens? Their opponent says "Oh bad luck" and the chap smiles and says "Bad play, I'm afraid, what".'

Penny giggled.

'And what they should do when they miss,' Ned went on, 'is

78

to cuss themselves silly. But that wouldn't be good form, so they bottle it all in.'

He took a huge swipe with a mallet at one of the balls lying at their feet and sent it shooting across the court and bouncing off the miniature chicken-wire fence at the edge.

'One day it'll all come out,' he said. 'And I'm going to duck.'

'Oh, I don't know, old chap,' Michael said. 'In a way you're right, of course. But there are other ways of letting off steam than cussing on the croquet court.'

'You should see Michael on the rugger field,' said Penny.

'Getting a bit of an old crock for that nowadays, but true enough I used to get rid of a lot of energy that way.'

'And you should see me when somebody puts on a jazz record,' Penny said.

'All right,' said Ned, I'll concede you two. You don't look as if you bottle things up all that much anyway, but not everybody plays rugger or jives. What about your old man, for instance, Penny? What does he do? Go out on a Saturday and get drunk as Chloe?'

Penny laughed.

'I don't think Daddy could get drunk,' she said. 'Not drunk as Chloe – whatever that means – anyway.'

'But what does he do? He's got more than a bit of steam to let off, if you ask me.'

Penny's eyes clouded.

'So you've noticed too,' she said.

'I notice things because I'm pretty much of a foreigner over here,' Ned said. 'I don't accept all the pretences and ready-ups you people put out.'

'I suppose Daddy works off his surplus energy over the firm,' said Penny.

She traced a pattern on the grass with the head of her mallet.

'All the same,' she went on, 'I'm worried about him. I think he's having some sort of trouble with Helen, and I don't know what it's all about.'

She looked up.

'I dare say that was why I got so batey last night,' she said. 'I reverted to my childhood. Do you know what I was going to do? I was going to go and hide in the place the boys keep their shoes.'

'The boothole,' Ned said.

'Yes. That's what I always used to do when I was younger. Went and hid in there and wept till I felt better. I was all set to do it last night, only I found the door was stuck for some reason. So I sobered up and came back and apologized all round.'

'How do you mean the door was stuck?' said Ned. 'There's no lock on it.'

'I know. That was what was odd.'

She smiled.

'I took it as a sign to behave myself,' she said.

Chapter Six

'It can't go on for ever,' Bert said.

He turned and paced back along the short length of the boot-hole.

Rosy sat on the bench watching him.

'That's what I keep telling you,' she said.

Bert stopped in his tracks.

'Who could it have been?' he said. 'Who was it?'

'It might have been anybody.'

'They've none of them any business in here.'

'I know, I know,' Rosy said. 'But there's no reason why any one of them shouldn't take a fancy to poke their nose in.'

'I tell you,' said Bert, 'I went cold. I stood in the corner there watching the door push up against that shoe under it and I went cold.'

'Come and sit down,' said Rosy.

Bert stood where he was.

'You could find somewhere else for me if you wanted to,' he said.

'Look,' said Rosy, 'Whoever it was pushing at the door didn't get it open, did they?'

'The trouble is,' Bert said, 'that you don't want to. You want me to stay in here and I know why.'

A flicker from Rosy's eyes in the gloom.

'You're quite safe with the shoe there,' she said. 'It jams the door hard. No one could get it open.'

'Yes they could. If they thought there was something funny going on they'd break down the door easy enough.'

'But – '

'Oh, shut up. It's easy for you to find reasons for keeping me here. Anything but the real reason.'

Rosy looked in front of her without moving.

'You hope someone will find me and get me sent back to that place, don't you?'

'No, Bert, no.'

Rosy jumped up and hung on to his arm.

'Honest, I don't want that to happen,' she said. 'Listen, I've been thinking about it all. If I do want you to go back I want you to go of your own free will.'

'Of my own free will? Don't make me laugh.'

'Listen, it's the only way. You can't escape them for ever. It isn't as if we were real crooks with plenty of lolly and a boat in the Channel. We can't hope to get you right away.'

'I can hide.'

'But not for ever. You know that really.'

Bert sat down heavily. The narrow bench creaked sharply.

'All right,' he said. 'I know I can't get away for ever, but I can get away for a bit. And every day I'm out is good.'

Violence of belief.

'That's what I'm telling you,' Rosy said. 'Have your time, have as long as you want – if we can manage it. But make up your mind that it's going to be over one day.'

'May be it won't be. Your luck can run on.'

'And it can run out. It might be running out at this minute.'

Bert jumped up and glared at the door.

'They'll have to fight me.'

Rosy came over to him and stroked the tense arm muscles.

'Don't do it,' she said. 'That's what frightens me. Don't do it.'

Gradually Bert relaxed.

'I'll try,' he said.

'I must go in a tick.'

'All right.'

'Will you promise to think about what I said?'

'About giving myself up?'

A mutinous look.

'Just think about it. That's all. You don't have to decide now.'

'All right, I'll think about it. I'll give it my consimderation.'

That morning there was also time for the game between Irene and Leonard. Leonard won 26-0. In the afternoon the semi-finals began. Ned met Sebastian and was beaten 26–3.

On the Monday Leonard was to play his daughter in the other semi-final. It was again a warm September day. The dense shadow turned the grass in the corner of the court which it shaded to a dark grey in contrast to the deep green of the area in the mellow sunlight.

Although there had been no rain since the tournament had begun the sun had never been strong enough completely to dry out the turf, and the court still gave a little underfoot. Before they began playing Leonard knelt on one knee and felt at the grass.

He stood up and looked at his fingers. There was a gleam of damp on them. The knee of his white trousers – he was the only one of the party to wear white – showed a faint green stain where it had pressed into the ground.

Leonard smiled slightly, flexed his shoulders and swung his mallet gently to and fro. He looked round the court. The whole party had assembled to watch the game.

Play was very even. Penny, it was obvious, had decided to go strictly on to the defensive. She took no risks. At the least difficulty she abandoned her breaks, set up as awkward a position as she could and left her father to do his best with it. It was seldom possible for him to do more than make things equally difficult for her.

After about an hour's play Cicely Ravell got up abruptly from her canvas chair at the edge of the veranda.

'I'm going in to write some letters,' she said. 'I can't think what's happened to Penny today. Of course, I taught her most of what she knows about croquet, and if there was one lesson I hammered in to her more than another it was the absolute importance of forward play. Go for it, I used to say. It used to be our motto in our games together. We used to dare each other to take longer and longer shots.'

She scooped up Peke Abou who had been lying watching the play with beady eyes.

'I can't think what's happened to her,' she went on. 'This game is simply appallingly dull. That's the only word for it. They've been playing for well over an hour already and haven't made half a dozen hoops between them. I've seen games finished twice over in that time.'

She marched off in the direction of the glass door leading from the playing-field into the house.

'All the same,' said Michael Goodhart when she had disappeared, 'Penny's holding her own. And there aren't many of us who can do that against Leonard.'

'In fact,' said Sebastian Skuce, 'there is only one of us. And I mean myself.'

'You certainly gave me a beaut of a beating yesterday,' said Ned.

He leant forward in his chair as Penny made a stroke. Her ball ran easily to join its partner in the corner of the court under the mulberry.

'See,' said Humphrey, 'she's left him only the ghost of a chance again.'

'I must say she's learnt a lot since last year,' said Irene. 'She couldn't have done this then. Leonard beat her 26–0.'

'No, no, bobbity. She put up quite a fight last year, 26–18 or something like that. You're thinking of the year before.'

'No, no, no. You've got it quite wrong,' Irene said.

Her bosom, in green again, swung towards her husband.

'Penny has never taken more than a couple of points off Leonard,' she announced.

'I'll get my records out at lunchtime,' said Humphrey. 'You'll see then. Last year she did quite well.'

'I expect you put down the wrong figures,' Irene said. 'But I can't stay here arguing with you. I must give the girl a hand with the lunch. She seems terribly slow these last few days.'

She sailed invincibly away.

'What Irene doesn't realize,' Humphrey said, 'is that Penny is growing up. She's learning that it sometimes pays to play a waiting game, to let the other fellow make the mistakes.'

He gave his shiny bald head a series of rapid little slaps, and watched Leonard play.

'Look, another complete miss.'

He heaved himself to his feet.

'I think I'll just go and check those figures,' he said. 'You see, Farran, I've got detailed records going back to the very beginning of our tournaments. Absolutely essential for settling arguments of this kind.'

He lumbered off.

'You know,' Michael said, 'if Penny goes on like this she'll sink her father. It's the game to play against him if you can. Patience is his weak point, he'll start making some really poor shots before long, and then . . .'

'Then he'll win,' said Sebastian.

Michael laughed.

'Never on the side of youth,' he said. 'A man with his money always on the battleships. You wait and see.'

'I'll take a bet on this,' Sebastian said.

Statistical confidence.

'All right. Half a crown?'

'Done.'

Ned gave Sebastian a curious look, and turned back to watch the game.

Almost at once Michael's prognostications began to work out. Leonard started walking quickly between shots and playing with only a moment's study of the situation. He left Penny a sitting break. She, true to her policy, abandoned it at the first danger, put her peg on the hoop and concentrated on leaving an awkward lie for her father, but she had notched up twelve hoops and was beginning to get into an advantageous position.

'She shows no signs of letting this go to her head,' Michael said. 'I think my money's safe.'

Sebastian smiled under his foxy moustache.

Leonard played again.

Michael winced.

'What a terrible shot,' he said. 'I didn't think he was capable of anything so bad.'

'Could Penny go out this turn?' Ned said.

'Yes, she could,' said Michael.

'But she won't,' Sebastian said.

Michael turned to him.

'How can you be so sure of that?' he said. 'Granted she'll probably continue to play safe and not try to win now unless it's very plain sailing. But there's no reason why it shouldn't be plain sailing.'

'You watch,' said Sebastian.

In silence they watched.

For the first time Penny seemed a little uncertain. She made one hoop without any difficulty and then looked round the court in an obvious dilemma.

'What's she worried about?' Michael said. 'It's quite a simple situ— Hallo, what's she doing now? Surely she can't be going that way? It's insane, and there's no advantage.'

He got up from his chair as if he was going to run down to the court and actually remonstrate with Penny.

Sebastian put a hand on his arm and he sat down again.

Penny played.

Michael buried his head in his hands.

'Of course she didn't do it,' he said. 'It was a chance in a million.'

He looked up.

'And now she's really let Leonard in. And he only needs one chance like this.'

They sat and watched Leonard playing. Ned occasionally took his eyes off the court to study his two companions. Sebastian sat impassively, twisted in his chair to ease his weak side, smiling slightly. Michael's face wore an expression of dismay so marked as to be comic. With every hoop that Leonard ran it got worse.

'A chance like that simply gave him back all the confidence she'd so cleverly undermined,' he said.

As Leonard's second ball hit the peg he groaned aloud.

'Well done, Daddy,' said Penny.

She ran up to Leonard and flung her arms round his neck.

Michael took half a crown from his pocket and tendered it to Sebastian.

'I thought it would be the other way about,' he said.

Sebastian laughed. A sharp bark.

'You thought she would let him lose?' he said.

Michael looked shocked for an instant and then said:

'Oh come, I don't think she would deliberately allow him to win. After all it's only a game when all's said and done.'

Sebastian smiled.

The four demolition men working on the roof of The Towers

that afternoon paused in their task of throwing down loosened tiles to watch the party come out on to the croquet court. Perhaps something in the attitudes of the eight people forty feet below them conveyed the extra tension of the tournament singles final. It was plain to the watchers on the ground that both Leonard and Sebastian were taking the affair seriously. Each wanted to win, wanted badly to win. There was something guarded in their attitudes to each other. Unexpressed hostility.

The game began slowly with neither player very ready to give anything away. Yet it soon became apparent that Leonard was the better player. He secured two small breaks and made seven hoops altogether, while Sebastian was able only to seize a couple of odd chances to score two points.

After the second of these he left Leonard a fairly long shot which Leonard rather unexpectedly went for. His ball hit Sebastian's almost at its dead centre. Leonard looked about with a more confident air and started to manoeuvre the balls to establish a four-ball break with every chance of adding considerably to his score. He was about to take his stance to run the first hoop of the break – from slightly farther away than the safest length – when Sebastian spoke.

'I gather the police still think he's hereabouts somewhere,' he said.

Leonard, without answering or showing in any way that he had heard, took his stance and played his shot. His ball hit the wire of the hoop a little too hard and bounced off it without going through.

'What was that you said?' Leonard asked.

Sharply.

'I was saying I met Superintendent Pinn this morning and he told me he thought the escaped Broadmoor man is still in the district.'

'So he may be. What of it? It's your turn to play.'

'Oh, so it is. I wasn't paying much attention. Did you miss that one? I'd have thought you'd have got it easily.'

'I missed it.'

'Ah well. Now let's see. Oh yes, this looks quite promising.'

Sebastian ran enough hoops to level the scores, but misjudged his effort to leave a difficult shot for Leonard at the end of the break. Leonard made no mistakes about taking advantage of this and ran four more hoops.

He was taking the lie of the land for a longish shot at one of Sebastian's balls when Sebastian said:

'Tell me, old man, I've always been meaning to ask you, this. What exactly is a transistor?'

'A transistor,' said Leonard. 'It's the key to our new radio.'

'I know, but what exactly is it?'

Leonard crouched for a moment and peered along the line between his ball and Sebastian's.

'Oh,' he said, 'it's the equivalent of the old-fashioned thermionic valve only it takes much less space and doesn't need to be heated to work. It's rather like the prehistoric crystal of the crystal set as a matter of fact.'

He addressed his ball and hit it. It ran across to Sebastian's and knocked it with exactly the right force to send it to the point where Leonard wanted it.

Leonard continued the break and added three more hoops.

Suddenly Sebastian shouted:

'Abou, get off, sir. Get off.'

Leonard's mallet tipped the ground an instant before it ought to have hit his ball and his stroke was much too weak.

'I'm awfully sorry,' said Sebastian, 'but I thought that dog was going to go right across your line of play.'

'He wasn't going to move an inch,' Cicely called from her chair near the bole of the gnarled old mulberry.

Sebastian smiled.

'Really,' said Cicely, 'anyone would think my dogs had never seen croquet played. The very first thing I do when I'm training them is to teach them not to cross the boundary wires when anyone is on the court. No dog of mine has ever dared to do it.'

'I must have misjudged the poor dear animal,' Sebastian said.

He took his stance, but there was little he could do and soon he was bound to concede Leonard an innings. Leonard began it with a daring long shot and soon was building up yet another break.

'You're certainly in form,' Sebastian said, 'but my turn will come.'

'Not if I can help it.'

Grim humour.

'Ah, hope springs eternal. Oh, by the way, that reminds me. You never said the other day when Humphrey challenged you over precisely that quotation whether you really knew who was the author. You implied that like any educated man you did know, but you were clever enough not to mention names.'

Leonard swung his mallet. Too much force in the stroke. A complete miss.

Sebastian was playing better now. The turn he had secured himself took him to within sight of victory with Leonard a few points behind. Sebastian had to abandon a risky shot with his first ball at the penultimate hoop but succeeded in leaving Leonard only a very slim chance of getting in again.

Leonard appeared to be made bolder by the nearness of defeat. He looked carefully at the shot he had been left, took his stance, swung his mallet and set his ball rolling at an even pace straight across the clipped grass. It struck its target ball fair and square.

The watchers round the court turned to each other in a flurry of admiration. Leonard ran two hoops and left himself with an easy shot for a third.

'You know,' said Sebastian, 'I don't like this one little bit. You've got a very nice set-up for the hoop after this as well.'

Leonard looked across to see the lie of the balls beyond his target, and then quickly addressed his ball for the easy hoop.

And missed it.

'Aha,' said Sebastian, 'there's many a slip. That's a common fault, you know, looking ahead and not concentrating on the matter in hand.'

Leonard was not out for long on this occasion. Sebastian had been left with no possibility of running any hoops and all he could do was to make the situation difficult for Leonard again.

And once more Leonard seized a faint opportunity with a fine long shot, although he left himself with a tricky set-up in a corner. Ned, who had strolled across to get a better view, squatted on his heels interestedly.

Very delicately Leonard manoeuvred the two balls. The stroke was a tricky one, but its result was just what he needed and he followed the balls across to their new positions with a springy step.

'Just a moment,' said Sebastian.

A sharp note.

'That was a double tap you gave your ball then,' he said.

Leonard controlled an angry jerk.

'No,' he said, 'there wasn't even a possibility of it.'

'I'm afraid I can't agree,' said Sebastian.

Cold politeness.

'But, my dear chap – '

'Don't you "my dear chap" me, if you please. That shot was obviously a double tap and it was your duty to give up your turn.'

'My dear chap – '

'I'm not your dear chap.'

Sebastian's eyes were gleaming under the fox-red eyebrows.

'Look,' said Leonard.

His face was growing whiter.

'Look, I know the rules as well as you do. If there had been a double tap I would have given up my turn. I'm not likely to do anything else.'

'Not unless you wanted to make sure of the game.'

'How dare you say that.'

Leonard's face went suddenly red.

'It means more to you to win than it does to me,' Sebastian said.

'I deny that.'

Leonard was shouting.

Ned strolled towards them.

'You know,' he said. 'I was watching that shot pretty carefully. If double tapping means hitting the ball twice it certainly didn't happen then.'

'Thank you,' said Leonard.

He turned still quivering with indignation to Sebastian.

'Now perhaps you'll apologize,' he said.

'Your shot, old chap,' said Sebastian.

He turned and limped away across the smooth grass.

Leonard looked as if he might follow him, but changed his mind and played his next shot, a comparatively easy one.

It did not come off.

Sebastian took both his balls painstakingly through all the rest of the hoops and pegged out one of them. Only a shot of about five feet to the peg with his second ball lay between him and victory. He took his stance carefully, swung his mallet, hit the ball cleanly. And completely missed the peg.

'I suppose,' said Humphrey from the veranda, 'you'd call that a case of pegitis – if missing a hoop from over-anxiety is hoopitis as it's sometimes called.'

'He won't do it twice,' said Michael. 'If Leonard has to let him in again at present he's got a six-inch shot to win.'

'Come what may he's only got to hit the peg from wherever Leonard puts him,' Irene said. 'And Leonard will find it pretty difficult to get at Sebastian's ball this turn. It's all but wired from him by the peg.'

Leonard walked slowly across to the nearer of his balls. He looked along the line between it and Sebastian's. Most of Sebastian's lay concealed by the peg. Very deliberately Leonard made his stroke. His ball ran smartly forwards.

'He'll hit the peg,' Ned said.

His toes inside the pair of rubber shoes twitching with anxiety.

'No, he'll miss it and miss the ball,' said Michael.

He got to his feet and craned forward to judge the ball's line better.

Chapter Seven

The ball passed the peg missing it by a hairsbreadth. A moment later it just grazed Sebastian's ball to give Leonard another shot and a chance of maintaining his innings.

A chance he did not fail to take. Inexorably he ran his remaining hoops, hit the peg with his first ball and then gave himself an easy shot at it with his second. Sebastian's ball had been left farther away but should Leonard miss in his turn Sebastian would have a reasonable shot for the peg to snatch victory at last.

Leonard took his stance, swung once or twice to and fro on the balls of his feet, settled himself, brought his mallet smoothly back, and shot.

The ball hit the peg bang in the middle.

Penny leapt from her chair and ran at full speed across the neat grass of the court and into her father's arms.

'Oh, Daddy, Daddy, you brought it off in spite of everything.'

Leonard, an irrepressible smile of triumph on his face, kissed her.

'Daddy, I know we're going to pull off the doubles between us too. I feel it in my bones.'

Leonard looked down at her.

'Don't be too confident,' he said. 'You can make mistakes that way.'

A warning.

Over the next two days Penny showed no signs of over-confidence. She and Leonard beat Irene and Cicely by 26–0 and won by 26–20 over the formidable combination of Sebastian and Michael. Against Humphrey and Ned they lost by the narrow margin of four points, 26–22.

Humphrey and Ned were the surprise of the contests. Combining Humphrey's mountainous knowledge of tactics and Ned's unshakeable natural skill they not only pulled off their game against Leonard and Penny but they too beat Irene and Cicely 26–0.

On Wednesday afternoon the last game of the doubles – Humphrey and Ned against Sebastian and Michael – was to be played. The whole party came out on to the veranda.

'Now,' said Humphrey, 'I hope everyone understands the full beauty of the position. It's one of the most exciting finishes we've ever had.'

The two ham hands floppily smoothing his billiard-ball head.

'Jeez,' said Ned, 'let's play it off. There are moments when I feel a fool doing this anyhow.'

'No, no,' said Humphrey. 'I want everyone to appreciate the situation before we begin, you see. Now it's like this. The prize for the doubles lies between my team and Leonard's, and of course if Leonard and Penny are the victors then Leonard has pulled off the two competitions and becomes the first to win the trophy.'

Leonard's compressed lips.

'Very well then,' Humphrey said, 'if Ned and I beat Sebastian and Michael we win the doubles by getting three outright victories, that's perfectly simple. It's when we come to consider what happens if Sebastian's team beat us that the full delight becomes apparent. Because then, you see, each of three teams will have scored two wins apiece and the doubles will go to whichever of them has most points.'

Cicely's fingers picking at the edge of her skirt.

'If only I hadn't played so appallingly,' she said, 'we wouldn't have been the team with no wins at all.'

'So listen,' said Humphrey.

He swung his arms wildly to and fro. An ecstasy of complication.

'Listen, Leonard and Penny have two wins at 26 points apiece and one loss when they scored 22: total 74. Now Sebastian and Michael get 52 for their two wins and their lost game brought them 20 points, so that their total is 72. Now with Farran's able assistance I have amassed 52 points so far, so if we lose against Sebastian and Michael this afternoon but nevertheless take 23 points off them we shall have a grand total of 75 and thus beat Leonard and Penny by one.'

'*Stupendo*,' said Penny. 'But my poor Daddy having to wait to see what happens.'

For the first time since the party had arrived at Ambrose House the weather was doubtful. The sunshine of the previous days which had eventually baked the ground hard had given way to heavy grey clouds and a strong south-westerly wind. The laden branches of the huge mulberry tossed and swung in it and the ripe fruit fell regularly on the smooth turf of the croquet lawn. Each time Humphrey had to wait to play he padded across to the corner of the court and bending cumbrously down began to pick up the squashy berries and toss them over the miniature wire boundary fence of the court.

Just as he was about to lower himself towards the ground for the tenth time a falling mulberry hit him fair and square in the middle of his shining bald head.

The deep red juice ran in three thick trickles off the smooth skin, one above his left eye, one above his left ear and one down the exact middle of the nape of his neck.

He let out a great roar of anguish and Ned, who was playing a delicate stroke, lifted his head, tipped the top of his ball and completely missed his target.

'Oh, confound and damn it.' Humphrey shouted.

Although none of the juice had actually entered his eyes he seemed to believe his sight was affected and staggered towards the house with his hands groping in front of him. A blind hippopotamus.

Irene grasped him firmly and led him to a chair.

'I'll get some water and wipe you up,' she said. 'Though at your time of life you ought to know better than to smear mulberries all over yourself.'

'But, bobbity, the wretched fruit fell out of the tree,' said Humphrey.

'Really,' said Irene, 'excuses like that would do no credit to a new boy.'

She marched into the house.

The game was brought to a standstill and everybody gathered

round Humphrey and stood looking down at the red mess squarely in the middle of his glistening bald pate.

'You'd make a good corpse for the school production of Hamlet, sport,' Ned said.

Humphrey groaned.

'Came at a good time for you, Sebastian,' Leonard said. 'Ned looked as if he had a nice break lined up there.'

'I'm afraid we gathered an unfair advantage,' Michael said. 'But we're scarcely out of port yet and we're down already.'

Irene reappeared with a bowl of warm water and a cloth and play began again. Sebastian screwed the last ounce of advantage from the situation Humphrey's sudden roar had presented to him. He and Michael ended their innings a little ahead of Humphrey and Ned.

Ned brought off a spectacular long shot to swing the game back in their favour. Humphrey, clean and quiet again, settled down comfortably to run a simple hoop.

'You know,' said Sebastian.

The offhand conversational tone.

'You know, I see this game as more than an encounter between two pairs of croquet players. I see it as a clash between two principles.'

Humphrey abandoned his stroke.

'Yes,' said Sebastian, 'I see it as a contest between you and Michael as embodiments of two different approaches to educating the young. You have been going for donkey's years and represent tradition – spare the rod and all that – while Michael coming fresh to teaching from the wider world represents all the new – it's all done by kindness, etcetera.'

'Indeed,' said Humphrey.

He smoothed a huge hand over his bald head. Put out.

'The interesting thing,' Sebastian went on, 'is which of you will prove to win the allegiance of the majority of parents – violence or softness, so to speak. After all Michael's establishment is not far off: there really is a choice between the two places.'

'Nonsense,' said Humphrey, 'there's an agreement that Michael had to set up at least a certain number of miles away from me.'

'Oh yes, I know all that. But that's out of date, really. Think of it from a parent's outlook. Does it matter from the convenience point of view whether their boy goes to school here or thirty miles along the coast? Of course not. What counts is the atmosphere of the school.'

Sebastian began to limp towards the tiny boundary fence of the court.

'Forcing it into them or drawing it out,' he said, 'The parents choose: the loser pays.'

Humphrey turned to take his shot, but seemed to lose heart and stood swinging his mallet above the ball aimlessly.

Michael laughed.

'If Sebastian's view is right,' he said, 'it looks as if the traditional way is winning. You should see my balance sheets.'

'It's kind of you to reassure Humphrey,' Sebastian said.

The plain note of irony.

Humphrey swung his mallet in earnest and ran his hoop.

The incident proved a crisis in the game. After it Humphrey and Ned began to draw ahead steadily. Part of their success came from Sebastian's increasingly poor play. The weakness in his leg and arm meant that he had to play the upright style with the mallet swung not between the legs but beside them. A position somewhat vulnerable to the effects of wind. And as the game progressed the wind grew stronger and stronger.

The falling mulberries, which up to now had plunked on to the grass near the tree, began to whip across the court in the stronger gusts. A little rain was carried in the wind and the clouds seemed to be getting even lower and darker.

Ned looked up at them.

'Do we go in?' he said.

Humphrey snorted with laughter and stamped his spreading feet on the ground in delight.

'What game do you think this is?' he said. 'Cricket? Let me tell you croquet players go on until play is really impossible. A drop of rain like this won't stop us. We wait till there's standing water on the court.'

He drew his clasped hands over the shining dome of his head and looked with beaming pleasure at the wetness of the palms.

'That's okay by me,' Ned said. 'Only if the rain comes on any heavier I reckon I'll nip in and change into bathers.'

Humphrey bent nearly double with laughter.

'You can play croquet in the altogether if you like,' he said. 'The only rule about clothing is that shoes with heels must never be worn. Naked feet should be quite all right, though I must seek official guidance on the point one day.'

'Well, naked feet would be nothing new to me,' said Ned. 'I never wore shoes at home as a kid, none of us did. The soles of our feet got so tough we used to make patterns in them with a needle and thread.'

'Hoo,' said Humphrey.

He pointed at Ned with his mallet.

'The wild man of Borneo,' he said.

And then the rain suddenly came down in buckets. In a moment all four of the contestants were drenched to the skin.

'We'll have to chuck it,' said Michael. 'You can't even see the hoops at the other end of the court.'

Humphrey pointed delightedly to a patch of ground near the mulberry tree.

'Look,' he said, 'standing water. In we go.'

They squelched heavily to the veranda and stood with their clothes clinging to them in its shelter. Humphrey went back to the court with a handful of coloured pegs to mark the positions of the balls. The rain cascaded from his bald head and beat on his broad shoulders as he lumbered round stooping to replace each ball with the appropriate peg.

With a startling crack an ancient branch broke off the mulberry tree in the tempestuous wind. Humphrey dashed back into shelter. The branch hung caught in the foliage of the tree leaving an ugly white scar on the trunk. The other branches heaved and tossed as more and more violent gusts of wind shook the old tree and hurled the heavy raindrops in swathes across the croquet court and the playing-field beyond.

They stood in spite of their soaking clothes and watched as the storm battered and lashed at the ground in front of them.

'We must be at the very centre of it,' Ned said.

'It's the effect of a violent depression, you see,' said Humphrey. 'We're at the point where it's growing in intensity. That's where the rain is always heaviest. It comes in a relatively narrow belt so this shouldn't last long, you see.'

They accepted the information in silence.

The wind gained in intensity and began veering wildly back and forwards. The leaves of the mulberry were suddenly turned inside out with a crack like the sails of a man o' war caught in a tropical squall. The rain in huge drops was being whirled to and fro. It drummed on the roof of the veranda like a continuous roll of gunfire.

'*Epouvantable*,' said Penny, who had been watching the game with her father and Cicely.

The rain drumming mounted to a new fury.

Cicely got up from her canvas chair and strode rapidly up and down the length of the veranda. Leonard sat without stirring looking out on the elemental chaos.

Now the wind was all but shrieking. Leaves left the mulberry tree with sudden sharpness, jerked off by an invisible and angry hand. Sticks whirled up into the air.

Peke Abou standing four-square on his feathery legs began to bark as hard as he could. The sound totally drowned by the frenzied beating of the rain and the howls of the wind.

'I say,' said Penny, 'oughtn't you lot to go in? You're utterly soaking.'

Humphrey raised his hands high above his bald head still gleaming with rainwater.

'Blow winds,' he shouted, ' "and crack your cheeks, rage, blow your cataracts and hurricanoes".'

A deck-chair near the mulberry left the ground, hung for a moment poised in the air with its canvas strained out, twirled round until it touched the branches of the tree and then suddenly fell back to earth.

A swarm of dust and rubble from the demolition work next door rose up in a twisted column and was swept away into the distance.

There was a sudden calm.

The watchers on the veranda stopped and looked at each other.

Then the rain began falling again, insistently but with less violence.

Humphrey, who had left his arms wide stretched after his outburst of poetry, suddenly dropped them.

'We must get in and find some dry togs,' he said. 'If Irene sees us in this state we'll never hear the end of it.'

Slowly Humphrey drew the blue curtains across the dining-room windows cutting out the view of the last calm light falling across the playing-field and the croquet court.

'You see,' he said, 'this is obviously one of those depressions in which the warm sector following the cold front brings a period of fine weather. It's a very common fallacy to think that a depression always means bad weather all the time. Look at this in the words of the poet, a beauteous evening calm and free.'

'We won't ask Leonard which poet it is,' said Sebastian.

He sat grinning in the depths of one of the large leather arm-chairs, twisted in a characteristic pose to ease his weak side.

'It certainly is calm now,' said Michael. 'I'm sorry the court didn't dry up a bit earlier. We might have finished the game.'

'I don't know why you didn't at least have a try,' said Leonard.

'My dear chap,' Humphrey said, 'there was standing water on the court until a quarter of an hour ago.'

'I agree with Leonard,' said Cicely. 'There's much too much waiting for the weather these days. I've played croquet when it's been absolutely foul. No one else would have played any other game, but I went out on to the court and got on with it.'

'But there were puddles,' Humphrey said. 'We couldn't have played, could we, Farran?'

'Until this morning I thought the sun had to be shining before anyone even touched a mallet,' Ned said.

'What nonsense,' said Irene.

She looked up from the enormous royal blue cardigan she was knitting for herself.

'You're making a great mistake,' she said. 'The whole thing about croquet is that you can play it in all weathers. Only one thing puts a stop to the game – standing water on the court. Hasn't anyone ever told you that?'

'It certainly stopped us this afternoon,' said Ned.

'Just as I felt I was getting back into form after that disgusting business with that mulberry,' said Humphrey.

'I was surprised you managed to swallow them at all at dinner this evening,' Sebastian said.

'Oh, do stop hinting things about the mulberries,' Penny said. 'Nobody ever has them anywhere else. I think it's jolly snob to get them here.'

'I was ready to cut down the tree this afternoon, I can tell you,' said Humphrey. 'I completely lost my form. And then the rain stopped me just as I was getting it back. There's only one thing for it.'

He heaved himself up from the sofa, squared his shoulders and stood resolutely facing the door of the room.

'You look as if you're going out to practise straight away,' Penny said.

Humphrey slapped his thighs and burst into laughter.

'Aha,' he said, 'even I couldn't do much in the dark. But I tell you what I am going to do.'

He stroked his shining bald head briskly.

'I'm going to get up at first light tomorrow morning and have a jolly good warm-up.'

'You can't do that.'

Leonard shot up from his chair and stood trembling with the violence of his objection.

Humphrey turned to him.

'My dear chap, why ever not?'

'It's – It's – Because it's obviously unfair to practise in the middle of a game.'

'There's no question of unfairness: the others are welcome to get up and practise too. There's plenty of room on the court for all four of us if need be.'

Leonard was getting very red in the face.

'I still think you're taking an unfair advantage,' he said.

'The trouble is,' said Sebastian, 'that Leonard knows quite well that nothing would induce me to leave my warm bed at dawn to practise croquet, and he is very concerned that we should do well enough to prevent Humphrey and Ned getting the doubles.'

'Not at all,' Leonard said. 'It's a matter of principle.'

'The conditions of the tournament are well know,' said Humphrey. 'There's an express agreement that anyone may practise if an interruption occurs in a match. Practice is only forbidden in the time before all the entrants have arrived.'

'I still say you've no right, no moral right, to do it,' Leonard said.

Humphrey swung his arms to and fro awkwardly.

'There's no point in saying things like that,' he said.

'Except that they happen to be true.'

The bald top of Humphrey's head suddenly flushed red. He glared at Leonard.

'You may be very good at business,' he said, 'but you've never had the faintest idea of the way a croquet week should be run, and that's flat.'

There was a moment of tense silence as Leonard looked at Humphrey with savage intensity. Penny half rose from the edge of the sofa.

Then Leonard abruptly glanced at his watch.

'I can't stay arguing here all night,' he said. 'You know my views. Humphrey, may I use the telephone in your study? I want to call Helen.'

'Certainly,' said Humphrey.

An air of dignity.

Leonard walked stiffly out.

Humphrey looked round as if he expected the room to be full of enemies to encounter. Finding nothing he sat down slowly. A deflating balloon.

Sebastian leant back in his chair and put the tips of his fingers together judiciously.

'Leonard never used to be ringing up Helen all the time,' he said.

'Why shouldn't he ring her up?' Penny said. 'After all she is his mistress.'

'We only have to read the papers to know that,' said Sebastian. 'But it was hardly my point. I only commented on the fact of your father's telephoning. As far as I remember on previous occasions he used to put his cares, his various cares, behind him when he came to Ambrose House.'

'I can't see what it's to do with you anyhow,' said Penny.

Sebastian smiled at her.

'The point was a little subtle,' he said, 'but nevertheless I thought your father's reference to Helen was plainly intended as a blow in his little encounter with Humphrey – and that was certainly conducted in front of us.'

'I don't know what you mean.'

'You must forgive us dons, my dear: we are apt to get rather too complicated thoughts. I simply meant that Leonard's dragging Helen into the conversation was his simple way of saying that he was a man of the world while Humphrey was incapable of even having a love affair with the matron.'

'Humphrey.'

Irene dropped the mass of royal blue knitting at her feet in hopeless confusion. She stood up.

'Humphrey,' she said. 'That I should find out like this. A chance remark in public.'

Humphrey peered at her.

'Bobbity,' he said, 'what on earth – ?'

'Now then,' said Irene.

Her purple prow rose high.

'Now then, it's no use trying to pretend I didn't hear, or that it wasn't said. Plainly said "Humphrey is having an affair with the matron".'

'But, no, bobbity – '

Suddenly heavy violent tears were coursing down Irene's square face. They fell on to her purple pullover and made a mottled patch of dampness.

'All the years,' she said, 'all the years we've been happy together and now this. Now I know why you said the other evening that divorce doesn't matter.'

She started to walk across the room in the direction of the door but her left foot caught in a loop of the royal blue wool at her feet and she was brought to a stop after two or three paces.

She looked down to see what was hampering her but apparently was unable to make out the strand of wool through her tears.

'Bobbity,' said Humphrey, 'this is all an absurd mistake.'

'It's too late to say that now. If you had come to me and told me you had made a mistake I might have understood and forgiven, but to hear it this way . . .'

'No.'

Humphrey shouted, sending the blood heavily into his face.

'No. You are making the mistake. Sebastian didn't say what you thought he did.'

Irene turned in the direction of Sebastian's chair.

'You said it, didn't you?' she said.

'My dear Irene, you must have heard what I said.'

'There.'

Irene turned back to Humphrey.

'It's the end,' she said.

She started forward again and was almost tripped up by the wool.

'Sebastian,' said Humphrey, 'for God's sake make her understand.'

His voice trailing away.

Sebastian spread his hands wide. The left one less than the right.

'My dear chap,' he said, 'no one has ever been able to do that.'

'But this is different. This is serious.'

'And Irene is the same,' Sebastian said.

Irene suddenly stooped, slipped the loop of wool off her foot, gathered up the rest of her knitting neatly and stood up again.

'It is the end, you know,' she said.

The quieter voice.

She walked slowly to the door, opened it and left them.

'Bobbity,' said Humphrey.

Nobody looked up.

Humphrey shook his bald head. A sea elephant emerging on to the ice.

'I – I'll go to her,' he said. 'What an absurd mistake.'

Promptly at 9 a.m. Rosalynn Peters rang, as she always did, the ship's bell that summoned everybody to breakfast.

As usual the party entered the dining-room all at about the same time. When Ned came in only Humphrey was absent. Ned looked round.

'Has anybody seen the paper?' he said. 'I'd like to know what's happening in Africa. It's a nasty situation they've got there.'

Michael Goodhart handed him the paper.

'It seems to be pretty quiet still, thank goodness,' he said.

'It isn't,' said Leonard, 'the very early news had more than the papers. There's been a lot of rioting.'

'Oh, this violence,' said Cicely, 'I can't understand it.'

'Rosalynn,' said Irene, 'draw the curtains. How often have I told you?'

'Sorry, madam,' Rosalynn said. 'I start in here before it's light outside and I kind of forget.'

'That's all right, my dear, but draw them now.'

Rosalynn went across to the window and reaching up as high as she could swished back the heavy blue curtains.

'Madam,' she said.

Everyone turned to look at her.

The two syllables conveying simply horror.

Rosalynn jerked her head towards the windows. They all stepped forward to look.

Humphrey Boddershaw was lying face downwards on the croquet court. His shining bald skull had an ugly bloody broken patch in its absolute centre. He could not have been alive. A blood-stained croquet mallet lay near him.

Chapter Eight

Ned and Michael Goodhart reached Humphrey at about the same moment. There could be no possible doubt close to that he had been murdered. A blow of considerable force had descended on the exact crown of his bald head.

A horrible parody of the effect the mulberry had made the day before.

Michael looked up.

'Hell,' he said, 'Irene's coming.'

He jumped to his feet and ran to intercept her. Ned ran back with him to the house. The others were standing in a bunch on the veranda.

'Keep everybody here, Seb,' Ned said. 'I'm going in to get the police.'

He pushed past them and in at the open french window of Humphrey's study.

Rosalynn Peters stood in the kitchen holding hard on to the edge of the big scrubbed table. Her face was completely without colour and shiny with perspiration.

She took a deep breath.

Slowly she relaxed her hold on the table and began to cross the big room to the door. A difficult journey. Dragging limbs.

She reached the door, fumbled with a sweaty hand at the knob, turned it and went outside. A few slow steps brought her round the house to the changing-room door and in. She leant against the door of the boothole for a moment and shut her eyes.

Then she heaved herself away from her support and tapped on the frosted glass of the door panel.

An impudent rhythmical phrase. The opening bars of 'Colonel Bogey'.

In a moment the glass panel was darkened by a shadow on the other side and then the door opened.

Rosalynn almost fell into the room and stood clutching at the shelf of one of the pigeon-holes. The linen name-tape glued to the edge of the shelf. Atkins.

She opened her mouth to speak but no sound came. Wearily she moistened her lips with her tongue. A duty to be performed against all inclination.

She tried to speak again.

'What – '

She forced herself to look at Bert.

'What did you do?'

'Do? What did I do?'

He came nearer her and peered down at her in the gloom.

She shrank away and then forced herself to look back up at him.

'Do you know what's happened?' he said.

'Bert, I saw him. Mrs B. told me to draw the curtains in the dining-room and I saw him lying there with his head ... Oh, Bert, what have you done?'

'Me?'

He looked down at her. Dully. Something too much to cope with.

'Why did you do it, Bert?' she said. 'Everything would have come out all right somehow.'

Hopeless regret. The moving finger writes and having writ ...

Slowly Bert shook his head.

'No,' he said. 'No, it wasn't me there. No.'

'Yes,' she said, 'you must have been out of your mind. It wasn't the real you. But this means you've got to be locked up for ever.'

'No,' said Bert.

'Oh, Bert, this was what I was afraid of all the time. That was why I – '

She began to cry. Quietly.

Bert put his hands on her shoulders. She did not flinch.

He spoke to her very slowly. A child piecing out a page of reading.

'I was in here,' he said. 'I was in here all the time. I was looking out. I was looking out of the window. I heard the noise of someone hitting the balls. It was very early. I looked out. I saw Mr B.'

Rosy was looking up at him between his outstretched arms. A look of pity.

'He was playing all by himself,' Bert went on. 'I stayed looking. And then I saw it.'

Rosy's eyes widened.

'Saw what?'

A whisper. Words too precious to say.

'I saw it.'

Bert shook his head. The spelled out lesson too difficult.

'Did you see someone else there?'

'Yes. That's right. Someone.'

'And was it them what – Was it them?'

'A hit on the head with one of the sticks.'

'One of the mallets?'

'Yes, that's right. Mallet.'

Bert stood in silence. Absorbing this.

Rosy stood, still between his thick arms, thinking.

'Bert,' she said, 'who was it?'

'Don't know.'

'Someone you've never seen?'

'No.'

A grudging admission.

'It was someone you knew then?'

No answer.

'Bert, you must tell me. Was it someone you know who did it?'

'I won't tell you.'

He turned away and stood in the far corner of the gloomy little room with his back towards her.

'But you have told me,' she said. 'You told me it wasn't a stranger. Isn't that what you told me?'

'All right.'

An admission.

Under torture.

Rosy was silent again. Then she said:

'Why haven't you told me who it was?'

Speaking carefully, humouringly.

'I won't.'

'But you must. It's – It's someone who's done a murder. You saw them. You must tell me who it was.'

Bert stood without moving in his corner. The obstinate angle of his shoulders.

Rosy looked at him. A glint of determination came into her eyes. Suddenly she ran across the little room, reached high up to Bert's shoulders and shook at them.

'Who was it? Who was it? Who was it?'

The squall beating on the cliff. Bert stood still and said nothing. After a while Rosy began stroking his back.

'I'm sorry,' she said.

Bert sat down on the slim bench running along the wall and put his head in his hands.

Rosy sat beside him.

'You don't want to speak about it,' she said, 'is that what it is?'

Bert nodded his head up and down without taking it from his hands.

'We'll leave it,' Rosy said.

Bert slowly looked up.

'We'll leave it for a bit anyhow,' Rosy said.

Bert shook his head.

'I can't say anything about it,' he said. 'Nothing never.'

The pale young man from *The South Sussex Trumpet and Messenger* looked diffidently into the bar.

'You're the chap,' said the up-and-comer from *The Daily Post*.

The pale youth stepped right inside.

'You're the chap who thought Bert Rogers wasn't violent. Good as told us we were wasting our time down here. What are you doing with the murder? Tucking it away as a village par?'

'No, we're giving it a good show. We can't lead with it, of course, there's the county council meeting.'

'Ah me,' said the man from *The Examiner*, 'we of the quality press have to pay for our privileges.'

'You aren't the only ones who have to pay,' said the old hand. 'That place is as hard to milk as an oyster. I don't like to think how much I've paid out in drinks to tradesmen and dear knows what else. And I haven't got much to show for it, to tell the truth.'

'Don't say *The World* is going to let us down tomorrow morning,' said the girl.

'It'll have a better story than you've got.'

The girl looked at her watch.

'They'll be eagerly examining *The Clarion* at *The World* offices at any minute now,' she said. 'I think it can be revealed that we've got an exclusive interview with Miss Rosalynn Peters.'

'I know,' said *The Examiner*, 'a film star.'

The girl lit another cigarette.

'Bert's girl friend as a matter of fact,' she said.

'Not bad,' said the up-and-comer. 'How did you get past the copper at the door?'

The girl smiled.

'There's times,' said the old hand, 'when I've thought of trying a bloody female impersonation act, only – '

'Only you haven't got the right curves, old sweet,' said the girl.

'Do you think I could get anything out of Rosy Peters?' said the pale youth. 'We were at school together.'

The up-and-comer from *The Daily Post* slipped off his stool and came and stood beside the pale youth.

'That's very interesting,' he said. 'What's she like?'

'I wouldn't bother,' said the girl. 'I didn't get much, but I did get a picture and every drop of background.'

'I'd have thought a girl like that would have been only too pleased to talk to *The Clarion*,' said *The Examiner*. 'Didn't you really get a lot?'

'You'll all hear when you ring your newsrooms,' the girl said. 'I got practically nothing that really mattered.'

The up-and-comer's eyes gleamed.

'Yes, yes, laddie,' said the girl, 'we know. There's something a bit fishy there like as not. We all start equal on that.'

'Fishy? You mean you think she knows something?' said the pale youth.

'Aren't you clever?' said the girl.

'Hid him up for a bit I dare say,' said the old hand. 'I wonder what the coppers will make of your piece in the morning, dear?'

'Don't know,' said the girl. 'They're not the Yard. It may not strike them that there was anything out of the ordinary. Anybody know anything about this chap Pinn?'

'He's got a bloody fine war record,' said the old hand. 'If you happen to see *The World* tomorrow you'll have the pleasure of reading all about it – M.C. and two bars. He led a bunch of commandos. Tough as you like.'

'But not a genius, as my old tutor used to say with a sad shake of his head?'

'He's jolly intelligent,' said the pale youth.

'My dear chap,' said *The Examiner*, 'I've no doubt the whole local police force is – er jolly intelligent. But it doesn't look to me as if a great deal of intelligence is going to be required. I should imagine the commando training will come in more useful.'

'Well,' said the up-and-comer, 'I'll be seeing you chaps.'

There was a series of bumps as the others slid off their bar-stools.

'If you're going to the police station,' said the old hand, 'we're coming.'

Dinner that evening at the long narrow table in the dining-room at Ambrose House was eaten almost in silence. Irene at the head of the table dished out large helpings to everybody but ate nothing herself. The others emptied their plates. There was nothing else to do. Afterwards they went and sat round the ugly stove for coffee. It was a cooler evening and Irene asked Rosalynn to light the fire laid in the stove. They sat and watched the flames take hold.

'Look, Irene,' said Michael Goodhart, 'are you really sure you want us all to stay?'

Irene glanced up from her sombre brooding in the chair nearest the fire.

'Yes,' she said, 'yes, please. I must have someone, you know.'

Leonard coughed.

'I think I mentioned this morning,' he said, 'that I may have to go. I've got to see Helen, or at least . . .'

110

'Of course, don't let me keep you if anything takes you away,' Irene said. 'I remember someone told me they might have to go. But – but I'm afraid I got in a muddle about who it was.'

Leonard looked as if he had something more to say, but he remained silent.

There came a tap at the door and Rosalynn came in.

'Please, madam, it's Superintendent Pinn, madam.'

Irene rose to her feet. Then she sat down again.

'No,' she said, 'show him in here, Rosalynn, dear. Perhaps some of you can help me if there's anything more he wants to know.'

Superintendent Pinn appeared in the doorway a moment later. His enormous frame blocking almost the whole arch.

'Good evening, madam,' he said. 'I'm afraid I've nothing much to report. But I thought I ought to keep you informed of the situation.'

'Thank you very much, Superintendent,' said Irene. 'It does help to know where one is. Will you join us in a cup of coffee?'

'Thank you, madam. That's very kind.'

The superintendent sat down. With care. His huge frame adjusting itself to the chair.

'Superintendent,' said Irene, 'are you sure that it was Bert? Has anything come to light?'

'No, madam, to be frank we've had no further information. Beyond some of a purely negative character. Our laboratories have examined the croquet mallet in question and confirm that it had been entirely wiped clean of fingerprints.'

'I see,' said Irene.

The superintendent stirred the tiny coffee cup nestling in his vast hand.

'No,' he said, 'Rogers must be found. That's the first thing. Until we've done that we've got nothing. It isn't even as if any of you heard anything to disturb you in the early hours, by what you have told me.'

He looked round the party. Nobody had any comment to make.

The superintendent drank off the little cup in a single swallow.

'Another cup, Mr Winn?' said Irene.

'Pinn, madam.'

'Oh, yes, of course, how stupid of me. Winn. Will you have coffee, Mr Winn?'

'No thank you, madam. I must be on my way. I was in course of making an inspection of my patrols. Thank you very much.'

The superintendent stood up. Towering towards the ceiling.

'I'll see you out,' said Irene.

'That's quite all right, madam. I am acquainted – '

But Irene had left her chair and stood waiting at the door. The superintendent followed her closing the door behind him with care.

'Yes,' said Sebastian, 'Irene with her usual directness has gone straight to the point.'

He leant his weight on his good elbow and eased his position in the deep leather armchair.

'The point?' said Leonard.

'Yes. The point being: is the superintendent sure that it was Bert? What if it wasn't?'

Chapter Nine

'What do you mean: if it wasn't Bert?' said Leonard.

Sebastian shifted in his chair again and smiled under the fox-red moustache.

'I only suggested that the superintendent isn't assuming necessarily that all he has to do is to catch his hare.'

'That was what he told us, though,' said Michael. 'His actual words were something like "Rogers must be found".'

'Yes, indeed,' said Sebastian, 'and he went on to indicate that he had to be found for questioning. And after that he said a very significant thing.'

'He was perfectly respectful, I was glad to notice,' said Cicely, 'but I didn't hear him say anything particularly significant. I remember thinking that it would be a good thing if more policemen had his manner nowadays. The young man who spoke to me while I was driving down here was positively insolent. I had to let him know a thing or two. Young man, I said, I was driving before you were born and everyone has always agreed that I'm a superb driver. He made some impertinent remark. I forget what it was.'

'Probably he told you he was going to give you another summons,' said Penny.

'Another summons. You speak as if I was one of those reckless modern drivers who ought to be kept off the roads for life. He may have mentioned something about a summons, but he was only trying to scare me. I know that type. They can see you're a lady and try to get their own back. When the summons comes I shall simply tear it up.'

Peke Abou jumped off her lap and growled menacingly at an imaginary figure in front of the ugly stove.

'Is nobody going to ask me what the superintendent's significant remark was?' said Sebastian.

'I certainly am,' said Ned. 'All this talk. Oh, jeez.'

'He asked us if we had been disturbed in the early hours,' said Sebastian.

'I can't see that that was particularly significant,' said Leonard.

'Oh, but it is,' said Ned. 'Don't you see that it is? He was actually asking us if we'd been up at the time it happened. We none of us said that we had. If Bert Rogers isn't their man it's good odds that one of us was lying, that one of us was up, that one of us is to blame.'

Rosalynn Peters, her face blotchily tear-stained, left her pert little high-heeled shoes at the door of the main kitchen and crept into the pantry. She went on tiptoe to the wide table underneath the serving hatch, tested her weight on it to see that it did not creak, and then carefully heaved her whole short body up on to it. She slid herself slowly across it until her ear, with its ear-ring in the form of a lantern, was touching the thin panel of the serving hatch itself.

She closed her eyes in relief. Every word that the superintendent was saying in the dining-room could be plainly heard.

'. . . afraid she almost certainly does know something, but she's got a will of her own and I could get nothing out of her. I'll give her a bit more rope.'

'I hope you treated her kindly,' came Mrs B.'s voice. 'She's such a tiny little thing.'

Rosy grinned.

'She may be small in stature,' replied the superintendent, 'but, if I may say so, she's too big for her boots. She knows something all right, but she'll use every dodge she can to keep it to herself.'

Rosy nodded silent agreement.

'But why have you suddenly started to suspect all this this morning? That's what I don't understand,' Mrs B. asked him.

'I don't suppose you've read today's *Clarion*,' answered the superintendent, 'but they carried an interview with the girl – about which I may say one of my constables is going to get into considerable trouble – and it was plain from that that Miss

Peters knew something and was going to say as little as she could in case she let out more than she meant to.'

'I thought there was something odd about that bit,' came Ned Farran's voice. 'I meant to tease the kid about it, but I haven't seen her all day.'

'She's keeping out of the way I dare say,' the superintendent replied. 'And she's just been spending a pretty uncomfortable half hour shut up with myself and a constable in the study.'

Rosy put her little pink tongue out.

'Very well, Superintendent' – Mrs B. again – 'if you're convinced of this you must act as you think fit.'

'Thank you, madam. I trust we shan't put you to any inconvenience.'

Rosy's eyes flicking to and fro with anxiety.

The sound of movement from the room on the other side of the hatch. Rosy began to ease herself off the table. Then she abruptly changed her mind and recklessly pushed her ear hard up against the panel once more.

The superintendent's voice.

'. . . sorry, sir, but I must refuse. I won't have any civilian nearer than I must, if we do find him I can't rule out violence.'

'All right, if you . . .'

Without waiting to hear anything more Ned Farran had to say Rosy slipped down, ran in her nyloned feet back to the kitchen and out again by the door leading to the changing room and the boothole.

As she tapped the 'Colonel Bogey' signal on the door she heard the long shrill note from a whistle somewhere just outside the house.

Bert was quick to let her in.

'What's up for crikey's sake,' he said. 'I saw a couple of rozzers out on the field.'

'They won't be the only ones,' said Rosy. 'It's a big search. That Pinn suspects something.'

Bert's eyes glinted.

'Let 'em come,' he said.

'No, no. That's not the way. We'll have to play it crafty or you won't last ten minutes. You'll never be able to fight your way out of this.'

'I'll smash a few first though.'

'No, Bert, don't say that sort of thing. Not now. Stick with me and we'll dodge the lot.'

A moment of doubt. Then Bert said:

'All right. I trust you, Rosy.'

'Come on, then,' said Rosy. 'They'll certainly want to poke their noses in here.'

She opened the boothole door and looked carefully either way. At the glass-panelled door leading to the playing-field a dark shadow appeared.

Rosy pushed Bert back and quietly swung the boothole door to again. They stood one on each side of it, flattened against the neat rows of empty pigeon-holes.

The sound of heavy steps. Regulation boots.

Bert lifted his hand with the index finger raised.

'Only one.'

Violently Rosy shook her head.

The steps came nearer.

Bert shrugged.

The constable stopped outside. The silhouette of his helmet easy to see through the frosted glass.

Bert moved a little away from the pigeon-holes and crouched slightly.

Rosy's eyes fell on the gymshoe doorstop. They had both forgotten to replace it.

A distant shout.

The constable moved quickly away.

Equally quickly Rosy opened the door and peered out after him. The moment he was out of sight round the corner she beckoned to Bert to follow her. They glided through the changing room and back into the kitchen.

'We'll have to get upstairs and do the same as last time,' Rosy whispered.

Bert ran across to the window keeping low to avoid being seen from outside. He stood at the side of the window and gradually moved his head until he could look out.

He drew back sharply.

'Three of them at the gate,' he said.

'It's upstairs or nothing,' said Rosy.

116

A fierce whisper.

'I'll go ahead,' she said, 'and if the coast's clear I'll sing something. You follow. Straight up the back stairs.'

'Okay.'

Rosy left him.

He stood behind the kitchen door waiting.

A long silence.

His eyes flicked nervously round the big room, coming to rest every time on the back door opposite to where he was standing. On the big scrubbed kitchen table there was a bowl of potatoes which Rosy had been peeling. A sharp little knife lay beside it.

Bert darted over and picked it up.

He listened.

Still silence.

He looked down at the short blade in his hand and back up at the door opposite. His grip on the knife handle tightened.

Suddenly Rosy's voice. High and slightly cracked.

> *'It's still the same old story,*
> *A fight for love and glory,*
> *A case of do-or-die,*
> *As time goes by.'*

For a moment Bert did not move. He glared at the back door. Then he turned swiftly to the door beside him and opened it. There was no one in sight. He ran almost noiselessly through to the bottom of the back stairs.

Where he had been standing in the kitchen lay the little sharp knife.

Bert listened again.

From the top of the stair well Rosy's voice floated down. Singing with effort.

> *'Tum ti ti ti tee*
> *And man must have his mate*
> *Tum ti ti . . .'*

Two at a time Bert began climbing the stairs. At the top Rosy was waiting for him, leaning in the doorway of her own room.

'It's okay,' she said. 'No one up here at all. Come on. '

Bert slipped into the room.

'Got something to hide my hands again?' he said.

'Same old bikini,' said Rosy.

'Okay.'

Bert went quickly to the window and looked out.

Slowly he turned back into the room.

'No go,' he said.

'What do you mean?'

'Half a dozen rozzers out there on the field,' said Bert.

Apathy.

Rosy went to the window and looked out.

'All right,' she said, 'we'll think of something else.'

Bert ran across to the door and jerked it half an inch open.

'A bit too late,' he said.

On the stairs the sound of several pairs of heavy feet.

At each landing one of the three constables climbing the back stairs called out quietly. Then they all waited until an answer came from the men coming up the stairs at the front. This and the thudding of their boots on the stairs were the only sounds they made. While they waited they glanced about, looking for the first unexpected movement.

Just as the signal came to mount the last flight of stairs up to the servants' quarters in the attics there was the noise of feet on the stairs in front of them. The three men stiffened and peered up into the gloom above.

A trim pair of legs in nylons. Above them the neat chocolate brown of the Ambrose House maids' uniform.

The constables relaxed.

The maid and the man from the school domestic staff in his matching chocolate brown uniform came on down the stairs. The constables stood aside for them to pass.

'Been hiding anybody under your bed?' said one of them.

The maid giggled.

The constables turned and went up the narrow stairs in single file. Grim-faced again.

They ate mulberries for lunch without remembering the berry that had hit Humphrey on the head.

Leonard helped himself to cream.

He gestured with the little silver jug over towards the mantelpiece.

'By the way,' he said, 'don't bother about that, Irene. I'll take it into somewhere in the town this afternoon and get them to do what's necessary.'

'I don't seem to understand,' said Irene. 'I generally grasp things without difficulty. I suppose I must be tired.'

'I don't understand either,' said Michael.

Sebastian leant across and took the cream jug from Leonard.

'He means the trophy,' he said. 'He is kindly undertaking to have his name engraved on one of those little shields on the base.'

'But he hasn't won it,' said Cicely. 'The terms of the competition were perfectly clear. I saw to that when we first decided on it all those years ago. It's terribly important always to be absolutely clear on a matter of that sort. Otherwise unpleasant squabbles always arise. But there's no danger of that this time. I was utterly firm.'

Taking advantage of her interest in something other than her food Peke Abou tried a tentative nibble at a mulberry. He choked.

'Abou, what are you doing, sir? Get down this instant. You bad, bad dog. If there's one thing I will not tolerate it's thieving from the table.'

Abou disappeared into the blackness under the table.

'You know,' said Sebastian, 'I think Leonard has actually won the trophy. He claims, I suppose, that Michael and I must be presumed to have won the last match of the doubles. That means that no partnership won three clear victories and thus with Penny he scored most points and can add the doubles contest to the singles.'

'But this is nonsense,' said Michael. 'I don't know why it's being discussed at all. Surely the whole doubles competition is called off.'

'No, I don't think so,' Sebastian said. 'Leonard has actually taken it for granted that Michael and I claim a victory, but in the circumstances I'm delighted to do that.'

'I'm afraid I must say that I'm not,' Michael said.

'Oh come,' said Sebastian, 'the spectacle of Leonard being so concerned about the trophy is surely worth risking a little bad taste for.'

'I don't think we ought to go on with this a moment longer.' Michael said. 'I do not claim any victory.'

'Ah,' said Sebastian, 'but I do. And I am the captain of our team. Well, Cicely, what do the rules you were so firm about have to say about that?'

'It wasn't an eventuality anyone thought of,' said Cicely.

She concentrated on her mulberries.

'I think Leonard is right,' said Irene.

She looked round at them all.

'Humphrey would have wanted him to have the trophy,' she said. 'It's always the custom for a game in which one of the players withdraws to go to the other. That's what would be right now.'

'My dear Irene,' said Leonard, 'I ought never to have mentioned the matter. I did it with the best intentions. I – I thought that things should go on as before. I thought it would be better that way.'

'Abou,' said Cicely.

Shocked tones.

They all turned to see what was the matter.

Cicely was peering underneath the table.

From near one of the legs a wide trickle was running towards the door.

Chapter Ten

Back in the boothole Bert slowly took off his old handyman's uniform.

'I'd rather have bashed all three of 'em,' he said.

'Fat lot of good that would have done,' said Rosy.

Brisk as a new broom.

Bert groaned.

'Walking right past three coppers in a row,' he said. 'Don't ask me to do it again. In another second there'd have been an exploseration.'

'Go on,' said Rosy. 'You never turned a hair. If you can do a thing like that and keep calm about it, I don't know what they want to go locking you up for.'

Bert looked round the boothole. He ran his finger over the linen name-tapes stuck under the pigeon-holes.

'Smithson,' he said, 'is that little blighter still here?'

'Getting quite a big boy now,' said Rosy. 'Leaving at the end of the year I dare say.'

'Always used to be on at me to play cards with him,' Bert said. 'Mad on cards he was.'

'They're always having these crazes,' Rosy said. 'It was marbles last term. Trod on the blessed things wherever you went.'

'I told him I couldn't play. But he kept on at me. In the end I gave in. Snap, that was what we played. We used to go down the bottom of the playing-field, behind the pavilion.'

He sat down on the narrow bench and rubbed his legs.

'Here,' he said, 'could you get us a pack of cards? If I'm going to be cooped up in here much longer I'll go stark raving mad without something to do.'

The implication of sanity.

Rosy smiled.

'All right,' she said, 'there'll be some in the games cupboard, but I haven't got time to come playing cards.'

'Oh, go on. You can spare half an hour or so sometimes. We could play Snap. I haven't played it since I was here.'

'I'll see,' said Rosy.

'What's up? You sound browned off all of a sudden.'

'I don't know.'

'What's there to be worried about? We got past them, didn't we? They won't come poking in here again. We're in the clear.'

'Don't be a fool, Bert Rogers.'

A blaze of anger.

'Don't be a fool,' she said. 'Do you think all our troubles are over just because we dodged past a lot of thick-head rozzers?'

'Well – '

'Well, you're wrong. They've only just begun. What happens next? Have you thought of that? Somebody killed old Mr B., don't you forget it. You can't put on a uniform and dodge past that.'

Bert stood up. Suddenly.

'Don't talk like that,' he said.

'And why not?'

'Because I might teach you a lesson, that's why not.'

'You teach me a lesson? I like that. Listen, without me you'd be finished in a day. In half an hour. Don't you try any of those tricks on me or we'll see how you get on on your own.'

'May be I'd get on a sight better on my own.'

'Oh yes, and how?'

'May be it would have been better if I'd had a bash at those rozzers on the stairs. I had 'em where I wanted 'em. Coming up those narrow stairs one after the other looking up into the dark like a lot of silly old women. I'd have been through 'em before they knew I was there.'

'Yes, and what then? What about all the rest of 'em? There must have been about fifty round the place. But I suppose fifty coppers is nothing to you.'

'There wouldn't have been fifty by the time I'd finished with 'em.'

'Oh no, Mr Cleverpants would go and do a copper. Not content with doing the only person whoever behaved decent to him he'd go and do a copper and swing for it.'

Bert wheeled round and caught her by the shoulders.

'What do you mean?' he said. 'What do you mean do the only person whoever behaved decent to me? Do you think I killed old Mr B., is that it?'

'Well, didn't you?'

Bert's grip tightened on her shoulders. She wriggled but his fingers merely closed harder on the thin cotton of her uniform.

'Let go. You're hurting.'

'Hurting? I've a good mind to – '

He dropped his hands and stood moving his head slowly from side to side.

'No,' he said. 'No. I wouldn't do that. I wouldn't.'

He looked at Rosy standing rubbing her right shoulder.

'You believe me, don't you?' he said. 'I wouldn't hurt you.'

'Oh, Bert,' she said.

She went to him and reached up to kiss him. He put his arm round her waist and lifted her. When he put her down again she said:

'I didn't mean all that.'

'I don't blame you,' he said. 'It's only natural to think that. But I didn't do it.'

He looked steadily at her.

'I didn't do it,' he said. 'I didn't do it. I didn't do it. You've got to believe that. I'm telling you I didn't kill him.'

'I have got to believe it,' she said.

Something in her quiet acceptance startled him. He turned away and peered through the frosted-glass panel of the door.

'What are you getting at?' he said.

'Just that I have got to believe you when you said you didn't kill Mr B. If I didn't believe you I wouldn't be able to go on with this. And somehow we're going to get away together. We must. So I've got to believe you didn't do it, haven't I?'

She walked across to him and pulled him away from the door.

'Oh, Ned,' said Irene Boddershaw, 'I don't know what I feel. If they had found Bert we might know. But what would I feel like? You never saw him, but he was really such a nice fellow. He was quite simple and always devoted to Humphrey. I can't believe he did that.'

'He had that temper,' said Ned. 'You've got to face facts.'

'Oh yes, I know. What he did to that man in the fight before they took him away was inexcusable, but he was learning to control himself. That was the pity of it. He was beginning for the first time to come to grips with his difficulties. It was wonderful in a way to see it. And has it all come to this?'

'We don't definitely know what it has come to.'

Irene looked up sharply from the miserable depths of her armchair.

'You mean it may not have been Bert?' she said.

'Listen,' said Ned, 'I'm not going around saying it wasn't him.'

'No. But you're not convinced that it was, are you? And I'm not either. I think that man, What's-his-name, Superintendent Winn – '

'Pinn. Pinn. Let's get that right anyhow.'

Ned pushed a hand through his wiry hair.

'Whatever he's called,' Irene said. 'I think he's got hold of the wrong end of the stick somewhere. I find as I go through life that that's half the trouble with the world: people get hold of the wrong end of the stick about so many things. They do violence to the facts, that's what it amounts to. And I'm willing to believe that it happens anywhere. Just because he's a superintendent of police he's no exception.'

'I can sympathize with that,' Ned said. 'It's something I've noticed over here. The way middle-class Englishmen always assume the police are right. I'm very happy to assume they're not.'

'Exactly,' said Irene. 'So I want you to see Mr Winn and tell him quite plainly that they're to stop looking for Bert. The poor boy's been chased and harried enough.'

'But – '

'Now there's no need to make difficulties. The only reason I'm asking you to do this is because when I mentioned the matter myself to Mr Winn – '

'Pinn.'

'Mr Winn wouldn't listen to me. Oh, he pretended to. But I could see quite well that he was just humouring me. I dare say he's one of those men that think all women are fools – when of course it's very much the other way about. In any case he'll listen to you. You're a sensible person, Ned. I've always thought so.'

124

'Jeez, but listen, Mrs Boddershaw, have you thought what it means if Bert didn't do it?'

'Certainly I have. It means someone else did. And the police are never going to find them if they go making poor Bert's life a perfect misery.'

'It means a bit more than that.'

Irene swung her formidable bosom towards him. Her black dress was old-fashioned and rather too small.

'You're beginning to humour me,' she said.

'You're too right, I am,' said Ned. 'Listen, just relax and let me do it. Let me persuade you to leave things as they are.'

'Don't be silly, Mr Farran. That might have been all very well when I had Humphrey to take care of things for me in his own clumsy way. But I can't let things slide like that now. I should never see daylight if I did.'

'All right,' said Ned, 'I guess I'd have had to have told you sooner or later, if you didn't see it for yourself.'

'Well?'

'Well, if Bert isn't the murderer, then it's odds on that it's one of the croquet party. We were the ones who knew Humphrey was going to be out there all alone early in the morning practising. One of us is the most likely person to have come up quietly behind him that way. Of course, it could have been a stray madman . . .'

'Do you think it was?'

'No.'

'Then who do you think it was?'

'I'll tell you who's quite likely to find out,' said Ned.

'Superintendent Pinn – no, that's not right – Superintendent Winn, I suppose.'

'Exactly. The police are in a position to find out about these things.'

'But all he's doing is to chase poor Bert.'

'He has to find out whether he's around, and if so what he was doing early yesterday morning. But I don't think that is all he's doing.'

Irene got up and walked up and down. The black dress stretched too tight.

'Whatever happens, how shall I know?' she said.

'There'll be a trial,' said Ned. 'That's the way they do these things – have a trial.'

'But they're so likely to get it all the wrong way round.'

'Not so likely. For heaven's sake, don't make it worse.'

'But almost everybody gets everything quite wrong. In these last few years I've begun to notice it.'

Ned smiled.

'Listen, in the end you have to accept the wrong for right,' he said. 'The majority view.'

'Of course you do,' said Irene. 'Haven't I been doing that over countless things every day of my life? But this isn't one of the countless things. This is who killed my husband. I want to know the truth about this.'

'We'll hope that you get to know it. I don't see what's to stop you. Take it easy.'

She halted her restless prowling in front of Ned and said:

'Ned, will you find out who did it!'

'No,' said Ned.

A statement.

'But you must.'

'How would you be sure in the end that whatever I happened to tell you was the truth?' Ned said.

'I think I can trust you,' said Irene.

Ned spread his arms wide.

'What about the first eleven cricket shirts?' he said.

'Oh,' Irene said, 'you were right about that. They did put them to the wash. Didn't I ever tell you?'

'There were other things,' said Ned.

'You're my best hope.'

Irene turned and walked back to her chair. She had to stop herself as she slumped into it and wait while she hitched up the tight black skirt to stop it splitting.

'I'll keep my eyes open,' said Ned.

He closed his eyes tight, and shook his head fiercely.

'You're very quiet this afternoon, chum,' said the up-and-comer from *The Daily Post*.

'Um,' said the old hand.

'Yes, you know,' *The Examiner* man said, 'you're quite right. He's not with us. The mind elsewhere, as my old – '

'I know what it is, chum,' said the up-and-comer, 'he's brooding. He got a rocket from his news editor over not getting an interview with that girl and he's taken it to heart.'

The old hand sank his face in his tankard.

'You want to take my example, chum,' said the up-and-comer. 'I got a rocket, but do I worry? No, I make up my mind to beat you all on to something good. So cheer up, chum.'

'Hm,' said the old hand.

'Come on,' said the girl, 'tell us about it. You've got a story.'

'Like hell – '

The girl kissed the old hand's ear as he bent to his tankard again.

'You're sweet,' she said. 'Like hell you'll tell us about it. All right. But don't go on pretending there's nothing to tell.'

'If you're so sure I'm on to something just look in *The World* tomorrow morning,' the old hand said.

'Oh, I say,' *The Examiner* said, 'do you mean I've been beaten to it again? You know when they decided to send me on this story I had grandiose notions of doing better than you people in your own field. But I seem to be doing rather badly on the whole. Tell me, this big thing you're on to, is it an *Examiner* story?'

The old hand thought for a moment.

'Yes,' he said, 'police inefficiency. I should think even *The Examiner* would like that.'

'Alas,' said *The Examiner*, 'they would.'

'Police inefficiency, eh?' said the up-and-comer, 'now I wonder . . .'

'All there in front of your eyes,' the old hand said. 'As far as I remember you all made the point this morning that there was only one maid at the school for this week. Any of you could have talked to the same bobbies as I did after the big search this morning. And if you had, they would have mentioned what they saw to you just as they mentioned it to me. And then you would have had this story too. Too bad.'

Sebastian Skuce had taken his deck-chair round to the side

of the house. He had carefully placed it in the most advantage-ous position and he had settled down comfortably to enjoy him-self.

Ned came and sat down beside him on the grass.

'Is this the next best thing to watching croquet, then?' he asked.

Sebastian turned and looked at him.

'Ah, Ned,' he said.

He turned back to his diversion again.

'Well,' he said, 'do you share my interest?'

Ned looked for a moment at the scene in front of him.

'There's something to be said for watching other blokes sweat their guts out,' he said, 'but on the whole I'd rather be doing something myself.'

Sebastian shook his head sadly.

'You haven't an idea,' he said. 'You may be an excellent schoolmaster – though somehow I doubt if you envisage spend-ing your life at it – '

'Too right,' said Ned.

'But you'll never make a building-site watcher,' said Sebastian.

They sat and looked at The Towers. Work had been going on fast since the roof had begun to come off at about the time the croquet tournament had started. Two men stripped to the waist were now standing on the top of the outer wall. One had a pick and the other a sledge-hammer and they were swinging heavy blows at the compact red brick under their feet. At the first blow the wall seemed hardly affected. A bright star of clean brick simply showed where it had been struck. The next heavy blow on the same spot sent a thin black crack running across one or two bricks and along the mortar between others. One more knock and a large piece of wall toppled easily over into the derelict interior of the house.

'My life is a very quiet one,' Sebastian said. 'I have the happi-ness to teach a dead language which fewer and fewer people are interested in learning. We do our best to liven things up with a few virulent little college controversies, but I must admit we seldom succeed in really stirring the surface of our almost stagnant pond. So to see people well and truly smashing something up is a rare pleasure.'

Ned looked up at him from the damp grass. From in front of them somewhere inside the ruined house a pneumatic drill suddenly broke into violent life.

Ned had to speak loudly to be sure of being heard.

'Did you get any pleasure out of seeing your old friend Humphrey smashed up?' he said.

Sebastian twisted sharply round in his deck-chair and then lifted himself slowly up a little to ease his weak side.

'No,' he said, 'of course I didn't. You aren't by any chance thinking, are you, that – '

The pneumatic drill stopped as abruptly as it had begun.

'That I killed him?' said Sebastian.

In the silence it sounded almost as if he was shouting.

'Okay,' said Ned, 'did you?'

'Bert Rogers is supposed to have killed him.'

'I'm asking if you did.'

Sebastian smiled.

'I may live a pretty quiet life,' he said, 'but that doesn't mean that I'm not in my own way quite tough. Bullying like that won't produce any dramatic confession.'

'Oh, come on, shake it up. Did you or didn't you?'

'No. As a matter of fact I didn't.'

A small piece of masonry from the top of The Towers fell outwards instead of inwards. It hurtled down on to a window frame lying propped against the wall. There was a huge crash of breaking glass.

'So you're not satisfied with the orthodox view of this business?' said Sebastian.

'Oh, cut that out,' Ned said. 'Neither are you. You were the one who suggested that there might be more to it than met the eye.'

'Ah, but that was only a little bit of mischief. I happened to notice that the deceptively unintelligent-looking Superintendent Pinn was guarding himself in case anything went wrong when he found Bert Rogers, and I couldn't resist drawing attention to it.'

'Then you think it was Bert Rogers? And no hedging. I can't stand this trick of never answering a straight question.'

'You don't have to tell me that.'

'There you are: you're doing it again. I don't want your comments on my feelings. I want to know if you think Bert Rogers killed Humphrey. Well?'

'I can't see any reason to think otherwise. Though given a chance I'd be happy to.'

Ned caught hold of a tuft of grass and jerked it savagely out of the ground. The drilling began again on the other side of the battered wall.

'I suppose that that's the nearest you can get to saying "Yes" right out,' he said. 'All right. Well, I can think of one very good reason why Bert Rogers isn't so much as an even money chance.'

With the noise of the drill still dinning in their ears Sebastian contented himself with raising an eyebrow.

'Did you hear what Pinn said about the mallet?' Ned asked.

An affirmative shake of the head.

'No fingerprints. Don't try to tell me that a poor dope straight out of Broadmoor is going to bother with fancy stuff like wiping off fingerprints. Don't tell me that.'

'I won't tell you.'

'Good. Then you can start thinking about who else killed Humphrey. Let's hear it.'

Sebastian leant back in his deck-chair and placed his fingertips slowly together. He sat in silence. Ned tore a blade of grass into minute fragments. The racket of the drill went on uninterruptedly. The men balancing on the wall swung away at it steadily. The noise of the falling chunks of brickwork could just be heard above the drilling.

Sebastian crooked his forefinger and beckoned Ned nearer. Ned leapt to his feet and dropped down to crouch with his head beside Sebastian's. He rocked up and down on his heels. Waiting for the off.

'You know what Humphrey is, or should I say was?' Sebastian said.

'Was. Was. Is. Is. What's it matter?'

'Perhaps it doesn't. And in any case I flatter myself that you don't know the answer to my question.'

'Come on, I'll buy it. I don't know. You win. Let's have it.'

Sebastian joined his fingertips again. Deliberately.

'He was the Fool King.'

130

'The fool what?'

'King.'

Ned shot to his feet.

'All right,' he said, 'I know you've got an idea behind it all. So stop the mystification. Give it to me straight out.'

Sebastian smiled.

'If only you wouldn't be so obviously impatient,' he said, 'I'd be able to refrain from teasing you.'

'Come on, shake it up.'

'Ah well. It is part of my duties as a lecturer in classics to be aware of the anthropological significance of a great deal of my material. So perhaps modern parallels to it are particularly easy for me to spot.'

Ned clenched his fists.

'And Humphrey,' Sebastian went on, 'provided a really startling instance of an age-old custom coming to life again in a contemporary setting. The dear chap was after all a clown. It is the only word, the obvious word. He was a physical fool. He couldn't do the ordinary things without breaking something or getting himself into some sort of trouble.'

'All the same,' said Ned, 'he was quite a bright boy. I'm not swallowing just anything, you know.'

'Oh, I know,' said Sebastian, 'Humphrey took quite a good degree and all that. But it doesn't alter the fact that he was physically and temperamentally a clown. He blundered into everything.'

'All right, all right. So he was a clown.'

Ned jabbed his forefinger at the top of Sebastian's chair. Above them a sledge-hammer blow sent rays of cracks shooting along the solid brickwork of the wall.

'You don't know about the ancient custom of electing a clownish character to be king for a limited period?' said Sebastian.

Ned frowned quickly.

'Yes, yes,' he said. 'I think I've read about it now you come to mention it, but – '

'Well, what used to happen to the king at the end of his short reign?'

'Oh yes,' said Ned. 'It comes back. They often killed him.'

'Exactly,' said Sebastian.

Chapter Eleven

Ned swung round in front of Sebastian. The drilling from inside The Towers ceased. From round the corner of the school behind them came the sound of a bird singing in the mulberry tree.

'All right,' Ned said, 'I admit Humph fitted into this picture of the clown being king over everything here for the week of the croquet. And he was killed right enough. So what does that mean? You've got to face up to your own facts. Are you telling me that you and everybody else banded together to sacrifice him?'

Sebastian's eyes gleamed under his foxy red eyebrows.

'Do you think I could convince Superintendent Pinn of that?' he asked.

'Okay, okay, okay,' said Ned. 'It isn't very likely. But what is likely? What's your idea? Let's have it.'

Sebastian leant back in his deck-chair again.

'It's going to be a little disappointing,' he said.

'Never mind, get on with it.'

'It had simply occurred to me that one of our party might have consciously or unconsciously taken on the role of executioner.'

Ned stood thinking for a moment. His lips moving impatiently.

'I suppose they'd rationalize it all,' he said.

'It would be a sensible precaution,' said Sebastian. 'Otherwise people would think they were mad.'

'Well, who are you thinking of?'

'Nobody, really. I contrived to entertain some suspicions of Leonard when he seemed so keen to get away, but I gathered from Irene not long ago that he has changed his mind. She told me he had dispatched some rather fierce telegram to his Helen and that he was staying on.'

'And that's the total of your suspicions?'

'Yess. I make it, in round figures, zero.'

Ned glanced at the men chopping away at the wall of The Towers opposite.

'I must be going,' he said. 'But you would agree that it would be no surprise if Bert Rogers turns out to have been nowhere near at the time of the murder?'

'That wouldn't create a very new situation to my mind, certainly.'

Ned ran quickly up the steps on to the veranda and headed for the french windows.

'*Grüss Gott,*' said Penny.

Ned stopped and wheeled round.

'Hello,' he said. 'I didn't see you there.'

Penny pushed herself up from the faded green canvas cushion tucked away in the darkest corner of the veranda.

'You weren't meant to see me,' she said. 'Nobody was.'

'If you're not meant to be seen you shouldn't go about saying things like that. What was it anyway?'

'*Grüss Gott?* It's German actually.'

'You surprise me. What's it mean?'

'God greet thee, I think.'

'You should have said "hello". You're all the same. You must make things complicated. Why do you do it?'

'You're quite right,' said Penny. 'You are different from the rest. That's why I spoke to you.'

Ned sat down on one of the deck-chairs littered about the veranda. Sun-bleached stripes.

'I take it you meant to say something more than *Grüss Gott,*' he said.

'Oh yes. Yes, I did.'

Penny stood looking at the dusty concrete. Gradually she fell into a gawky attitude, her weight all on one foot and her hands swinging loosely.

'Look,' Ned said, 'I'm sorry, but I hate this. Spit it out. Shake it up. If you've got something to say, say it.'

'It's a bit difficult to think of how to put it.'

'Then don't think. Just speak, say words, talk.'

The flicking impatient gestures.

'All right.'

A decision arrived at.

Penny walked towards Ned's chair and stood leaning against one of the posts that supported the veranda roof. Poised.

'I've been worried,' she said. 'Terribly worried.'

'Yes?'

Ned looked up at her.

'Oh, Ned,' she said, 'you're the only one I can talk to. You don't know how worried I've been.'

'All right. Talk then.'

'Ned, I think you can help me.'

She flopped forward on to her knees and down into a sitting position at his feet. She glanced down and flicked her skirt out into a swirl.

'Will you help me?' she said.

'Yeah, yeah. Of course. But come on, what's the trouble?'

'Oh, I knew you would.'

Big eyes blinking up at him.

'All right. Give, shoot, fire away.'

She looked down.

'Ned,' she said, 'do you remember that awful row I had with Humphrey when he wouldn't do anything about those shares?'

Ned jumped to his feet.

'Oh, that's it, is it?' he said. 'Hell, you needn't trouble yourself about that. Everybody has rows. Just because the bloke you had one with gets killed, you don't have to go torturing yourself. Cheer up. Cheer up.'

'Oh, don't be a sausage.'

Penny jumped up. She failed to notice now that her skirt had got caught up on itself at the hem.

'A – a sausage?' said Ned.

'Yes. Well, I mean of all the idiots. Oh, but I suppose you were right really. I say, I'm awfully sorry I called you that. Only I thought I was doing it all so well, and then you go and get the wrong end of the stick. And it was difficult.'

Ned sat down again.

'Look,' he said, 'suppose you try it without the trimmings. What is the trouble?'

'It was what I said to him. Don't you remember?'

'You were pretty sore, but I don't remember anything outstanding.'

Penny's eyes widened.

'But I said to him "I could kill you for this".'

A near wail.

'Yes, I suppose you did. Something like that anyway. I remember thinking at the time that there must be a bit of devil under that English miss look.'

'Oh.'

Penny blinked.

'Oh, Ned,' she said. 'Ned, now you see what a terrible situation I'm in, you will help me, won't you, Ned?'

Ned shot up from his chair. He thrust his face towards Penny's and stuck out his tongue.

'Hey,' she said.

'All right, but don't break into that routine again. You're not bad at it, but I've seen it all before.'

'Oh, all right. But it wasn't bad, was it?'

'Listen, just how worried are you? Give it to me straight.'

The light faded from Penny's eyes.

'Yes,' she said, 'I am worried. I really am. That's why I was sitting in a huddle there keeping out of everyone's way – when I said *Grüss Gott*.'

'And you were worried because you said what you did to Humph? Nothing else?'

'No. But when you think of it, that's enough, isn't it?'

Ned plunged his face into his hands and sat for two seconds in thought.

'Yes, ' he said, 'it's a pity you used those words. Or it may turn out to be.'

'If what Sebastian said about Bert Rogers is true?'

'Correct weight.'

'And is it true? Or do you think he did do it after all? Is he still lurking about somewhere?'

'We'll find out, sport. He won't last for ever. He was put away because he wasn't very bright: he isn't going to dodge the whole police force for too long. We've just got to wait, that's all. And then we'll know.'

Ned looked up at her. Ruefully.

'As if I'm the one to give lessons in patience.'

'And if – If they find for some reason that Bert didn't – didn't kill Uncle Humphrey, what then?'

'Then it looks as if one of the party here might have done.'

'Almost must have done, isn't it? Because of knowing he'd be out on the lawn so early.'

'Yes.'

'And then if someone tells the police I said what I did.'

'Someone will, you know.'

'Sebastian? He's terribly cruel at times, but – '

'Probably not Sebastian. He'll be getting too much pleasure out of seeing who's first of the others to tell them.'

'And when the police do know?'

'They'll want to talk to you.'

Ned looked up at her sharply.

'What'll you have to tell them?' he said.

Penny's unsmiling face. Woebegone.

'All I can tell them is that it was because I absolutely lost my temper,' she said. 'And that's worse than nothing. If I can lose my temper like that, they'll say – '

'No, I don't think so. Not if that bloke Pinn is as bright as I think. He'll probably reckon you're all the safer for having an occasional bust-up.'

'Do you think so?'

Penny flopped to the ground again. Not with grace.

'I feel a bit happier now,' she said.

'You were worrying all right,' Ned said. 'I wouldn't, if you can be tough with yourself. It only wears you away. I should know.'

'I'll try not to.'

'After all you've got nothing to worry about really, have you?'

Ned stood up and looked down at her. Looked hard down at her.

Slowly Penny raised her head till her eyes met his.

'No,' she said, 'I haven't got anything to worry about really. Do you believe me?'

Ned stood without answering.

'Don't you believe me?'

Penny scrambled to her feet. Awkwardly. Hurriedly.

'But don't you?'

Ned smiled at her.

'You don't sound as if you're putting on an act,' he said. 'But I only met you a couple of days ago. How in the hell can I know for sure?'

The instant Rosy tapped the opening rhythm of 'Colonel Bogey' on the glass panel of the boothole door Bert jerked it open.

'Come in quick,' he said. 'I've got something I want to ask you. Something desperate.'

'Give me a kiss first then,' said Rosy.

'No. No, listen. I want to know this.'

'Come on, give us a kiss.'

'I want to talk to you.'

'Talk as much as you like only give us a kiss first.'

'Why?'

Sudden suspicion.

'Why? Why give me a kiss? Why do you think, stupid?'

Bert looked at her.

'All right,' he said, 'I need to feel I can implace trust on you.'

Rosy put up her face provocatively. Bert's enormous shoulders blotting out her diminutive body.

'All right,' she said, 'now what do you want to know?'

Bert was silent.

'Come on,' said Rosy, 'I haven't got all day. I'll have to be thinking about getting their dinner soon.'

'What are they all doing?' Bert said. 'I see some of 'em sometimes, walking about round the croquet lawn.'

'Was that all you wanted to know?'

'No, that was something else. But I think about what's happening in the house too. What about old Ma B.? How's she going on? You couldn't tell her she has my condecencies, I suppose?'

'Don't be more of a fool than you are, Bert Rogers. How could I go to her and tell her you were hiding here? She thinks you were the one who hit Mr B.'

'Does she?'

'Of course she does. Everybody does.'

'Do you?'

Rosy's eyes flicked up to his face.

'That's what I was wanting to ask,' he said. 'Only I got all twisted up about it – till it came out unpromptu like.'

'You didn't have to ask that, you silly,' said Rosy.

Bert's eyes widened.

'Because you're certain sure I didn't?' he said.

Rosy tossed her head.

'I don't have to tell you,' she said.

Bert's hand flashed out and caught her by the wrist.

'Oh yes, you do.'

'Oh no, I don't.'

'We'll see about that.'

Bert began squeezing the tiny wrist, scarcely thicker than the heavy fingers of his hand.

Rosy looked at him pertly. He squeezed harder. Her face suddenly betrayed the pain.

'Let go.'

'No.'

'Let go, I tell you.'

'Not till you answer my question.'

'I have, stupid.'

'Not properly, you haven't. I don't want any of your invasions.'

He squeezed again.

'Oh, all right. But let go first.'

'Say it first.'

'I'll say it when you let go and not before.'

'All right then.'

Bert dropped her wrist. He looked at her hard.

'Now say it.'

'All right. I don't believe you did.'

'Did what?'

'Did kill Mr Boddershaw. There. Now are you satisfied?'

Bert sat down slowly on the narrow bench. It bent into a curve under his weight.

'All right then,' he said.

'Why do you want to make such a fuss?' Rosy said.

'There's something I want you to do.'

'Yes?'

The quick look. The trace of doubt in the voice.

'I've got to get away.'

'But we've been over all that. It's too difficult just yet.'

'I've got to get away. I've got to.'

'But why? Why do you start this all of a sudden?'

'Never mind why. Just start telling me how I can do it.'

'Oh yes, that's precious easy, isn't it? Where do you want to get away to, I should like to know. You going to fly to Paris by private plane?'

'Cut that out. I want to get away and I want to get away fast.'

'But why?'

'You believe it wasn't me who did the murder, don't you?'

'I told you I did.'

'Yes. Yes, I made sure of that. Well now, get me away.'

'But why?'

Slowly she brought her eyes round till she was looking at him full in the face. Searchingly.

'Bert, you haven't been lying to me, have you?'

'I told you I didn't do it. I told you I was in here and I saw it happen.'

'Very well then, if you saw it, who did it? Who did it?'

'I won't say.'

'You must say. You must.'

'I won't.'

'How can I believe you when you won't tell me who did it? How can I believe you aren't tricking me? Bert, did you do it?'

'You promised me you believed me. You promised. Why, you little – I made you say that you believed I didn't do it. You said it. And now you go back on it all. You think I killed him, don't you?'

'No.'

'Oh yes, you do. Well, get out. Get out quick, if you think I'm a killer. Get out while you're still safe.'

'I'm going, Bert Rogers. I'm going all right. I won't stay here to be talked at like that. Don't you think so.'

The quivering panel of frosted glass as the door slammed.

*

In the early dusk of the September evening Ned spotted the tall figure of Leonard walking swiftly round the playing-field.

He looked at him for a moment and then went quickly across to the french window, jerked it open, and hurried out into the chilling air. He intercepted Leonard at the corner of the field where on the other side of the chestnut paling the demolition team were still working on The Towers.

'Hello there,' Ned said. 'I hear you're staying on with us for a few days after all.'

'Yes,' said Leonard.

He stood and looked at the activity next door mounting to a climax in the fading light. The main effort was centred on a stack of masonry left at what had once been one of the corners of the house. The walls on either side of it had been knocked down to ground level but the solid block at the corner had resisted the picks and hammers. Now a man was perched precariously on top of it fitting round it a thin wire hawser running down to a crane with caterpillar tracks on the ground below.

'Yes,' said Leonard. 'Helen wanted me to leave here as early as I could and spend this weekend with her in town. But I told her I couldn't leave until the tournament was over.'

'That was before you came down then?' said Ned.

'And of course her first reaction to the news about Humphrey was that I should go up and join her at once. So I decided the time had come to take a firm line.'

He dropped into silence. The man on the top of the pillar of masonry had fastened the hawser to his satisfaction and began carefully making his way to the ground.

'They're working late,' said Ned.

'Yes,' Leonard said, 'the time to take a firm line. That's the way, you know. Decide exactly what you want and then get it. You ever been in business?'

'I had a clerk's job for a few weeks once.'

'Well, if you ever get into business, that's my advice to you. Decide what you want and then get it. It sounds easy, doesn't it? But believe you me, it isn't. You've got to have the right qualities.'

The man who had fixed the hawser jumped the last four feet

to the ground. A puff of brickdust hovered in the air where he had landed.

'That's a favourite thesis of mine,' Ned said, 'that it isn't the brains you need but the right attitude.'

'You've got to be tough, damned tough,' said Leonard. 'To reach up and take it, take just what you want.'

'Still, you're going too far on that,' said Ned. 'You're going to extremes. It isn't practical.'

'That's what's the trouble with that policeman,' Leonard said.

He turned full towards Ned and looked at him fiercely.

The engine of the crane on the pulling end of the hawser suddenly revved up violently. The hawser began to tauten switching to and fro.

'The policeman?' said Ned.

'Superintendent Pinn. He's not going after this man for all's he's worth.'

'He seemed quite a go-getter to me.'

'He's got to catch this fellow,' said Leonard. 'That's what he wants. He must get him.'

The hawser was fully taut now. The crane engine roared even louder. Ned and Leonard watched.

The caterpillar tracks slipped a little. Then they gripped.

Ned looked quickly along the line of the hawser up to the top of the column of masonry where the remains of a drain pipe stood up in the air silhouetted against the pale blue evening sky like a chimney. The wire loop was fast round the bricks. It bit into them, then slipped and jerked upwards.

'It'll come off,' said Ned.

The loop gripped again, slipped again.

'The fool,' said Leonard. 'Do the job properly.'

The loop caught under a slight projection in the brickwork. The crane engine roared. The hawser twanged with the strain. The loop held. There was a moment of poised stillness.

Chapter Twelve

A sharp puff of dust came out of the old drain pipe which pointed upwards like a chimney at the top of the column of masonry. Then slowly at first, but with gathering speed, the whole pile tumbled over. There was an enormous crash. Large pieces of brickwork were flung through the air and bounced up as they landed. Piles of rubble cascaded down. A heavy cloud of dust rose up, hung in the air and gradually swirled away. The site slowly settled down to quietness. Someone blew a long note on a whistle. The workmen put down their tools and started to get into their coats. The noise of the crane engine throbbed into silence.

'Were you there the other evening when Sebastian made that absurd suggestion?' Leonard said to Ned.

'Absurd? You mean – '

'Well, perhaps you weren't. I'll tell you what he said. He had some notion that this man Rogers didn't kill Humphrey but that one of us did. Utter nonsense. Typical piece of donnishness. Never satisfied with the simple solution.'

He turned and looked at Ned.

'You've only got to consider the facts,' he said.

The old hand flopped down his copy of *The World* on to the breakfast table.

'They didn't use it,' he said. 'They didn't use a blind word of it.'

'There's no room this morning for anything but the I.R.A. story, chum,' said the up-and-comer. 'Was this your police inefficiency stuff that got crowded out?'

'It was. The best news to come out of this so far. Something with a bit of meat in it. If they sacked the lot in our subs' room and put in the copy boys you wouldn't notice the difference.'

'Still,' said the girl, 'you should worry. There's damn all besides the bomb outrage stuff in any of them today.'

'I rather cared for our book review page,' said *The Examiner*. 'I thought we were rather good on this thing they're making all the fuss about, "The Seeds of Violence". A nice piece of deflation, my old tutor would have called it.'

He turned to the old hand.

'Didn't you think so?' he said.

'I don't read book reviews,' said the old hand. 'Features just take away from good hard news space. Look at our centre page today. Bloody flam the lot of it. Of course, the truth is they don't want news any more. They ought to turn this lot in, if they're not going to use the stuff we send.'

'You could be right,' said the girl. 'I reckon my news editor only keeps me here out of spite because I said the place was a dead-and-alive hole. The story's gone on too long, you know. To all intents and purposes it's dead.'

'Trouble with you,' said the up-and-comer, 'is that you believe everything you read in the papers.'

'Well,' said the girl, 'the ever-lively *Daily Post* was so dull this morning you had to believe it.'

'What you forget,' the up-and-comer went on, 'is that there may be developments in a story without there being a word to file. I don't think I'll be called back to my office just yet awhile.'

'Guff,' said the old hand.

'All right, I'll tell you, chum. I can give you the gist of it witout putting you on to anything as it so happens.'

'Beaten to it again, alas,' said *The Examiner*.

'Who do you think I happened to bump into last night?' the up-and-comer said.

'The editor of *The Daily Post* coming to give you a gold medal,' said the old hand.

'No, I know,' said the girl, 'laddie's dear old tutor.'

'All right, chum, be clever. Only you'll kick yourself when you know.'

'Then my dear chap, as my old – Then my dear chap, let's hear.'

'Rosy Peters,' said the up-and-comer.

'Okay,' said the old hand, 'that's something. It's a bit. I

wouldn't have minded a chat with her myself. Where did you find her?'

'Came hurrying out of the school about eleven, just as I was having a last look round.'

The old hand picked up *The Daily Post* and made a face at it.

'She gave you some pretty decent copy,' he said.

'You'll have to wait till tomorrow for that,' said the up-and-comer. 'She said she wanted twenty-four hours to think about it.'

'Think about what, laddie?'

The up-and-comer grinned.

'I can't be sure,' he said. 'We called it her problem when she told me last night that she was worried stiff. What a break for her to run into a tough newspaperman who knew all the facts of life.'

'Don't make me throw up,' said the girl.

'Be bitter, be bitter, I don't mind. She may have enjoyed her woman-to-woman chat with you the other day, but when she wanted advice she came to yours truly.'

'But, not wanting to appear too naïve, old man, what exactly was she wanting advice about? Wouldn't the dear old *Examiner* have been more avuncular?'

'I'll tell you what she wanted advice about. Mind you, she never told me anything that I could pin down. But I reckon there can't be anything else. She's hiding Bert Rogers somewhere and can't decide whether to turn him in. But when she does, it'll be to *The Daily Post*, don't you worry.'

They no longer all came down to breakfast in a bunch. When the ship's bell rang as usual Ned left his room, but the only person he found in the dining-room was Michael Goodhart.

'Good morning,' Ned said.

'Good morning, good morning,' said Michael.

He cast a weather eye on the view from the windows.

'Looks as though the sou-wester's holding,' he said. 'We should get a spell of fair weather.'

'Listen,' said Ned, 'I've been wanting a word with you on the quiet. This is a good time. I want to know what you think about Bert Rogers.'

144

'Rogers? The killer?'

'All right. That's as good an answer as any.'

A slight frown appeared for an instant above Michael's bright blue eyes.

'You think I'm prejudging the issue?' he said. 'I don't want to do that, but really is there any other answer?'

'Sebastian thought there might be,' said Ned.

'Sebastian's a good chap, I know, but he stays cooped up in that college of his all the time. He's a bit inclined to see things as being more complicated than they are.'

'People are always telling me that,' said Ned. 'But just because Sebastian's arrived at a point – in whatever twisted way he works – it doesn't mean that that point's wrong.'

'Oh, I grant you that,' said Michael. 'There's no reason why he shouldn't get at the truth coming round astern as it were. But in this case you get a very different answer if you go straight forrard.'

'In short that Rogers killed Humph.'

'Look,' said Michael, 'you haven't got any ideas that people are giving this chap a raw deal, have you?'

A sharp glance from the bright blue eyes.

'That's what I like,' said Ned. 'You don't beat about the bush, sport. And you're too right. I do think he's getting a raw deal.'

'Just because he's a lower-deck type?'

'No, not entirely. But lower-deck types, as you call them, do get a raw deal pretty often in this country.'

'They more often get away with a hell of a lot – on shore at least. No, until I hear something to the contrary I shan't worry myself looking for something that isn't there. The chap's a lunatic, it's a very poor show but you've got to face facts.'

'There are one or two facts on the other side,' said Ned.

'All right. Let's hear them.'

Michael looked straight in front of him. Enemy dead ahead.

'Okay. First, Superintendent Pinn isn't completely neglecting the possibility that one of us is involved.'

'One of us?'

'Yes. If Bert didn't do it, we were the ones who knew Humph would be out on the croquet lawn so early.'

'Well, no doubt Pinn's a thoroughly efficient type. He's bound

145

to keep an eye open for the unlikely, the very unlikely I should call it. Anything else?'

'There is. Did you know there were no fingerprints on the mallet that was used?'

'Yes, I think I heard that. Don't these criminal chappies always wear gloves?'

'If the bloke had been wearing gloves there would have been other prints on the mallet handle.'

'All right then, criminals know about fingerprints. This fellow wiped them off. He'd been trained to do it.'

'In Broadmoor?'

'Now look here,' said Michael, 'this lower-deck lawyer stuff's all very well, but it doesn't alter the facts. The chances that Bert Rogers is the man the police want are pretty well a hundred per cent.'

'That's all I wanted to know, sport.'

'All right, you've got my views for what they're worth. But they ought to get ahead and catch the chap. They must. This waiting business can't go on much longer. It can't.'

A bright glint in the hard blue eyes.

In the gloom of the boothole Rosy and Bert sat silently on the narrow bench.

'I'm sorry,' said Bert. 'It was all the fault of the tensing.'

'Oh, Bert.'

Rosy scrambled round till she was kneeling on the bench beside him and put her arms round his squat neck.

'Oh, Bert, I know. I should have realized. It was bound to get you down.'

'That was all,' said Bert.

'I know it was. I was silly to think it wasn't.'

'All the same, I still don't know what happens next.'

'We've got to wait for our chance. That's all we can do.'

'But all the time the tensing will go on mounting and mounting up inside me.'

'Try not to let it.'

'I try. But it goes on.'

Silence again. The bright morning light coming through the opaque glass of the louvres.

'Bert,' said Rosy.

'Yes?'

'Bert, about that time.'

He stiffened.

'What about it?'

She put her arms round him more tightly.

'Bert, who was it you saw?'

'No.'

He jerked away from her and stood up.

'It's no good,' he said. 'I can't tell you. I can't think of it. I can't bear to see it again. It's something psychlelogical.'

Rosy came and clung to his arm. Her head not reaching much above the elbow.

'I think that's what's making you feel so bad,' she said.

'Yes.'

Dull acquiesence.

'So if you made up your mind to it and just told me, you'd feel better.'

'No.'

She stroked his arm.

'I – I'll think about it,' he said.

'Just try to bring yourself round to it. It'll help you. I'm sure of that. And it might be the way out of everything. Don't you see that?'

'What do you mean?'

'Because if you first told me what you'd seen, I could go and tell the super, and then when he found out you were right they wouldn't put you back in that place, not when you'd shown them you were so sensible.'

'They wouldn't believe me if I did tell.'

'If you really saw it, it's the truth. And they'd have to believe you. Who was it, Bert? Who was it?'

Bert stood in the middle of the room. His head slightly lowered, his eyes clouded. He seemed oblivious of Rosy still holding on to his arm.

'They came up very quietly with the mallet,' he said. 'I wondered what they were doing and – '

His hands shot up and covered his face.

He said no more.

'Bert, who?'

A whisper.

Bert did not speak.

'Bert, who was it? You do know the name.'

'I wish I didn't. I wish I didn't. I wish I didn't.'

Bert went across to the louvred window and hauled himself up on the pigeon-holes until he could see out. He stayed there in silence. Rosy stood looking at him. The quick movement of her eyes. Calculating.

'It must seem funny looking out there,' she said.

Bert half turned.

'Seeing the field where you used to work so much and all that,' said Rosy.

'Wish I was out there now,' Bert said.

'Do you? What's happening?'

'Nothing. The whole place is desertified.'

'Do you remember of an evening behind the pavilion?'

Bert turned and jumped down from his perch. He came toward her.

''Course I remember,' he said. 'I'm not likely to misremember that.'

He rummaged in a corner and produced his chocolate brown handyman's uniform. He held it up in the dim light.

'I had some good times in you, I did,' he said. 'Some good times.'

He sat down on the flexible bench and rested the uniform on his knees.

Rosy stood watching. Waiting.

'I learnt to play Snap in you,' said Bert. 'The first thing I ever done for just enjoyingment.'

'I never brought you those cards,' said Rosy.

Bert looked up.

'Will you bring 'em?' he said.

'Will you do something for me if I do?'

A sudden suspicion in the tilt of his head.

'Do what?'

'Oh, nothing much. Just have a little bet with me when we're playing.'

'A bet.'

148

Bert's eyes gleamed.

'I like betting,' he said. 'I'm a born gambleleler really. Did you know I once won sixpence off old Mr B. in a bet?'

'I remember.'

In the gloom Bert could not see the look of softness in Rosy's eyes. And the look of pain.

'It was over the weather, wasn't it?' she said.

'Yes. He told me it was going to rain, and I told him silly bastard. He said it must rain, scientififically. I said it wouldn't, flat. And he bet me. And it stayed dry as old boots. That's the way I won my sixpence. He paid up all right, old Mr B. I don't know how you do it. Gaius Sempronius Gracchus, he says.'

'So you will have a bit of a bet when we play Snap?' said Rosy.

' 'Course I will. What do you want to bet? Want to bet it's going to rain?'

'No.'

'What do you want to bet then?'

A moment's silence. A moment of decision.

'I want to bet the name of the person you saw.'

'Bet that? No.'

'I won't play unless you do.'

Bert sat looking straight in front of him. Slowly he bit his lower lip in calculation.

He breathed deeply.

'All right,' he said, 'I'll do it.'

Rosy's eyes gleaming. She came and stood in front of him and looked into his face.

'You promise?' she said. 'A bet's a bet, mind.'

'I promise. I ain't never gone back on a bet yet, and I don't never mean to.'

'All right. We play Snap and when one or the other of us gets the two packs all into their hand then the game's over. And if you win I won't ever ask you the name again or mention it at all. But if I win, then you look straight up at me and you say the name out loud there and then. Is it a bet?'

'It's a bet.'

Ned and Cicely rounded the corner into the playing field.

'That's very interesting,' said Ned.

Cicely Ravell paid no attention.

'. . . and of course it was a perfectly foul thing to do and I told him so. In front of the whole club. You should have seen his face. He won't do that again in a hurry. To play on right round without once stopping to consult your partner about laying up. Damnable, perfectly damnable. Of course, that was before the war.'

She tugged at the sleeve of her cardigan.

'Yes, yes, I see. Now look, Mrs Ravell, I – '

'Oh yes, you don't know the game as I do, Mr Farran, but if you did you'd be surprised, utterly surprised, at the ghastly standard of play you sometimes get. And not only in private games, but at tournaments, positively at tournaments. Of course, the men are the worst. Did I ever tell you about that perfect pig at Budleigh Salterton?'

'No, but – '

'Oh yes, of course I did. I was just telling you that, wasn't I? Stupid of me.'

'Jeez, I thought you meant someone else, someone new, I know who you mean now.'

'Yes, exactly. But that isn't the worst. There's the sort of man who will insist on captaining any doubles pair if he's playing with a woman. Now, of course, these days I'm a pretty high bisquer. I've had some perfectly damnable luck. But before the war I was a superb player. I tell you that quite frankly. I know I was: people were always telling me so. You're a superb player, Cicely, they used to say. I only tell you that so that you know just how good I was.'

She started to rub the top of her left leg with vigour.

'I see. It must – '

'And as I was saying there was this Captain Prodgers – not a Naval captain, mark you, an Army man. Of course, if he'd been a Naval captain the whole business could simply not have occurred. I do think the Navy's so fine, don't you? Look at Michael. A splendid man, a perfectly splendid man.'

Ned reached out and grasped her firmly by the elbow. He leant forward until his mouth was close to her ear, and speaking very deliberately he said:

150

'I had one hell of a row with Michael before breakfast this morning.'

'What?' said Cicely. 'What was that you said? Did you say you had had a row with Michael?'

'Yes. Do you want to know what about?'

'Really, you must be a most extraordinarily argumentative young man, Mr Farran. I've never had a row with Michael, and there aren't many people I can say that about.'

'This was over something special.'

'Of course, I know I have rows,' Cicely said. 'I have rows perpetually, but it's all the other people's fault. That's what I keep telling John – that's my husband you know – I keep telling him that it's not my fault if I have to tell people what they're doing wrong. And if you don't tell them in no uncertain manner, they don't listen, Mr Farran, they simply don't – '

'Murder. Murder. It was about murder.'

'Really, Mr Farran, you and I are going to quarrel. If there is one thing I will not put up with it's being interrupted – '

'He thinks he knows who killed Humphrey, Mrs Ravell.'

Cicely stopped her excited pacing of the playing-field as if she had butted into a solid wall of air. The two hectic spots of colour on the pommels of her cheeks drained away.

She turned full round on Ned.

'Who killed Humphrey,' she said, 'he knows who killed Humphrey. In heaven's name, who was it?'

Ned smiled sharply.

'Then you wouldn't be surprised if it turned out to be someone else than Bert Rogers?' he said.

Cicely looked at him.

She was silent.

The sound of a fool thrush singing its head off in the mulberry tree.

'On the contrary, Mr Farran, I can't imagine who else could possibly have killed him.'

'That's what Commander Goodhart thinks,' said Ned.

A rueful smile.

'That's what we had our row about, in fact,' he went on. 'Not really all that much of a row either, come to that.'

Peke Abou who had been trotting behind them suddenly growled wheezily.

'Quiet, sir,' said Cicely.

Peke Abou barked.

Cicely wheeled round and bent forward to glare at the dog. Peke Abou sat down and scratched.

Cicely thrust her face towards his.

'Of course,' she said, 'it's an excellent thing. You know the man was absolutely unfit to be here at all.'

Ned looked at the back of her head. The frizzle of many-shaded grey hair.

'If you mean what I think you mean,' he said, 'turn around and say it properly.'

'Good boy, good fellow.'

Cicely patted Peke Abou on his neat head and looked up.

'I hope you're not going to disagree with me,' she said. 'It's been perfectly obvious for years that Humphrey should never have been in charge of children. And now by the mercy of providence they're safe from him. It's a blessing, a perfect blessing.'

'Look, the last time you said all that about Humph I told you fairly politely that you were mad as a two-bob watch. All right, it didn't sink in. So I'll tell you again. You're just crazy to think a thing like that. Of course, old Humph used to shout a bit and fool around, but the kids loved it. It did them good. It worked some of those repressions out of them.'

Cicely drew herself up. A bundle of erect skin and bone.

'I'll be perfectly frank,' she said. 'That's the most arrant nonsense I've ever heard. You should be ashamed to have even thought it. And it convinces me more than ever that you're unfit, absolutely unfit, for the position of trust you hold. And I shall – '

'Hey,' said Ned, 'what was that about being convinced "more than ever"?'

'Of course I said "more than ever". It was obvious to me the moment I set eyes on you that you had no business to be here at all. An Australian in an English school. I always knew Humphrey was mad.'

On the last word her voice rose almost to a shout. Ned looked at her. Peke Abou turned round from his business with a flea somewhere in the region of the base of his tail and looked at her too.

Then suddenly he began yapping. Standing squarely on his four short legs with his head lifted high he yapped.

'Stop that damnable noise, sir,' said Cicely.

Peke Abou went on yapping.

'Stop it this instant, you damn brute,' Cicely said.

Peke Abou ignored her.

She wheeled round on Ned.

'It's all your talk about violence,' she said. 'The dear little boy's adding his voice to mine in protest. He's a very sensitive soul. He knows what I feel about this subject and, when he hears anyone being so stupid as to disagree with me, naturally he has to put in his little say. Don't you, darling?'

She bent down towards the dog.

Peke Abou went on yapping.

'I won't stand for it,' said Cicely. 'I won't stand for this continual cult of violence. I'm a woman of peace and I mean to see that the peace is kept.'

She flung herself on her knees face to face with Peke Abou.

'Stop that infernal noise, can't you?' she said. 'Stop it. Stop it, do you hear me?'

Peke Abou could not have failed to hear her, her face was so near to his. But he had obviously decided not to take her request with any great seriousness. He went on yapping.

Cicely straightened up. Suddenly. As if a spring had been released with a snap.

She looked round her wildly.

Ned took a pace backwards.

Abruptly. Cicely strode towards the pavilion a few yards away. She stooped just outside the door and stood up again holding half a broken cricket stump.

'Now sir,' she said.

Ned watched her warily. A certain ambivalence in her threat.

She advanced towards Peke Abou. Ned relaxed. Peke Abou slightly turned his head so that he had her in good view. He went on yapping.

Cicely advanced.

'Stop it, sir,' she said.

Peke Abou went on.

Cicely advanced again.

When she was within two inches of striking distance Peke Abou snaked round and began haring away as fast as four short legs working in not very good rhythm would carry him.

Cicely tossed away the stump.

'That's the only way with a dog,' she said. 'Let them know who's master. Beat it into 'em.'

'Yes,' said Ned.

Cicely looked round at the rapidly diminishing form of her pet.

'Abou, Abou,' she called. 'Here, boy, here.'

The fast moving fawn object on the dark green of the playing-field. Nearing the house now.

'Come here this instant, sir,' called Cicely.

Peke Abou scrambling up the steps towards the door into the changing room.

Cicely set out in pursuit.

'Have to keep an eye on him,' she said. 'He's a dear little thing, of course, all my dogs are. But he's a bit temperamental at times. He has to be watched.'

'Oh, yes,' said Ned.

He hurried along beside Cicely.

They found Peke Abou just inside the changing room. He looked perfectly calm. At the sound of their steps he raised his head for a moment. Then he returned to what was absorbing him – the bottom of the boothole door.

Ned and Cicely looked at him.

'Seems to have found a rat or something,' said Ned.

He went across and pushed at the door.

It stayed firmly shut.

Ned pushed harder.

Chapter Thirteen

'Something seems to be jamming up this door,' Ned said.

'Where does it lead to?' said Cicely. 'I don't think I've ever been through it, though of course I've been visiting the school for years and years.'

'It's what they call the boothole,' Ned said. 'Where the boys keep their outdoor shoes. Jeez, the happy hours I've spent making sure the little devils had the right sort of shoes on at the right time.'

He pushed at the door again.

'Think I budged it,' he said.

'If it is a rat stopping up the opening, I wish you'd leave it alone,' said Cicely. 'I don't want Peke Abou to go eating it.'

'Why not?' said Ned.

He rested his shoulder against the door and pushed steadily. Without success.

'Why not?' he said. 'Might do him a bit of good to get some good dirty meat between his teeth.'

'That shows just how little you know about pekinese. No doubt you're one of the people who consider them effeminate. But let me tell you, you couldn't be more wrong. In China they're renowned for their fierceness and absolute bravery. They're the most lion-like of all the breeds. It makes me simply furious to hear ignorant people go about running them down. I've been breeding them for years. In the old days I used to have champion after champion, only of course I never show now. The standard of judging is absolutely appalling, absolutely –'

The boothole door burst open.

Peke Abou gave a startled yap and backed away to the far end of the changing room.

Standing fair and square in the middle of the little room now flooded with daylight was Bert Rogers.

'Who the – ' said Ned.

With a rush Bert came forward charging full at Ned with the whole weight of his body.

Ned went down as if a prop had been pulled sharply away from under him. Cicely flattened herself against the wall and let out a shrill scream. Peke Abou squirmed under Benthorpe Major's locker.

The very violence of Bert's attack stopped it being completely successful. Had he been content to push the unsuspecting Ned sharply back he would have been out of sight before Ned had recovered. As it was Ned fell backwards so suddenly that Bert tumbled head foremost on top of him. It was only an instant before Ned recovered his wits. Before Bert could scramble to his feet and run off Ned had gripped him hard round the chest holding their two bodies fast together.

'It must be the Broadmoor bloke,' Ned said,

The words gasped out between fought for breaths.

'Run for the police, you silly fool,' he added.

'That's where you're absolutely mistaken, let me tell you,' said Cicely. 'I'm by no means a fool. Many people – many people far more intelligent than any Australian – have made that mistake.'

With a terrific effort Bert rolled both Ned and himself sharply over. With a heavy thud they landed against the wall where Cicely was standing, pinning her fast.

'Let me go at once, both of you,' she said.

She fell forward on top of them. Her sharp skinny fingers scrabbled at Ned's neck.

'I'm surprised at you, Bert Rogers,' she said. 'I thought you at least knew how to behave.'

Ned forced his leg up and slowly moved it round until it was pinioning Bert.

'Listen, Cicely,' he said, 'forget all that about Australian accents. This chap's wanted by the police, badly. In a moment I'm going to roll him off you. When I do, run for it.'

'Except you won't,' said Bert.

Ned smiled slightly.

'We'll see about that,' he said.

He jerked his face quickly forward and nipped Bert's ear with his teeth. Bert moved his head swiftly back and slightly relaxed his grip. Ned heaved and they rolled away from Cicely.

But Ned had reckoned without the full effect this manoeuvre would have on Bert.

A look of blind rage came into his eyes and with a violent effort he sent the pair of them banging back against Cicely with twice the force of their first impact. Now Bert was full on top of Ned again and his legs were no longer pinioned. He began heaving himself up off the floor and dropping down again with his full weight on Ned.

Under the repeated blows Ned began to look glassy-eyed. His hands, still tightly clenched together behind Bert's back holding the two of them fast, began to lose their grip. With a fierce twist and a grunt of triumph Bert broke the hold. He put a foot on the ground beside Ned's head and half staggered to his feet.

But the release of his weight sent cool air flowing back into Ned's lungs. His battered head cleared and he shot out a hand and clutched with all his might at the collar of Bert's shirt. Bert heaved back but succeeded only in pulling Ned up with him.

For a moment they half-stood half-knelt side by side, too exhausted to do more than look at each other with implacable anger. Near them Cicely lay in an open-eyed daze. Then Bert brought his free hand round and banged it down with all his force on the place where Ned was gripping the tough stuff of his shirt. A sharp jab of pain shot all the way up Ned's arm but he kept his grip as tight as ever. Bert raised his free hand for another blow, but Ned shot his other hand with the fist doubled up hard into Bert's face.

Bert looked dazed for an instant, but Ned had been unable to get enough length into the blow to make it really effective. Bert simply staggered back a pace.

Then suddenly he fell over backwards as, trying to regain his balance, his foot came into contact with Cicely's skinny leg where she lay stretched at full length on the floor beside them. This was all Ned needed. As Bert fell he twisted his grip on the shirt with savage force and then planked his legs astride Bert's, holding him in an unbreakable grip.

'Here, here,' he began calling out. 'Here somebody. Here. I've got Bert Rogers. Come and give us a hand. Here somebody, here.'

Only Peke Abou heeded his shouts. Cautiously he emerged from under Benthorpe Major's locker. Slowly he walked across to where Ned and Bert were lying on the floor. Deliberately and viciously he sank his sharp teeth into the hand with which Ned was holding Bert's shirt collar so firmly.

Ned let out a yelp and involuntarily flung Peke Abou away with the hand he had bitten.

In an instant Bert was up. Ned went sprawling and Bert was out of the door leading from the changing room to the playing-field before Ned had even begun to get to his feet.

'Damn it,' said Ned.

He jumped up, pushed the fiercely growling Peke Abou away with a foot, and ran to the door. He flung it open. Bert was running across the playing-field for all he was worth.

Ned set out after him.

Bert had not got a very long start and an expression of grim delight came into Ned's face as he ran. There were not many people whom he could not catch up from this distance.

In less than fifty yards Bert's captivity in the boothole began to show its effects. He slowed down a little and then staggered as he ran.

With a visible effort he forced himself on again at his former pace, but it could not last. He slowed again, and Ned with a slight smile lifting the corners of his mouth launched himself forward in a classic low rugby tackle.

He brought Bert down faultlessly and was up himself and sitting pinning Bert down before he had had a moment to recover.

'This time,' he said, 'you'll get no help from a cross-brained pekinese.'

Bert groaned.

For a moment or two Ned sat on him considering. Then he got a firm hold on Bert's right wrist and jerked him to his feet.

'I think a spell locked in the pavilion would do you no harm,' he said. 'I'm certainly not going to call for help again and get bitten for it. On you go.'

Ned marched the silent and cowed Bert across the few yards to the pavilion, fished a key-ring out of his trouser pocket with his free hand and fitted the pavilion key into its slot. He swung the door open, shoved Bert hard in, banged the door to and made sure it was relocked.

'You cool your heels off for a moment, chum,' he said. 'I'm going to call the police.'

Suddenly weary he trudged off across the playing field towards the door into the changing room, still gaping wide where he had flung it open as he set out after Bert.

Walking quietly and drooping with exhaustion he mounted the steps and entered the house. As he did so Rosy Peters appeared in the doorway of the boothole. The expression on her face told him everything.

'If you want to know where your boy friend is,' he said, 'I just locked him in the pavilion.'

Rosy turned on him.

'Why do you want to go poking your nose into things that aren't none of your business?' she said. 'I suppose you think you've been no end clever catching a poor fellow who never did no harm to no one and handing him over to the rotten stinking police.'

'Easy, easy,' said Ned. 'He did harm to someone all right. He nearly battered the life out of me when he had me on the floor just there – if that's any satisfaction to you.'

'I bet you asked for it,' Rosy said. 'And I suppose you think he ought to go back to Broadmoor for the rest of his life because he dared to touch you.'

'Now, now. Of course you're sore. But, believe me, I just got rushed into this. That noble beast of Mrs Ravell's smelt something in the boothole there and I was just sticky-beaking when I came across your boy friend. And he started the rough stuff first, note that.'

'Well, and what do you expect him to do? You come barging into the place where he thinks he's safe and you expect him to say "Come in, have a cup of tea" or something. I hope he hurt you.'

Ned smiled.

'He did all right,' he said.

'Good.'

'Now look,' said Ned, 'I don't want you to think I'm not on

159

your side. Come on, sit down on that bench there and we'll talk about it.'

He guided her back into the boothole and sat down beside her on the narrow bench. It curved down beneath their weight.

'How did the police miss him when they went over the place?' Ned said. 'They seemed pretty thorough to me.'

Rosy turned and looked at him.

'We had a bit of luck really,' she said. 'He dressed up in his old handyman's uniform and the rozzers we met didn't recognize him.'

'Good on you,' said Ned. 'That was pretty smart. And otherwise he was in here all the time, eh?'

'Yes, he was,' said Rosy.

Returning belligerency.

Ned sat silent for a moment.

'Jeez,' he said, 'let's stop this dodging around. Did he do it?'

Rosy held on to the edge of the bench tight with both hands.

'I don't know.'

'What's that? This is no time for muttering.'

She looked up.

'I don't know, and there's the truth.'

'He wouldn't say anything, is that it?'

'He said he saw it happen and he won't tell me who he saw there. He did see it happen too, because he knew all about it when I came to see him later that morning.'

A rush of words.

Ned looked at her steadily.

'He could have known about it because he did it,' he said. 'It's no use not facing that one.'

'Do you think I haven't?' said Rosy. 'Do you think I've been sleeping easy in my bed these nights? Do you think I haven't been over and over it in my mind? What do you take me for?'

'All right, all right. I – '

'I've been over and over it, but I can't see how he did it. Every night Mr B. used to lock the door between the changing room and the rest of the school, didn't he?'

'Yes, yes, I think he did.'

'You think – '

'Okay, I know he did. He made a fuss about it. But that doesn't – '

'And every night I stuck one of them silly mallets under the knob of the door on to the field so no one could get out. You all came out after the first night just as I was putting it away and I didn't half feel a fool standing there holding that thing.'

'Yeah, I remember. Old Humph was tickled pink because you told him you'd been dusting it.'

'What else could I say? You think of some fine excuses if you're so clever.'

'Quiet, quiet. I wasn't saying anything against you. You're a pretty bright kid. You thought of that uniform dodge, didn't you? And you passed off that mallet business all right. Take it easy. No one's trying to get at you.'

'Thanks for nothing,' Rosy said. 'You think yourself no end tough, don't you, catching an escaped loonie like that? Then you come all over big and tell his girl she's been very clever hiding him away like that, quite a bright little thing. Well, I don't fall for it. You stuck your nose into my affairs and took my chap away from me when all the police in the country couldn't find him. All right, you're marvellous, but don't expect me to thank you.'

Ned sighed.

'I didn't expect you to feel anything else but the way you do,' he said. 'All the same I'm going to tell you something, and perhaps one day you'll realize it's sense. What's happened is the best thing that could have happened. You were pretty clever to hide him for a week, but you wouldn't have lasted much longer, believe you me. Sooner or later he'd have had to have given himself up. What he did in breaking out of Broadmoor was no solution to his troubles, and you ought to know it.'

'Thank you very much,' said Rosy. 'Now can I go? I've got work to do in this house besides everything else.'

Ned got up.

'I'm sorry,' he said. 'You won't believe I mean it, but I am sorry. If there could have been any other way out I would have been glad.'

Rosy took hold of his hand.

'Of course you would,' she said. 'You mustn't mind me. I get a bit shirty at times, but I know all what you've said's been the truth really. That's what made me so furious.'

Ned smiled at her.

'All for the best?' he said.

'All for the best.'

The man from *The Examiner* burst into the bar.

The girl from *The Clarion* nudged the old hand from *The World*.

'Look at laddie there,' she said. 'He's on to something.'

The man from *The Examiner* hung his umbrella from the edge of the bar with punctilious care.

'What are you people having?' he said. 'Make it the same again, my dear.'

'Could I have a Guinness this time,' the pale young man from *The South Sussex Trumpet and Messenger* said. 'I think Guinness is more of a journalist's drink.'

'Do you, my dear chap? Then I think I'll have a Guinness too. To tell you the truth I feel a little like a journalist today.'

'Come on, chum,' said the up-and-comer from *The Daily Post*, 'out with it.'

'My dear fellow, you needn't think I'm going to succumb to crude bullying of that sort.'

The up-and-comer turned back to the bar with hunched shoulders.

'Listen, laddie,' said the girl, 'we've always been friends, haven't we? I mean I've kept these sharks in their place for you and all that. Shall we . . .?'

She slipped from the barstool.

'We shall not,' said the man from *The Examiner*.

'Look, mate,' the old hand said, 'there are ways and ways of handling a big story and if you don't know the ropes you can make a muck of it as easy as falling off a log. Now I'm willing to make a deal. My experience and your information. How about it?'

'Right in front of our faces,' said the girl. 'The Street's going down, there's no doubt about it.'

'It's a very decent offer,' said *The Examiner*, 'and I'm sorry to disappoint you, but the fact is that this is the sort of thing I'm ideally equipped to handle.'

A deprecating half-smile.

'Then you might as well tell us all about it,' the old hand said. 'I don't want to be rude, old boy, but if you're ideally equipped to handle this, quite plainly the subs at *The World* aren't.'

'There's a modicum of truth in what you say, my dear fellow. And in point of fact there's no reason why you shouldn't all hear the whole fantastic tale.'

'That's jolly decent of you,' said the pale young man.

The old hand swivelled round on his stool and looked at him without speaking.

'Then, laddie, for heaven's sake, tell,' said the girl.

'Well,' said *The Examiner*, 'I was mooching about up at the school just now – I felt I ought at least to be able to say I'd looked at the place, you know – when who should I see but – '

He broke off and looked suddenly thoughtful.

'Do you know,' he said, 'there was a hell of a row going on just as I was leaving, a lot of shouting and all that from the playing-field, I wonder ... But, no, it couldn't have been.'

The girl leant along the bar and grasped him by the tie.

'Who should you see but ...' she said.

'Oh, yes, of course, I'm so sorry. As I was saying, who should I see but ... You'll never guess. None other than my dear old tutor.'

The old hand gripped his glass with all the strength he possessed. A fixed point in a whirling world.

'Your old tutor?' he said.

'Yes, the very man. You must have heard me mention him. Old Skuce, *le vrai* Sebastian. It turns out he was one of the croquet party. He's been on the spot all the time. I'm having tea with him at the Grand later on. I'll be able to do the whole thing. The atmosphere story. He'll have everything I want. Nothing could be better. And to think if I hadn't happened to stroll past the place I might never have known he was there.'

The enormous figure of Superintendent Pinn strode across the playing-field beside Ned. His large face remained its usual shade of uniform deep pink and was as placid as ever.

'I shall be relieved to have the prisoner in custody again,' he said.

'You want to watch the way you open the pavilion door,' said Ned. 'It's a good job there are bars on the windows.'

'I don't think any difficulties should arise,' said the superintendent.

They stopped outside the pavilion.

'Now, sir,' Superintendent Pinn said, 'if you'll kindly open the door and step aside, I think you can leave the rest to me.'

Ned looked at him. Six foot six in height, shoulders like a brick wall.

'All right,' he said.

He took the key from his pocket, slipped it in, turned it, pushed the door wide and stood back.

The dark doorway.

'Come on now, me lad, look lively,' said the superintendent.

No movement. Silence.

'Now then, that's enough of that. Just come along quietly.'

The open door. Dimly swimming into view as their eyes grew used to the gloom a row of cricket bats in a rack. Above them the outline of a photograph frame. The first eleven.

'All right,' said the superintendent.

He took one enormous pace into the darkness of the little building.

Ned waited outside. Slightly crouching. Ready.

'Would you step in a moment, sir?'

The superintendent's stolid voice.

'The pavilion appears to be empty.'

Chapter Fourteen

Ned stepped into the pavilion. A faint smell of mustiness and the sweetness of linseed oil.

He looked round at the single room. The diffused light coming in from the drawn sunblinds over the two small barred windows. Nowhere for anyone to hide. The rack for bats, a pile of half a dozen stumps in a corner, a rickety scorers' table against one wall, a narrow cupboard with its door open showing an untidy collection of pads and gloves, the framed pictures of first elevens. Nothing else.

No one.

'Now, sir,' said Superintendent Pinn, 'the prisoner was locked in here, wasn't he?'

'Yes, he was,' said Ned.

'I have to make full inquiries, sir. You're certain that you actually relocked the door?'

'It's on a spring.'

'Could the snib have got pushed back before you reclosed the door?'

'No, it couldn't have. Look, superintendent, I know what's happened. That girl of his, Rosy, she's let him out.'

'That's Rosalynn Peters, an unsatisfactory witness. How could she have released him?'

'Oh hell, it was easy enough,' said Ned. 'There's a spare set of keys hanging on a board in the study.'

'We'd better make an immediate inspection,' said the superintendent.

They set off back again across the field to the house. The superintendent's walker's stride taking them along at a cracking pace. They went straight to the french windows leading into the study.

The keyboard behind the door. The rows of little screw-hooks, each neatly labelled. The faded ink of the writing. PAVILION. And the bare hook under it.

'I trusted her,' said Ned. 'I suppose I ought to have thought about the keys in here, but it never entered my head. I thought she would never think of trying anything.'

'I don't think you need blame yourself unduly, sir,' said the superintendent. 'Now we know where we are we should have the pair of them to hand within a reasonable time.'

He lifted the telephone receiver off its rest and said simply: 'Police.'

*

Lying flat against the chestnut paling that ran along the bottom of the playing-field Bert and Rosy watched, each through a different crack, as Ned and the superintendent went back to the house.

Until they were well out of earshot neither of them spoke. But as soon as it was safe Bert scrambled into a crouching position.

'So they know it was you,' he said.

'Of course they do. Do you think they'd believe it was fairies or something?'

'I thought it mightn't be all that oblivious. I didn't want you to get in it too.'

'Well, I am in it. And I'm glad I am. So that's all there is to it.'

Bert crouched in silence peering through the wooden paling. The superintendent and Ned vanished into the house.

'I don't know what to do,' Bert said.

'But I do,' said Rosy. 'Hide, and hide quick. He'll be on that phone before you can cross your fingers and the place will be swarming with 'em in no time at all.'

'We could get away down to the beach,' said Bert. 'It's not above a quarter of a mile. We might pick up a rowboat there.'

'What, with me in this,' said Rosy.

She glanced down at her trim chocolate brown uniform.

'And you still look as if you'd been dragged through a hedge,' she said.

'It was only a suggesting,' said Bert.

'Well, we've got to think of something better than that or we might as well walk straight down to the copper shop. Come on, let's move anyway.'

Rosy got to her feet and they began to move cautiously across the piece of waste land bordering on the school towards the road on the far side of it. They reached the tall hedge next to the road without any alarms. Rosy pushed aside some branches and looked through on to the road.

Quickly she drew back her head.

'Police car,' she whispered.

'Better get clear,' said Bert.

He began running back away from the road keeping low and looking back at every few strides. Rosy ran hard to keep up with him. A bramble tore the thin chocolate-brown cotton of her skirt.

The sound of the police car's engine grew louder and then died away. Bert stopped.

'We better try the road again,' Rosy said. 'If we don't get over it soon, we never will.'

The beginning of desperation.

'All right, come on.'

But before they had gone very far they heard the sound of another car. And this time the engine noise did not die away. There was the sound of rapid braking and sharp voices giving orders.

They stopped running.

'It's them,' said Bert. 'They're putting a cordrum round the place.'

'We can't stay here,' said Rosy.

Tears in her voice now.

Without any consultation they began to run back towards the school. They reached the paling together and leant their heads against it peering through the cracks to see what was happening on the playing-field. Panting with exhaustion.

Four policemen were marching sedately across the dark green grass.

From the other side of the waste land there came the sound of a second car drawing up on the road.

'More of em,' said Rosy. 'They'll come through the hedge in two seconds.'

Again they began to run. Bert kept low; Rosy was able to stay in the shelter of the paling without crouching. They stuck close to it until they got to the corner. A moment's pause while Bert flung himself to the ground and looked round the edge of the fence.

'It's okay,' he said. 'Come on.'

The waste land was broader here as the grounds of The Towers next door to the school were not as large as those of Ambrose House. Bert and Rosy ran along the side fence of the school until they reached the hedge at the bottom of The Towers garden.

'We'd better go through if it's safe,' Rosy said. 'We won't last a minute here.'

The hedge was a loose mass of rhododendrons with a rusted swathe of chicken wire running through the middle. They had no difficulty in pushing their way through.

The garden of the derelict house was deserted. They looked at each other in relief.

'Nobody much to see us where we are,' said Bert.

'No, no,' said Rosy. 'Come on, we can't wait about here for ever. Let's push on while we can.'

She darted out of the big hedge into The Towers garden. Coarse fast-growing weeds already filled the deserted flower-beds and choked back the clumps of perennials still blooming to order. The grass of the lawns was ankle-high and tussocky.

Followed cautiously by Bert, Rosy approached the silent remains of the house itself. A film of pink brick dust covered the grass, the luxuriant weeds and the paths already starred with outbreaks of dandelions.

They got to the ruins of the house itself.

'Nobody,' whispered Rosy.

Bert pulled at her sleeve.

'Watch it,' he whispered.

'All right, but come on. We've got to get under cover. Some-one's bound to poke their silly head out of a window at the school in a moment, and then we've had it.'

'All right.'

Bert clambered into the house through a gaping hole where a window had been taken out. He turned and lifted Rosy in after him. Easily into the air.

They stood silent for a moment looking up into the sky

through the roofless space above them. Big puffy white clouds were slowly moving across the blue.

'We'd better lay up here,' Rosy said. 'It's too late to go anywhere else, I reckon. There'll be cops all over the school and in the road outside.'

'What do we do then? They'll look over here all right.'

'I know. But we've got one chance. When the men come back this afternoon, and they've worked every Saturday afternoon so far, you take off your shirt, rub a bit of dust on your face and see if you can pass yourself off as a labourer.'

'But what about you?'

'I'll be all right.'

'No, Rosy, I won't let you do it. I won't let you make the scaryfice.'

'Don't be silly. Nothing's going to happen to me if they do catch me. But if they get you it might be Broadmoor again. That's what I couldn't bear to think of after Ned Farran told me where he'd locked you up.'

'So that's – '

'Never mind that. We've got to find somewhere to hide a bit till we can see a good chance to get you in with the men.'

'Listen, I – '

'Oh shut up, for heaven's sake, you and your listen thises and listen thats. Come on.'

Rosy set off on a quick exploration of the ruins of the big house. It was obvious that there was only one place left to hide in in the shell of the building, the remains of one of the towers. It had been left almost untouched and stood up above the rest of the building, for the first time a real, solitary tower.

They stood looking at it.

'It'd make a hidey hole all right,' said Bert. 'If we could get up there.'

Rosy looked up and down.

'We could do it,' she said. 'Look, we clamber up as far as there. Then we look about a bit and if the coast's clear we get up on the outer wall on that side and climb into the old window there. We wouldn't be long out where we could be seen.'

Bert looked at her. Her head at the level of his solar plexus.

'Could you do it?' he said.

'Yes.'

His eyes gleamed.

'Come on then,' he said.

The climb up to the top of the partly demolished outer wall was easy. At the top Bert peered over.

'Lucky we got off the waste when we did,' he said.

'Cops? Could they see us now?'

'There's about half a dozen of 'em. But they're lining the bottom fence of the playing-field and looking at the house. Come on, quick.'

He caught hold of the top of the wall and heaved. A sliver of brick came away under his right hand. He tossed it aside and scrabbled with his feet on the inside of the wall. The wallpaper still stuck to the plaster. A pattern of fleur-de-lis.

Bert's left foot came up to the top of the wall. A heave and he was lying straddled on the bright red of the broken bricks. He reached down inside the house as far as he could. Rosy reaching up to her full four foot eight just clasped his hand.

'Hup,' he said.

She scrabbled in her turn at the fleur-de-lis wallpaper. The marks of Bert's boots and of her pointed black shoes. And she was up. Leaning on her tummy across the wall in front of him.

'Come on, if you can,' he said.

'All right.'

They swung themselves round till they were kneeling on the wall and then began climbing using hands and feet. Two apes.

The silent midday. No outbreak of shouting. Neither of them dared look at anything but the crumbling wall directly under them getting steeper and steeper as they approached the tower itself.

And then Rosy reached the window gap and a moment later had stepped into the tower. Bert was at her heels.

They stood and looked at each other.

'I don't hear nothing,' said Bert.

'I think we've done it,' said Rosy.

Suddenly they both sank to the floor of the little octagonal tower room and lay on the dusty boards exhausted.

Slowly Bert patted something in his pocket.

'I got the cards you brought,' he said. 'Both packs of 'em.'

*

'All the same, Superintendent,' said Irene, 'once you'd caught him I don't understand why you let him go.'

'In point of fact, madam,' Superintendent Pinn said, 'the prisoner was never officially taken into custody again.'

They were standing in a group near the giant mulberry tree which the superintendent was using as an al fresco headquarters for his search operation. At intervals of a few minutes hot and bothered constables came up to report from the various sectors of the campaign. Reports of failure.

Irene had come out to ask if there was anything she could do to help. Ned had accompanied her and Sebastian and Penny had spotted the group from the house and had come to join them.

'Exactly,' said Irene, 'you let the prisoner out of your custody and one never seems to hear an adequate explanation.'

'It was all my fault,' Ned said. 'I found him and locked him up in the pavilion, but like a fool I told his girl where he was and she pinched the key and ran off with him.'

'But what was the policeman on guard doing?' said Irene.

She directed her prow bosom at the superintendent. Aggressively.

The superintendent sighed massively. His large strawberry-pink face lugubrious.

'We were not informed of the prisoner's whereabouts until too late, madam,' he said.

'Well,' said Irene, 'it's not for me to teach you your business, but I should think the man on duty at the pavilion deserves a thorough speaking-to.'

The superintendent looked towards the house where a constable had just appeared at the french window.

'Come on, man, double up,' he shouted.

The constable ran heavily towards them.

'Get a move on there,' Superintendent Pinn shouted.

The constable spurted ponderously, came to a halt in front of them and saluted puffing.

'Well?'

'Nothing, sir.'

'All right then, don't stand there blowing and snorting like that. Get back to Inspector Jarvis pretty sharp and tell him to get his men regrouped in the road outside. Double.'

The constable turned and ran off with heavy strides.

'And tell him to help out next door – in among the demolitions.'

The constable turned his head to acknowledge the order, but evidently did not trust himself to speak. He went into the house, leaning picturesquely for a moment on the edge of the french windows.

They turned to look at the search party working at The Towers.

'I nearly had industrial action on my hands,' said the superintendent. 'I wanted the men to stop work so that we could go over the place in a thorough manner, but apparently they're on piecework at overtime rates and the foreman wouldn't even consider a temporary halt.'

'I say,' Penny said, 'supposing he's in there and he disguises himself as one of the workmen. It would be quite easy to do: he'd only have to take off his shirt really.'

'I have considered that possibility,' said the superintendent. 'But I don't think it's likely to arise. I've thrown a cordon round the whole site and I've got the foreman waiting at the only point of egress to carry out a personal check on any man going out.'

'You think of everything, Superintendent,' Sebastian said. 'I must see that your thoroughness comes to the attention of a young friend of mine who, I discover, is reporting this affair for one of the papers.'

'Indeed, sir,' said the superintendent. 'I regret to tell you that my relations with the press in this affair have not been entirely satisfactory. There's been at least one instance of pressure being brought to bear on one of my constables to secure information and one case where a reporter has claimed to have information and refused to divulge the nature of it.'

'Oh, I think my protégé would be blameless,' said Sebastian. 'He writes for *The Examiner*. I gather that all he has sent them so far is what he calls a backgrounder – a little essay on "The End of Season at a Bathing Resort".'

'Hm,' said Superintendent Pinn.

They watched the double entertainment on the other side of the fence. At that moment the demolition work was providing the more thrills. The search consisted merely of the occasional sight of a despondent-looking policeman scrambling over the remains of a wall; but the demolition men were using a large iron weight swinging from a crane to knock down the last length of the outer wall of the house. An impassive workman sitting in the cabin of the crane swung the jib back through an angle of ninety degrees and then brought it round again with gathering speed. The iron weight – it was shaped like a cottage loaf – swung clumsily through the air and landed askew against the wall.

'Ineffective, though impressive,' said Sebastian.

'You wait till they catch it a really good bash,' Penny said.

'I'm prepared to spend some considerable time in expectation of that happy outcome.'

'Well, I'm not,' said Ned. 'If they don't manage to give it a decent whack in a minute I'll give up.'

The crane jib swung back again. There was a pause. And then it whirled slowly forward. The weight swayed crazily. A cracking impact and a small piece of brickwork from the corner of the wall was sent hurtling through the air to land with a crash in the middle of a bed of battered yellow chrysanthemums in the deserted garden.

'I hope they weren't hiding in there,' Penny said.

The superintendent glanced down at a notebook cradled in his vast hand.

'The garden of The Towers has been dealt with,' he said.

'Thank goodness for that,' said Irene. 'I don't like to think about that girl Rosalynn. She was one of the best workers we've ever had. I know she dresses a bit flightily in her time off but after all they're young and you have to make some allowances. How she could have been so silly, I can't think.'

'There was apparently a strong relationship between the two of them,' the superintendent said.

'Oh, I know. I encouraged it. Of course, Humphrey hadn't an idea of it. But it was so good for Bert to feel someone was taking an interest in him, and she was a really sensible girl at heart. How could she have done this?'

The crane swung forward once more. This time the weight kept its chain at full stretch.

'It's going to hit,' said Penny.

They all watched. Poised.

The weight landed fair and square in the middle of the wall. A thick black crack shot across its full length and the whole large section of masonry quivered visibly.

A sigh from every one of the watchers. Pent-up tension released.

The impassive crane operator swung the jib slowly back again.

Sebastian rubbed his hands together.

'Now,' he said, 'if I'm to be of any use to my young friend over the criminal affair I must get the details of this latest fiasco straight. Tell me exactly what happened.'

'I suppose the fiasco refers to letting that girl free Bert,' Ned said. 'Why can you people never speak straight out?'

'My dear chap,' said Sebastian, 'there have been no other fiascos, I hope.'

'All right,' said Ned, 'I'll tell you just why it happened. It was because I was stupid enough to trust young Rosy.'

'We're not interested in your stupidity as such,' said Sebastian. 'But the reason for it does intrigue us.'

'I don't think you are stupid,' Penny said.

'Thanks,' said Ned. 'But I guess I was. I told Rosy where Bert was locked up. Everybody knew where the key hung. The only thing was that I was convinced she was actually happy to think that Bert was under lock and key again.'

Superintendent Pinn, who had reverted to keeping a stern eye on his searchers, turned and took notice.

'That was not the impression I gained when I questioned her,' he said. 'I should be interested to know why you thought differently.'

'I'll tell you,' said Ned. 'It was because of what she said to me about the door leading into the changing room. You know –'

'Oh, look,' said Irene, 'they'll smash it this time.'

They all jerked round to watch the crane. The cottage-loaf weight was swinging forward in a full circle again. There was a moment of doubt and then it hit the wall with a resounding thwack on the exact spot scarred by the previous impact.

Slowly the whole large section of brickwork keeled over.

There was a thunderous crash and a heavy cloud of dust rose into the afternoon air. The crane operator unmoved swung the jib clear.

'Excellent,' said Sebastian, 'that leaves the one tower standing in splendid isolation, remote and unapproachable. I wonder if there's any chance of them blowing it up? I suppose not.'

He rubbed his hands briskly together again. The sunlight catching the reddish hairs on the backs of them.

'However,' he said, 'all that is neither here nor there. We were investigating the curious mental processes of Mr Farran. You were saying something about the changing-room door.'

'Yes,' said Ned. 'Rosy told me she put a croquet mallet under the handle of it from the outside every night. Do you see what that means?'

'Of course we don't,' said Irene. 'Heaven knows what nonsense you're talking. Everybody must be perfectly aware that that door has no lock on it. Humphrey was always fussing about it, but he never got a lock put on. I can't think why.'

'It was because the door was almost all glass, Aunt Irene.'

'Exactly, no reason at all. So he used to lock the door from the changing room into the rest of the house. It was a fearful nuisance because there's only one key to that lock.'

'Yes,' said the superintendent, 'we found the key in his pocket.'

'Too right,' Ned said, 'so you see what that means. The changing room and the boothole leading off it were completely cut off all night. The windows there don't open. They're just those glass louvre things. And one door was locked with the key in Humphrey's pocket and the other door was jammed with a croquet mallet.'

Penny's face went slowly white.

'So Bert was really locked up every night,' she said. 'He was locked up at the time of the murder.'

Chapter Fifteen

They trooped out of Superintendent Pinn's office. The girl from *The Clarion* turned to the pale young man from *The South Sussex Trumpet and Messenger*.

'You know this place,' she said, 'where's the nearest pub? I need a drink, but quick.'

'Just round here actually,' the young man said. 'But I'm afraid it's not very nice.'

'This is no time for footling about,' the old hand said. 'As long as they sell something alcoholic.'

They went in.

When they had got their drinks the man from *The Examiner* said:

'So our friend from *The South Sussex Trumpet and Whatnot* is right after all. Bert Rogers is not a murderer. This puts a somewhat different complexion on the matter.'

'You're bloody right, chum,' said the up-and-comer, 'unless the super's fooling us.'

'No point,' said the girl. 'If he wants to avoid trouble he's not going the right way about it. Look at the story we're left with now. Mysterious murder of host at croquet party and the implication that it's almost certainly one of the guests what done him in. We're on page one for days.'

'Provided there's a bit of action,' the old hand said. 'If nothing happens for too long some assassination in the Middle East or whatnot will steal our thunder.'

'Yes, but there's bound to be bits, chum,' said the up-and-comer. 'You know, I think we've been misjudging this Pinn chap. He seemed a go-getter all right just now.'

'Yes,' said the girl, 'I'd guess there'd be some copy about in the next few days. Comings-and-goings stuff at the very least.'

'But the question is,' said *The Examiner*, 'who ultimately is going to be the one to go? I trust, oh I trust, dear old Sebastian isn't going to let the college down.'

'It's anybody's guess,' said the old hand. 'Take your dear old tutor, for instance. He's been a friend of the family for years, right?'

'I gather he's been coming to this croquet week since before the war. He never let out that he played. He said to me when I bumped into him here that he was always so busy in college that he hadn't time for anything serious. The wonderful old fraud.'

'Do you know anything about his disability?' said the girl. 'It could have affected him in some way.'

'I know, I know,' the pale young man said.

Honest excitement.

'How about if the deceased had been responsible for crippling him and he thirsted for revenge?'

'Thirsted for revenge is good,' said *The Examiner*, 'only he certainly never complained to me that his life had been – er blighted.'

'But did he actually tell you he'd been born with this paralysis or whatever it is?' said the girl.

'No.'

'Then we'll bear him in mind, if only for the honour of *The South Sussex Trumpet*,' she said. 'Now what about the wife? If we're going to think in real life terms it's almost certainly the wife.'

'Sex,' said the up-and-comer. 'I dare say he was mad over Rosalynn Peters. She's a dish all right, even if she isn't exactly a giant.'

'From what I gather from old Skuce she's quite likely to have got hold of the wrong end of the stick anyhow,' *The Examiner* said. 'And I suppose she could get just as worked up over a mistake as she could over the truth.'

'I tell you who it won't be,' the old hand said. 'It won't be Leonard Driver. Having a murder done by a name the public know would be much too easy. Breaks like that don't happen to journalists.'

'Old Driver's a ruthless devil, chum,' the up-and-comer said.

'Oh, come off it,' said the girl. 'He's not the only successful businessman in the country. All of them can't be murderers.'

'Not personally anyhow,' said *The Examiner*. 'And while we're on the subject I rule out the Driver girl. She's only fourteen.'

The old hand laughed.

'Only fourteen,' he said. 'Listen, mate, nice little middle-class girls of fourteen may act like children, but there are plenty of kids of that age who behave as if they knew the facts of life. Haven't you ever covered a basement strip-clubs story?'

'I did "The Training of a Choirboy" once,' *The Examiner* said, 'but that's about my total experience in the juvenile field.'

'Then take it from me,' the old hand said. 'The kid counts.'

'And her old man counts, chum,' the up-and-comer said. 'All businessmen may not be killers, but they're not all plaster saints.'

'Granted,' the girl said. 'And the same can be said for naval heroes. There's a lot of drooling saliva behind those stiff upper lips.'

'Do you mean Lieutenant Commander M. Goodhard, R.N., retired?' the pale young man said.

'Yes, yes. I do as a matter of fact.'

'Then I can tell you something about him.'

'You can?'

'Yes. He's a headmaster too. A rival. He used to be only a teacher at Ambrose House, and then he set up on his own farther along the coast – out of our area.'

'Pity,' said *The Examiner*.

'All right,' said the girl, 'melodrama aside, if a man's tough enough to sink a battleship he isn't really so worried about human life.'

'And he did that?' said the up-and-comer.

'Of course he did,' the old hand said. 'Don't you youngsters ever do your homework nowadays?'

'Oh, we find things out, chum, don't you worry. Happen to know anything about that Australian up there?'

'No,' said the old hand.

Caution.

'You want to read the files of *The South Sussex Trumpet* then,' the up-and-comer said.

'Yes,' the young man said, 'I did a diary par on him when he first came over.'

'All right, all right,' said the up-and-comer.

The old hand smiled.

'Shall we hear all about it?' he said.

The up-and-comer turned to his drink.

'He's had a jolly interesting career,' said the young man. 'He isn't really a teacher at all. He just took the job here because he was broke. He's done all sorts of things since he graduated from university in Australia. He fought as a free-lance against the communists in Laos, he served as a merchant seaman on a pretty tough Liberian freighter and he was in Cuba for a bit with Fidel Castro. He's jolly interesting about Castro. Apparently he's not such a – '

'Okay, okay,' said the girl. 'We just want the facts: we don't want all the flim-flam feature stuff.'

'I say, you don't think Humphrey Boddershaw was really an agent of the dread Dominican dictator, do you?' said *The Examiner*.

The girl patted him on the cheek.

'No, I do not,' she said. 'I just think that Mr Ned Farran is capable of committing a murder, nothing else.'

'And of course there's that mad woman,' the old hand said. 'What's her name?'

He began pulling a battered notebook from his mackintosh pocket.

'Mrs Ravell,' said the girl. 'Mrs Cicely Ravell, the breeder of pekinese. Don't you old codgers ever do your homework?'

'You've dug up a story on her?'

The girl grinned.

'After many hours of patient research,' she said, 'our wonderful library discovered the fact that she once won a minor prize at Crufts.'

'All right,' the old hand said, 'I promise not to use that important fact. I know all I want to know after just one glimpse of the old haybag. She's capable of anything.'

'A little nervy certainly,' said *The Examiner*. 'What my dear old tutor would describe as "of a fine febrile nature". Only, come to think of it, when he's sneaking off for a quiet week's croquet my dear old tutor cuts out most of the fancy phrases.'

*

'Well,' said Sebastian, 'I think we are to be congratulated on our calm nobility of character.'

'I ought to take no notice,' Ned said, 'but, hell, I want to know what the fancy phrase is for?'

'Fancy phrase? I suppose so. A bad habit. I try to confine it to undergraduates who after all don't matter, but occasionally something slips out in company. Do mention it if you notice, my dear fellow.'

'But what Ned wanted to know was why we're all so noble,' Penny said.

'Oh, that. Simply because in spite of our complete lack of domestic aid we are all sticking it here. Yes, sticking it.'

'Oh what nonsense,' said Penny. 'I thought I'd actually done something clever for once. Anybody would be prepared to stay here.'

'Only until Monday morning, I'm afraid,' said Leonard. 'I've got a meeeting in Scotland at lunchtime and I can't afford to miss it.'

'I simply can't leave John later than I said I would,' Cicely said. 'He's hopeless in the house, perfectly hopeless. Heaven knows what an absolute mess I shall find when I get back, and if he tries to start cooking for himself the house will never be the same. Do you know I left him to it once before when I was ill, and he tried to cook himself tripe and onions. And naturally I refuse to have any such thing in my kitchen. Of course, he ruined the pan I keep specially for green vegetables.'

'So you are also to cease being noble on Monday?' said Sebastian.

'I have to go home then, that's all. I simply must.'

She jerked sharply at the edge of her cardigan.

'Nobody seems to be condemning them for running away,' said Sebastian. 'I wonder if I should invent some excuse for leaving? A very important academic controversy or something.'

Sitting twisted as usual to one side in the big leather armchair he grinned round at them all.

'If you want to go, Sebastian,' Irene said, 'by all means go. I thought you said you would like to stay and – what was the phrase? – "see the fun". But if I misunderstood and you want to leave, I shall manage. Don't you worry.'

'That's very kind of you, Irene,' Sebastian said. 'But of course I shall stay, and we won't go into my reasons.'

'I wish you'd let me take a turn in the galley, Irene,' said Michael. 'I can boil a pretty fair egg if I'm put to it.'

'No thank you,' Irene said. 'You're all being most helpful. And in any case I like doing the cooking. It takes my mind off things.'

For a moment she looked crestfallen. The enormous bosom deprived of its aggressiveness.

'I'm not really sure that I want my mind taken off things, though,' she said.

She looked round at them all.

'Tell me someone, is it true what that man Winn or Finn, or whatever his name is, keeps saying to me?'

No one answered.

'If you mean is it true that the police believe one of us killed Humphrey,' said Sebastian, 'then the answer is that they do. There's no getting out of it.'

'Thank you, dear,' said Irene.

She got up and walked slowly to the door. When it had closed there was a moment's silence.

'But why?' said Cicely. 'I can't see why they persist in this absolutely stupid idea. I knew the police weren't to be trusted any more – you've only got to motor on our ghastly roads today to find that out – but I didn't realize they were quite so stupid. You've only got to look round this room to see that they've gone hideously wrong. The fact of the matter is that every one of us is a sahib.'

She looked round the room. When she got to Ned she stopped.

'At least . . .' she said.

'What nonsense, Cicely,' said Leonard. 'People don't refrain from murder because they've been brought up as gentlemen. You've got to face facts. They refrain from murder because they've got good reason to.'

'And I take it you had good reasons to refrain from murdering Humphrey,' Sebastian said.

The quick dart of contempt.

Leonard flushed.

'I don't think that's a matter we can valuably discuss,' he said.

'I don't think it's a matter we ought to discuss,' Cicely said. 'I don't think it's a matter we ought even to consider. It's all very well for you, Leonard, to go about pretending to be a hard-faced businessman, but anyone in their senses knows the real facts. And that is simply that no one in this room would ever have killed Humphrey. I don't even think Mr Farran would.'

Ned sitting perched on the arm of the big settee leant forward in a bow.

Sebastian rubbed his hands together and shifted his position in his chair.

'Let me explain the police reasoning to you, Cicely,' he said.

'There's no need to, thank you very much. I dare say the police can waste their time inventing theories to account for the impossible, but I don't need to have my time wasted hearing them.'

Peke Abou lifted his head from his doze in her lap and slipped to the floor. He waddled straight across to Sebastian and sat looking at him with large limpid eyes.

'I'm almost constrained to recognize the existence of the brute,' Sebastian said.

'Abou,' said Cicely, 'come here this instant, sir.'

Abou remained motionless.

'While you are disciplining him,' said Sebastian, 'permit me to tell you one thing. Humphrey was killed very early in the morning, before anyone could reasonably expect him to be up and about. Anyone, that is, except us. Because we and we alone had been told by Humphrey that he intended to do an unprecedented thing and get up as soon as it was light to practise on the lawn. Are the police and I really so very foolish?'

'I suppose you're meaning to tell me that no one else knew he would be there?' said Cicely.

'Exactly.'

The foxy moustache twisting under the smile.

'But it didn't need to be anyone who knew he was there,' Cicely said. 'It could have been anybody just passing by.'

Triumph.

'And of course,' said Sebastian, 'people just passing by so very often biff anyone they happen to see with the nearest croquet mallet. We all believe that, naturally. Only unfortunately in the present instance no one was likely to be passing by. The croquet lawn can't be seen from the front of the house, and on either side and at the back, as you well know, there are no public ways.'

'Very clever,' Cicely said, 'only what you and your policemen friends haven't taken into account is that we weren't the only ones to know that Humphrey was going to practise early.'

Everybody looked at her.

'Is this some joke?' said Ned.

'How dare you suggest such a thing,' Cicely said. 'I suppose you don't understand this is a serious business. I've no doubt that in Australia people don't particularly notice one murder more or less, but let me tell you that in some parts of the world the sanctity of human life is still valued.'

'All right,' said Ned, 'who else knew about Humph's idea?'

'Almost anybody might have done.'

'But who did? Come on, I want names.'

'I don't see that you've any right to question me in this dramatic manner. It may do very well in – '

'Okay, okay,' said Ned. 'You don't have to do the whole business each time. I know what you think of Australia. Let's just take it as read, shall we? And if you don't want to tell us who knew about Humph, don't. Only, have you told the superintendent?'

Cicely stood up. Regally.

'As a matter of fact I haven't,' she said. 'I may do so in due course.'

Ned covered his face with his hands.

'And in the meantime he thinks one of us committed a murder,' he said. 'Holy cow.'

'Come along, Abou,' Cicely said. 'You need some nice fresh air after all this sitting about chattering.'

Peke Abou looked at her over his shoulder. Ineffable contempt.

Sebastian heaved himself out of the big chair and went crookedly across to the door. Cicely inclined her head towards him.

Sebastian turned round and leant firmly against the door.
He smiled.

'You're not actually leaving this room,' he said, 'until you've told us what you know about this. And when you have told us you're going straight to Superintendent Pinn to tell him.'

Cicely drew herself up.

Sebastian's smile widened. Both ends of the foxy red moustache curling.

Cicely looked round the room. Nobody moved.

'Very well,' she said, 'if you must be so childish.'

Sebastian bowed.

'It's perfectly simple,' said Cicely. 'I happened to mention Humphrey's plans to that girl, the maid, whatever her name was.'

'To Rosalynn,' said Ned. 'She told me once that you said good morning to her the first time you saw her each day and you never said a single word afterwards.'

'I don't believe in hobnobbing with the domestics, certainly,' said Cicely. 'But I happened to meet the girl and I said something to her. I thought she ought to know Humphrey would be about so early. And what is more she was just going out of the house. For what she called a breath of fresh air. So I dare say she told half the people in the town. You know what these girls are.'

Sebastian stepped aside and opened the door wide.

Cicely went through.

A toss of her head.

'No,' said Rosy, 'I never did take to that Mrs Ravell. I always said she never had a word to say to you except good morning.'

'Yes,' said Bert. 'She never said much to me for all she's so chatterish.'

'Snap,' said Rosy.

Bert's face fell.

Rosy reached forward and gathered her haul into the pile of cards in front of her.

'I'm half-way through getting the second pack,' she said.

'You ought to stop when we're talking,' Bert said.

'Go on, don't be a sissy. Can't you even play and talk at the same time?'

'No,' said Bert, 'I can't. I'm not naturally double-headed.'

'Oh, all right. Only I like a bit of chat. It's a sight better to be sitting up here talking about them down there than rushing round after them seeing to their every want.'

'Snap,' said Bert.

He scrabbled up the small central heap of cards and added it with care to his own decreasing supply.

'Snap,' said Leonard. .

'Yes,' said Ned, 'but – '

'Snap,' Leonard repeated, 'that's what's lacking everywhere today. That's why my business thrives; because I insist that everything in it from top to bottom is done with snap, smartness, efficiency. No hanging about. Even when perhaps there's no hurry. The thing is to keep everybody up to the mark.'

'Do they like it?' said Ned.

'And that's what's wrong with this investigation,' Leonard said. 'I dare say Superintendent Pinn's quite an intelligent man. People keep telling me so, and I'm willing to believe them. Because intelligence isn't what matters. What matters is snap.'

'He gets after his men all right,' Ned said.

'You think he does. But he doesn't get results. Remember he let that man get right away under his nose once. And what's he doing now? Time's passing and he's made no arrest.'

'Right now I'd guess he was having one hell of a headache,' Ned said. 'Cicely's little piece of info must have come as quite a bombshell.'

'Then he should find the girl and get to know just exactly who she told,' said Leonard. 'Get on with it. Push and press. Push and press.'

'I bet you find he's doing just that,' said Ned. 'We can't know the half of what he's done. For instance, I don't know if he's asked you about those shares.'

'Shares? What shares?'

Leonard stopped his forceful pacing of the flat surface of the playing-field. He looked at Ned.

'The shares you believed Humph's sister was keeping from you on Humph's advice,' Ned said. 'That's obviously something the super will have to go into sooner or later.'

Leonard turned and walked on. Their path took them under

the wide shade of the old mulberry tree. Leonard's heavy feet squashing the fallen fruit.

'That's absurd,' he said. 'The whole business of the shares was a complete triviality. Just a matter of tidying up the holdings. Not a thing that mattered one way or the other. You weren't thinking that I might have killed Humphrey because of a handful of shares, were you?'

'Certainly I was,' said Ned. 'Jeez, it's only natural. Until Cicely came out with this business it looked almost certain that it was one of us who killed him. You have to think of all the possibilities.'

Leonard looked at him.

'And you thought of me?' he said.

'I thought of everyone,' said Ned. 'Didn't you?'

'Yes, yes, I did. Of course I did. It's only natural in the circumstances.'

'All right. So who do you think killed him?'

'I – I really cannot say.'

'You must have some opinions one way or the other.'

'I don't see – And in any case it now looks most likely that a rumour got about the town and someone took advantage of it and came up here early and . . .'

'Sounds most likely, I must say.'

'Well, it may not sound very possible on the face of it, but it's the only reasonable explanation, and there it is.'

'Listen,' said Ned, 'before there was this off-chance you had someone in mind. Who was it?'

'I don't see – '

'Oh come off it. Who was it?'

Leonard came to a stop. He looked cautiously at Ned. He glanced round about. No one to be seen on the whole wide field. He leant his head nearer Ned's.

'I've always suspected,' he said, 'that Cicely is mad.'

Chapter Sixteen

Ned glanced sharply at Leonard.

'Mad?' he said. 'I don't think you can say that just by seeing her about. People aren't bits of litmus paper: you can't dip them into a test solution and see whether they come out red or blue.'

'Yes,' said Leonard, 'Poor Cicely is mad. There can be no doubt about it.'

He caught hold of Ned's sleeve.

'The question is,' he said, 'is she so mad that she might have killed Humphrey?'

He seemed to expect an answer.

Two-way communication.

'It's certainly possible,' said Ned. 'I don't mind telling you she as good as told me Humph ought to have been killed.'

'She did?' said Leonard.

He looked round again.

'Don't you see,' he said, 'if she did murder Humphrey all this business about telling the girl that he was going to be up early is a blind?'

Ned found Irene staring sombrely at the demolition work still going on at The Towers.

'I hear the cops have given up,' he said.

'Yes,' said Irene, 'Superintendent Winn – I've got his name right at last – came and told me they think the pair of them must have got out beyond the town somewhere. I don't know what to think about it.'

'Hell, neither do I. I thought I had Rosy buttoned up. I thought she was a sensible kid. And then she went and did that to me. It's a poor cow right enough.'

'And Bert didn't kill Humphrey?' Irene said.

'No. That's definite anyway. The super seems quite satisfied.'

'Now, what about this thing of Cicely's? If Rosalynn knew Humphrey was going out early to practise, what does it mean?'

'It means for one thing that you've got to add Rosy to the list of suspects. That may have been the reason why she skipped. I don't know.'

'Well, that's nonsense for one thing,' said Irene.

Ned smiled.

'It's a relief to hear someone who thinks that something's definite,' he said. 'And I think you're right. I don't see that four foot nothing slamming out with a croquet mallet. But if she was just going out that night as Cicely said she was, then it's certainly possible that she told someone. It means the field is more open certainly.'

'Yes, but who could it have been?' Irene said. 'It's utter rubbish to think of the town as being full of Humphrey's mortal enemies.'

'Somebody might have got some crazy idea that he had a lot of money on him.'

'But he didn't. The police told me what they found in his pockets. One handkerchief and one bunch of keys. Nothing else at all. He just got up and put on a few clothes and crept out without waking me. He didn't bother to put everything in his pockets.'

'Yes, yes, I know. But the idea could have got about.'

'No, you can put that right out of your head. Humphrey did not have any money on him. I know that.'

'But – Hell, it doesn't matter anyway. That wasn't what I wanted to ask you. I wanted to hear something about Cicely, Mrs Ravell.'

'What about her?'

Ned held on to the top of his head with widespread fingers.

'I don't know,' he said, 'I guess that's stupid, but what I want is for you to tell me all you know about her, in case there may be something.'

Irene wheeled her prow bosom towards him.

'In case there may be what?' she said.

Ned looked at her from the corner of his eye.

'In case she killed Humph,' he said.

'Well, she didn't,' said Irene.

'That's great. That's one less to think about. How did you find out?'

'Find out? I didn't find out. I know. You can't suspect Cicely of murder: I've known her for years.'

Ned reached forward and clutched the top of the paling between Ambrose House and The Towers. It shook.

'Listen,' he said, 'you told me you didn't trust the police, do you still feel the same way now as you did then?'

'I told you then,' said Irene, 'that I wanted to know the truth. Of course I still want to know it. There are too many mistakes and misunderstandings in the world, Mr Farran. This mustn't be one of them.'

Ned let go of the fence. Cautiously.

'Then you will have to stop telling me that people didn't kill Humph because you've known them for a long time,' he said.

'My dear Mr Farran, let us get this one thing clear. If you think Cicely is in any way responsible for this then you're utterly wrong. That's simply all there is to be said about it.'

Ned looked at the palings.

'As far as I can see,' he said, 'there can be only one reason why you . . .'

He looked at his hands. They were stained with pink brick-dust. He looked up at the three-parts demolished house.

'They seem to be knocking off over there,' he said. 'They're getting along at a pretty smart rate. They'll be bashing the old tower down before we know where we are. Likely as not first thing on Monday morning they'll come along, whip a bit of wire round the top, give it a yank, and – bingo – the whole bloody thing will come cracking down.'

'Very interesting,' said Irene. 'And now suppose we go on talking about who killed my husband?'

Ned turned and looked at her full in the face.

She stood looking squarely back at him, her feet as often a little apart. Solidly on the ground. Her large eyes unblinking, her wide mouth set in its accustomed determined line. Only a little extra depth in the furrows running down the edge of her cheeks showing the experience she had passed through. She wore as she had done since the day after Humphrey's death a plain black dress noticeably too small for her. Three stitches had given at the waist.

'All right,' said Ned, 'tell me who you think killed Humphrey?'

'If I knew the truth about it, I wouldn't ask you to help me find it.'

'All right, there'll be nothing you can prove. Maybe you never will be able to. Perhaps you can't even begin to see the why and wherefore of it all. But who killed him, Mrs Boddershaw?'

Irene's unflinching face.

'It was Sebastian,' she said.

'Sebastian?' said Ned. 'You know, I've got a feeling he isn't really the violent type. This was a crime of violence. If it wasn't that, it didn't happen, it just didn't happen.'

'He's nurtured a grudge against Humphrey for very nearly a whole lifetime,' said Irene.

'This crippling business. I'm not quite sure – '

'Nothing Humphrey could do could ever repay the debt Sebastian felt he was owed,' Irene said. 'He had to pay it with his life. I didn't want to tell you this. I hoped you would see for yourself that it was so. I would have felt I had some corroboration then. So often I'm the only one to be right. Oh, I know that's only over the little things, the minor worries of running a school. But it's a strain. To be on your own like that so much. Humphrey was no help to me over that. He was a dear kind soul and I'm totally lost without him, but he was always desperately muddle-headed. I had to keep things straight.'

She looked down at her feet. Steady as rocks.

She looked up again.

'I hoped that with something as overwhelming as this I was not going to have to set the pace yet again,' she said. 'But it was not to be. It fell to me to say it. Sebastian Skuce killed my husband.'

'Just tell me one thing,' said Ned.

Quietly.

'Yes?'

'Why did he wait so long? If he hated Humph like that for all those years – if he did – why did he wait till last Thursday

190

morning to kill him? Why Thursday? Why in the morning? Why last week? Why this year?'

'It was because he had waited so long that he waited till Thursday morning,' said Irene. 'Don't you see that?'

'Hell, no, I don't,' said Ned.

No longer quiet.

'People are so dense,' Irene said. 'Everybody is. I can't understand it. This is perfectly simple. Circumstances at the time prevented Sebastian revenging himself as he wanted to straight away. I don't know how it happened. I heard very little about the episode. It was something buried in Humphrey. Buried deep. But that doesn't matter. What does matter is that Sebastian had to wait. He wasn't able to kill in hot blood, so he had to kill in cold blood. He didn't want to pay the penalty, Mr Farran. He wanted to have his revenge and then to start his life afresh, where he thought it would have gone on from before this obsession came upon him.'

Ned's eyebrows rose.

'Bert?' he said.

'Ah,' said Irene, 'you see it now at any rate.'

The overbearing bosom loomed.

'That's exactly it,' she said. 'Sebastian waited until there was someone to take the blame for Humphrey's death. He waited just for that, year after year after year. And now there may be no way of proving him guilty. He may have left no trail. No trail at all.'

'Look,' said Bert.

Rosy wriggled over beside him on the dust-stained boards of the isolated tower room. She peered over the edge of the empty window.

Below them in the gathering dusk the figures of Mrs Boddershaw and Ned Farran were still clearly visible.

'Old Ma B.,' Bert said.

'And look at Mr Farran,' said Rosy. 'He seems to be watching this very spot. You don't think he's spotted something, do you?'

'Don't be a scaredy,' said Bert. 'He couldn't see nothing, not with there being no light in here. There's nothing for us to show up against.'

Rosy stayed where she was.

'I suppose he can't have done,' she said. 'He'd be racing off like mad, if he thought he'd seen us. You know what he is: something comes into his head and off he goes.'

'What they call impressive,' Bert said.

'Impulsive,' said Rosy, 'that's just about what he is. I like it though. I hate the cold calculating sort. Makes me feel sorry I had to do what I did to him. He was trusting me, you know, really. But all of a sudden I thought of you back in that place and I couldn't bear it. I think he'd understand that all right.'

She half sat half leant against the wall under the window still looking out.

'I wonder what they're talking about,' Bert said. 'You can almost hear what they're saying.'

'There's no need to hear what they're saying to know what they're talking about,' said Rosy. 'It couldn't be anything else but the murder. They must know by now that you didn't do it.'

Bert laughed.

'And you thought I did,' he said. 'When all the time you had that mallet up against the door and I didn't know it.'

'I'm sorry,' Rosy said. 'I seem to have made a proper muck up of everything. There wasn't no one I could turn to.'

Bert put his arm round her.

'You're a muggins, that's what you are,' he said, 'I couldn't no more have got out of the changing room without smashing something than what I could fly.'

'Oh, I know. I ought to have known all along really. But I got muddled. Fancy being such a fool as to talk to that man from the papers. It was you seeing the murder and not being able to talk about it that I couldn't bear.'

'I can't help it.'

'I know you can't. I don't mind if I don't ever know now.'

'Yes, yes.'

Hoarse urgency.

'I want you to know. But I can't tell you. Not unless something makes me. That's why I don't mind even though you're winning at the Snap.'

'But perhaps I won't win in the end.'

'Then it's decided for us. I've been thinking about it. We'll finish the game tomorrow, one way or the other. Then if you've won I'll call out and say we're stuck up here as soon as I see anybody.'

'Look,' said Rosy, 'there's old Mrs B. tramping into the house. Just the way she always does. I bet she's been laying down the law about something.'

'She's given that young chap something to think about by the look of it,' Bert said.

'What if I don't win?' said Rosy.

'I'll have to climb down the tower in the middle of the night,' Bert said. 'It'll be a bit dodgy but I think I'd manage.'

'If you go I go,' said Rosy.

Bert squeezed her more tightly.

From behind the door of the dining-room there came a high insistent whining sound. Ned paused for a moment in the darkness of the corridor and listened.

Then he walked quietly up to the door in his bare feet. Pyjama legs flapping round his ankles.

He opened the door.

'Oh,' he said.

The room was in complete darkness with the heavy curtains drawn. From the far end where the television set stood between the two boards painted with the names of head boys and scholarship winners there was a faint light. The set was switched on and although the television programmes had long ago closed down the radio in the set was uttering a very subdued stream of jazz.

Without bothering to put on the light Ned padded his way across the familiar room to the set, reached forward and switched it off.

'Hey,' said a sharp voice from low down behind him.

Ned started.

Lying on the floor in the shadow of the large sofa Penny Driver laughed.

'You jumped a mile,' she said.

'You bet I did,' said Ned. 'I didn't know there was anybody in here. It's after midnight. I was prowling around and I heard a noise in here. I thought it was that bloody dog of Cicely's.'

'And what were you prowling around for at the terrible hour of after midnight?' said Penny.

'I couldn't sleep if you must know,' Ned said.

Penny sat up.

'Neither could I,' she said. 'I wonder if all the rest of them are lying awake. I listened at Daddy's door on my way down, but I couldn't hear anything.'

'You're very fond of your old man, aren't you?'

'Well, Mummy wasn't really very satisfactory,' Penny said. 'How Daddy came to marry her I can't think. They had simply nothing in common.'

'Which probably redoubled the violence of their mutual attraction,' said Ned.

For a moment Penny was silent in the darkness of the room.

'Yes,' she said, 'I expect you're right. Anyhow by the time I was taking notice they were poles apart. I suppose I ought to have sided with Mummy. It isn't as if she isn't my type or anything. She's really awfully nice, like Uncle Humphrey, only she doesn't go biffing about the way he does.'

'But you didn't back her,' said Ned. 'You backed your old man.'

'Yes. So when the break-up came eventually it was agreed that I should more or less stick with him.'

'And that worked out very well for you?'

'We've always got on terribly well. I honestly sometimes feel more like a sister to him. I really do understand him. That's why I'm so sympathetic about Helen.'

In the darkness Ned smiled.

'I know what you're getting at,' said Penny.

Ned stopped smiling. The wary eyes.

'All right,' he said, 'did you think you understood that he wanted your Uncle Humphrey out of the way? And did you do it for him?'

Penny got to her feet. Ned could just make out that she was wearing a dressing gown, woollen, in some plain colour, school regulation.

194

'If I had done that for Daddy,' Penny said, 'I'd have to go through with it, wouldn't I? It would be no use committing a murder to make him happy and then going and making him twice as miserable by confessing to it.'

Chapter Seventeen

Penny stood silently in the dark dining-room with the school-girlish woollen dressing gown knotted firmly round her.

'What makes you say that?' Ned asked her.

'Well, it's true, isn't it?'

'Depends what you mean by truth.'

'I mean the truth, what really is. If I had killed Uncle Humphrey for Daddy I couldn't let anyone find out: that's true.'

'If the moon was made of green cheese we could eat it,' said Ned.

Penny suddenly sat back on the floor. In one lithe movement.

'I wouldn't mind having the wireless on again,' she said.

Still watching her, Ned reached behind him and clicked the switch. Quite soon the thin stream of violent music spread into the darkness.

'It's New Orleans,' said Penny. 'I hate cool jazz.'

'Good on you.'

They listened.

Penny's head nodding to the fierce beat of the music. Her hair just visible.

The nodding stopped abruptly.

'She didn't.'

'Who didn't?' said Ned. 'And if you don't want to drive me insane, you'd better tell me what she didn't at the same time.'

'Cicely,' said Penny.

Slowly.

'Cicely didn't tell Rosalynn about Uncle Humphrey.'

'No?' said Ned. 'Are you sure? You're not kidding?'

'No. It's just come back to me. She couldn't have done because I was with her when she went to bed that night. We went up together. She went straight to her room. She never saw

Rosalynn on the way to bed, the way she described it to us. She even put out her light almost straight away. I went to the bathroom and I noticed it on my way back.'

'She couldn't have left the room and then met Rosy when she was on her way to bed for the second time?'

'No. For one thing she made quite a thing about going straight to bed. You know what she is.'

'I've an idea.'

'And then as I passed her door I heard Peke Abou snoring. He makes a fearful row. And he never will stay in the room if Cicely goes out. It's quite a joke. If she goes along to spend a penny in the middle of the night Peke Abou goes too.'

'I'm going to have a talk with Cicely right now.'

Penny laughed.

Ned looked down at her.

'I wouldn't if I were you,' she said. 'Not unless you want to catch rabies.'

'All right,' said the old hand, 'but I'm not going to stay up twenty-four hours on end for any lousy night-news editor. At my time of life I need my beauty sleep.'

The girl slipped off the bar stool and peered closely at his face.

'You do,' she said.

'There's no point in staying up anyhow, chum,' the up-and-comer said. 'Nothing's happening. I'm beginning to get sick of the myth of Superintendent Pinn.'

'Yes,' said *The Examiner*, 'we've been passing it to and fro all afternoon and evening. Let's have the myth of the stupid police now for a bit of a change.'

'It's all very well to make jokes,' the pale young man said, 'but the super's done some jolly good work down here. He's been commended by the bench three times.'

'Oh well, we didn't know that,' said the girl.

Ned stopped suddenly.

His foot on the first tread of the stairs.

He frowned slightly and peered backwards into the darkness. Through the uncurtained windows of the corridor behind him the dim light of the moon coming from behind a thin layer of cloud allowed him to make out the shape of the walls. A thin black line painted along them about five feet from the ground, below it serviceable green paint, above it slightly dingy white. Two fire extinguishers clamped side by side.

Still frowning slightly Ned retraced his steps. He went along the corridor. At the end he suddenly raised his eyebrows.

The door cutting off the changing room from the main body of the house was open.

Ned crept forward.

He stood beside the open door and waited. Silence.

He slipped into the changing room. In the faint obscured moonlight he could make out the rows of empty lockers. Without taking his eyes from the far end of the room where there was space, he knew, for someone to hide, he sidled along to the boothole. Its door was shut.

Ned listened.

Nothing.

With a quick jerk he threw open the boothole door and ducked back.

But this time no hurtling figure came out. Ned cautiously looked in. There could be no doubt even in the darkness that the room was empty.

Coming out Ned noticed that the lockless door to the playing-field was an inch ajar. With a final quick glance at the far end of the changing room, sleeping still in the faint light, he went up to the outside door.

Standing beside it he counted up to ten while he strained his ears.

The sound of the slight wind stirring the leaves of the mulberry tree. Too much noise in the quiet night to make it possible to distinguish any other minute sounds. Ned moved round and looked through the gap between the door and the jamb.

The steady draught which had first caught his attention as he had begun to climb the stairs.

He could see a segment of the playing field. The grass black in the half moonlight. He looked up at the sky. A jagged rent in the clouds was slowly sailing towards the brighter patch of light where the moon was. Quickly Ned slipped out of the door before the full light of the moon flooded the playing-field.

And immediately he saw the end of his trail.

Standing on the croquet lawn within a yard of the place where Humphrey Boddershaw had been killed the unmistakable twisted figure of Sebastian.

He was standing still looking down at the hoop which Humphrey had been practising at and which with the others had been left in place since his death.

Ned stood quietly watching Sebastian. For a long time he gazed down at the hoop at his feet. Then he crouched on the ground and stayed motionless.

Inch by inch Ned edged away along the veranda to a place where he could watch Sebastian from the deep shadow thrown by one of the supporting pillars.

He was only just in time. Abruptly Sebastian rose up, turned and limped awkwardly towards the house. Ned eased his body forward ready to follow quickly. But on the veranda Sebastian stopped. He peered round in the moonlight. Ned held himself rigid. Sebastian bent down and picked something off the floor. As he straightened himself Ned could see what he was holding.

In the dark shadow of the pillar he frowned quickly.

A pair of croquet balls.

Ned kept his eyes firmly fixed on the silhouette of Sebastian. He saw him go decisively to the rack of croquet mallets near the door to the changing room and take one out of its holder.

The faint ping of the springy metal as the mallet was jerked out.

Quickly Sebastian went back to the croquet lawn. He carefully placed the balls about a foot away from the hoop. Then he stood up, took up position carefully, swung the mallet two or three times in the air, bent forward a little and with the greatest delicacy played a stroke.

The tap of the mallet on the first ball and immediately afterwards the click of the two balls meeting. The sounds loud as pistol shots in the night.

Ned craned forward.

The first ball ran neatly between the wires of the hoop.

Sebastian slowly straightened himself up. He let go of the mallet with one hand and rubbed the small of his back.

'Not a bad shot, was it, Mr Farran?' he said.

Ned grinned.

'I didn't really have too much cover,' he said.

He came down the veranda steps and joined Sebastian on the close-cropped turf of the croquet lawn.

'I hope you're wearing shoes without heels,' Sebastian said without turning round. 'You know how strict Humphrey is about that particular rule.'

Ned wriggled his naked toes. The clamminess of the grass on the soles of his feet.

'Is,' he said, 'so Humphrey wasn't killed after all?'

Sebastian turned towards him.

The full light of the moon on his face. The reddish hair distinctly visible. The twist of his moustache as he smiled.

'The feel of a mallet in my hands brought him back,' he said. 'I suppose this is the only time in the rest of my life that I shall handle one.'

He swung the mallet back and forth in the chill night air.

'A midnight farewell,' said Ned.

'No.'

Indignation.

'I'm not exactly a sentimental old spinster,' Sebastian said.

'I thought it wasn't entirely in character,' said Ned, 'but you take such care to present your character by the light of day that I wondered if you weren't relaxing just for a moment.'

Sebastian laughed.

A fox's bark.

'Your psychology is a bit too simple, my dear chap,' he said. 'Life isn't like that. When you're dealing with flesh-and-blood people the mask is the face. They grow fast together.'

Ned's rueful smile.

'So Humphrey is dead,' he said.

'Of course,' said Sebastian, 'why else do you think I'm here?'

'The old anthropology angle, eh? Did you get anywhere?'

Sebastian stooped and picked up the two balls. He grunted as he straightened himself up.

'There was nowhere to get,' he said. 'One becomes a trifle foolish in the middle of the night when one can't get to sleep.'

'Yes,' said Ned.

'But not quite so foolish as to turn into a sentimental old spinster,' said Sebastian. 'There aren't any fairies in the moonlight.'

As he spoke a sharp edge of cloud passed in an instant over the face of the moon. The light withdrawn.

'In which case,' said Ned, 'I have to take a twist at the mask myself.'

The soft double thump as Sebastian let the two croquet balls fall.

'What made you into a cripple?' Ned said.

Sebastian laughed.

'I do believe Irene has been talking to you,' he said. 'You didn't really believe that story of hers, did you? About the terrible thing that Humphrey did to me at school. Of course, I'm not supposed to realize she talks to people about it, but you know Irene. I'm sorry to tell you that the truth of the matter is that I'm just that much younger than Humphrey was, and although we were at the same school he left the term before I went there.'

He chuckled and rubbed the palms of his hands together. The reddish hair on their backs invisible in the dim moonlight.

'A matter susceptible of verification,' he said. 'Schools preserve their documents, if Humphrey's is anything to go by.'

'I had to check on that business,' Ned said. 'Irene can't be at cross purposes over every blamed thing.'

Sebastian smiled.

'You've missed the point of Irene,' he said. 'She is at cross purposes over everything. It's her nature.'

He looked down at the two balls lying on the short grass, black in the half-light, at his feet.

'I hope she doesn't change after all this,' he said. 'She needs somebody to look after her. It was only having Humphrey that let her grow so luxuriantly. And it's her great charm.'

The cold diffused rays of the moon and the chill breeze stirring the leaves of the giant mulberry.

Sebastian picked up the balls again.

Ned looked up at the house, the colour of its red bricks just emerging in the pallid light. The white-painted windows of the classrooms and the dormitories – Passchendaele, Ypres, Somme, Mons, Aisne, Vimy.

'I'll tell you one thing,' he said. 'Somehow or another someone has got to satisfy Irene that she knows who killed Humphrey.'

Sebastian tucked the croquet mallet under one arm and began hobbling back to the house.

'I suppose so,' he said.

'You know so,' said Ned.

Sebastian stopped and looked back at Ned.

'What if I do?' he said. 'We may never know. And if we do, it's a hundred to one that Irene will decide everybody else is wrong. It's beyond me, it's all too much.'

He limped on again.

Ned caught him up as he was restoring the mallet to its clip.

'What about the Fool King?' he said. 'You had ideas enough a couple of days ago.'

'My dear chap, if you believed that you'd believe anything.'

'All right then,' said Ned.

The spurt of anger.

'All right then, who did kill Humph? Don't pretend to me you haven't got some name in your head. Who was it? For once in your life just answer straight out.'

Without speaking Sebastian trickled the two croquet balls back into their box.

'Answer up,' said Ned.

Sebastian looked at him briefly.

'My dear fellow, you sound as if you might use violence.'

Ned's shoulders dropped. Sudden relaxation.

'I sound like that, do I?' he said. 'Well, you're too right, sport, I will use violence. Answer my question or I'll hit you just where you stand.'

'Hit a cripple? Hardly cricket, old man.'

'Only Pommies play cricket that way. Now answer up.'

'I do believe you would stoop to violence.'

The crooked smile a bit forced.

Ned took a pace forward.

'All right,' said Sebastian quickly, 'if you can't think of it for yourself. But isn't it obvious? Who had just learnt something about Humphrey that changed their whole attitude to him? Are you that much of a fool?'

'Cut the insults,' said Ned.

'Gently, gently. I'll spell it out for you if I must, though you disappoint me. I had thought you showed a certain astuteness. Just think a minute. Wasn't it Irene who had learnt only a few hours before Humphrey was killed that he had been deceiving her with the matron? Isn't it plain as a pikestaff?'

Ned shook his head.

'I suppose I was a fool,' he said.

Sebastian turned and began to limp away towards the changing-room door.

'I ought to have known better,' Ned said, 'than to think I could get an answer out of you. But you might have credited me with more sense than to fall for that cock.'

Sebastian showed no sign of having heard.

He went back into the house.

In an instant Ned was standing at the changing-room door peering into the darkness. He could just make out the twisted form of Sebastian passing the boothole.

'I've been remembering my anthropology,' Ned said.

The quiet, carrying voice.

'I remembered that it was the rule that whoever killed the Fool King succeeded to the throne. Do you know any good Jokers around?'

At the corner Sebastian stopped. He turned slowly to look at Ned in the doorway. Then he hurried on into the darkness.

Penultimate

The next morning, Sunday, was the first day of autumn. The sun was shining but, low on the horizon, it had lost its power to warm. The wind, though light, was from the east and chilly. One or two leaves on the mulberry tree had yellowed in the night.

Cicely Ravell swung open the wide panelled oak front door with 'Ambrose House School' painted above it. Peke Abou darted out with a concerned expression and made for the nearest rhododendron bush.

'There's a good old man,' said Cicely.

Ned stepped forward from behind the corner of the house.

'Good morning,' he said, 'I wanted a word with you.'

'Good gracious,' said Cicely, 'have you been waiting for me here? What an extraordinary thing to do. You might have caught a dreadful chill. It's decidedly cold this morning. This isn't – hem – down under, you know.'

Ned turned up his jacket collar.

'This was important,' he said.

'Abou, Abou,' said Cicely. 'Leave that alone at once, sir. It's filthy, filthy, do you hear me?'

Peke Abou came out of the rhododendron bush with his tiny teeth clenched firmly on to a discarded toffee apple. He was growling hard.

'Would you like me to get it from him?' said Ned.

'He certainly mustn't be allowed to have it,' Cicely said. 'Sweet things are terribly bad for him, and this is bound to be full of the most awful germs as well. Abou, let it go at once.'

Abou looked up. For once he seemed disposed to obey. He attempted to drop the toffee apple.

His jaws were totally stuck.

Cicely rushed forward.

'My poor little darling,' she said. 'Did he hate the horrid toffee apple? Has he got his little mouth stuck on it? There, there. Let Aunty Cicely do it for him.'

She tried to haul open Peke Abou's jaws. After a moment he produced a squeal of agony from behind the toffee apple.

'Did she hurt him? Well then, he must be a brave old boy and let her have just one good pull. Now then.'

With a violent wriggle of his whole body Peke Abou escaped from Cicely's grip and took up a position in the depths of the rhododendron bush.

'Well,' said Cicely, 'can't you get him out, Mr Farran?'

Peke Abou growled. Miniature thunder.

'I'm wearing a good suit,' said Ned.

'Really, I should have thought an Australian wouldn't have been put off by a little dirt. Besides it's perfectly good mould under there. It's excellent for growing things.'

Ned went down on his knees. He approached Peke Abou. Peke Abou retreated.

'I don't want to grow anything,' Ned said.

'What was that?' said Cicely. 'You shouldn't mutter like that.'

'Nothing,' said Ned.

'And in any case you should try to learn to like growing things. Gardening's a wonderful hobby, and teaches you patience.'

Ned lunged forward viciously and caught Peke Abou round his middle. He backed out of the rhododendron holding firmly on to the wriggling dog.

'Oh, you mustn't hold him like that,' said Cicely. 'That's completely the wrong way to hold any dog.'

Ned looked down at the squirming creature in his hands.

'He seems to have forgotten his toffee apple anyhow,' he said.

'Then give him to me this instant,' said Cicely.

Ned extended his hands. Cicely put one hand carefully under Peke Abou's chest and the other under his back legs.

'There,' she said.

In a flash Peke Abou was back under the rhododendron.

'So long as he doesn't get that terrible toffee apple again perhaps it would be better to leave him there,' said Cicely. 'He needs a few moments perfect quiet to recover in. You may not know, Mr Farran, that a thoroughbred pekinese is much more sensitive than the majority of human beings. There, there, Abou darling, you just stay there and have a good rest. The horrid man won't touch you again.'

'Listen,' said Ned, 'why did you lie to everybody when you told them you had passed on the information about Humphrey going to practise? Why was it? What did you do it for?'

Cicely stood quite still.

For almost the first time since Ned had seen her she was bereft of violent jerky movement. She stood looking at a point somewhere beside the rhododendron bush without the constant darting glances that she was generally incapable of suppressing. Her hands hung limply at her sides instead of restlessly fiddling with whatever they came into contact with.

She was silent.

'Come on,' said Ned, 'shake it up. I know you lied: what did you do it for?'

Slowly Cicely turned her head and looked at him.

'Yes,' she said. 'Of course I invented all that.'

Ned relaxed.

'But what did you do it for?' he said.

Cicely's eyes darted a quick glance at the rhododendron bush. No sign of Peke Abou.

'What else could I do?' she said. 'I simply had to say something. I couldn't bear it a moment longer. I wasn't going to put up with it: the thought that one of us – a croquet player – had done a thing like that. It was unendurable, utterly unendurable. So I told everybody that it wasn't so.'

A simple declaration.

Ned remained silent.

After a moment he whistled sharply and Peke Abou came frisking out of the rhododendron bush.

'Come on, boy,' Ned said. 'It's time we all went in to breakfast.'

Peke Abou rushed to the door.

Ned went to open it for him. Cicely followed.

At the door Ned said:

'You know you couldn't have changed the truth of the matter, don't you?'

'It was very silly,' said Cicely.
A whisper.

Bert and Rosy woke early.

Rosy groaned.

'I feel awful,' she said. 'It's so cold. I'd be hungry if I wasn't so sick.'

Bert looked at her. He rubbed his shoulder where it was stiff from lying all night on the bare boards.

'Want to turn it in?' he said.

'When we've almost done it? Don't be stupid.'

A flash of the old fire.

Bert stood up, stretched, and flapped his arms vigorously across his chest.

'That's better,' he said. 'Starts the old circumlation going again. You try it.'

'No thanks. I feel too sick.'

'Go on, try it. It'll warm you up, then you'll feel better. It's no use sitting still feeling miserable. You got to do something, if it's only move about a bit.'

Rosy stood up and leant against the wall. The bright contemporary wallpaper. A pattern of veteran motor-cars. Her face, the last traces of make-up gone, without colour.

'Come on,' said Bert. 'You got to do something. Something violent.'

Rosy shook her head.

Bert seized her hands in his and began pumping them backwards and forwards as hard as he could go.

'No, no. Stop. Stop, Bert. I'll sick up. Bert, stop. Really I will.'

The colour coming back into her face.

'Oh, you devil,' she said. 'Wait till I get my hands free. I'll slap your face for this, Bert Rogers.'

Bert laughed. Backwards and forwards, backwards and forwards.

Rosy laughed.

Bert dropped her hands.

'That's better,' he said. 'Now come on, on with the old Snap while we're a bit warm.'

'Okay,' said Rosy.

She sat cross-legged on the boards pink with brickdust.

'And if I win . . .' she said.

'And if you win I lean right out of that window and holler till someone comes,' said Bert. 'And the first thing I do down there is to tell 'em the name I'll tell you.'

He began flicking the cards one by one from his turned-down pile into the centre.

'Snap,' said Rosy.

Ned and Penny stayed on after breakfast to clear the table.

'Well,' Ned said, 'and when did you get to bed eventually last night?'

'Oh, I went up about five minutes after you left me. I suddenly felt terribly sleepy. I was so quick I thought I'd catch you up on the stairs, but you must have whizzed up.'

'No,' said Ned, 'I went for a little moonlight stroll.'

'For heaven's sake, I thought I was mad enough. It must have been awfully cold at that time of night. I felt a fierce draught in the hall whistling in from somewhere.'

'I guess I must have left the playing-field door open,' said Ned.

'Have you had your talk with Cicely?' Penny said. 'I thought she was rather subdued at breakfast and now she's disappeared somewhere.'

'She's off to see the super,' said Ned. 'She wants to tell him she invented that piece about Rosy.'

'Invented it? But in heaven's name why?'

'She had her reasons, of a sort.'

Penny thought for a moment, and then she said:

'I say, I'm awfully sorry I said all that last night about never confessing if I'd done a murder to help Daddy. It was green cheese, you know.'

Ned paused. Two toast racks clutched in the fingers of his left hand, an empty milk jug with a cup perched in it in his right.

'That's the line you'll have to take,' he said. 'You'll have to stick to it from start to finish. "It would never have entered my head to do a thing like that." You just keep on saying it. It's the only way.'

He grinned.

'You pig,' Penny said.

Ned carried the dirty dishes to the serving hatch. With care.

As he was leaning through to dump them on the table on the far side Penny said:

'All the same that doesn't solve anything, does it?'

Ned backed out of the serving hatch.

'I didn't catch that,' he said.

Penny put down the crumb brush which she had just begun to use.

'Ned, who killed him?' she said.

Ned looked at her.

'It isn't going to be easy whoever it was, is it?' he said.

'That's what was keeping me awake last night.'

'And I thought it was a guilty conscience.'

Penny smiled. Half-heartedly.

'You're the outsider really,' she said. 'You'd be the one who could look at us all and see us as we really are. Ned, do you know? Have you any idea really?'

'Look,' said Ned. 'I'm not going to go telling you a name or anything. I could be wrong.'

'Then you do know.'

'Hell, no, I don't.'

'You must. You wouldn't have said what you did, if you hadn't got a name in your mind.'

'Listen,' said Ned, 'whoever it is it's going to hurt you. Correct weight?'

'Correct weight,' said Penny.

The sad parody of Ned's accent.

'Oh, even Sebastian,' she said. 'Especially Sebastian in some ways.'

'Well,' said Ned, 'just try to think of that. Try to be ready whoever it is.'

He picked up the crumb brush and began pushing the crumbs round the table in a series of violent jerks.

'And remember,' he said, 'you're the favourite, odds of about two to one on.'

'The awful thing is,' said Penny, 'there's no real reason why you shouldn't think that. After all everybody can see that I'd do anything for Daddy – I did even threaten Uncle Humphrey – and I knew all about how serious Daddy is about those shares of Mummy's. If he doesn't get absolute control of the company, he's convinced it'll go bust. That's why it's been so sickening of Helen to go on about them getting married when he had all this other worry. You've got a terribly good case against me.'

'Well,' said Ned, 'I'm not the detective around there. If you've got any confessions to make Superintendent Pinn's your man. He's very approachable, you know, you've only got to take a little walk and – '

The door opened breezily.

'Oh, hello, Michael,' said Penny.

Her voice a little unsteady.

'Not butting in on anything am I?' said Michael Goodhart. 'You look a bit serious.'

'Oh no,' said Penny, 'we were just talking.'

'You want to watch that,' Michael said. 'Nothing like talking for getting you into trouble.'

'Silent service, eh?' said Ned.

'That's the ticket. Well, Penny, what dark secrets were you giving away? You want to keep an eye on this chappie. He's a bit of a Q-boat type if you ask me. Looks innocent enough, but at any moment out will come those guns and he'll go into action dead ahead.'

Ned grinned.

'I'll tell you what we were talking about,' he said. 'Bit of a delicate subject in a way. We were wondering how Irene would take it if anyone played croquet. I'm rotting here.'

Michael looked serious.

'I don't know,' he said. 'My first instinct is to say "Don't do it" but it might be the best thing when you come to think about it. You have to go belting into the centre of a hurricane sometimes, you know.'

'That's what I had in mind,' said Ned. 'I'll think about it.'

'Of course,' Michael said, 'it all depends to some extent on Irene's plans. I haven't liked to ask her if she's thought of the future at all, but if she's decided to leave here pretty soon it would obviously be best not to start anything by using the croquet lawn.'

'She hasn't told me anything,' said Ned.

'Nor me, or Daddy as far as I know,' Penny said.

She picked up the crumb brush where Ned had left it when Michael came in and with a few deft sweeps she finished clearing the table.

'You're more likely to know than me anyhow,' said Ned. 'You've known her some time and worked here a good while and all that.'

'Yes,' said Michael.

The bright blue eyes narrowed a little.

'To tell you the truth,' he said, 'I've been a bit shy about asking her anything. You see, I'm personally involved in a way. If she does decide to pack up here, I'm afraid I stand to benefit. A good many of the boys would come to me. You know, more or less friendly with the parents and all that.'

'I wouldn't let that worry you,' Ned said. 'You'd be doing Irene a favour as much as anything. She'd worry about the boys' education being shot to hell. If most of them went to you they'd get continuity – for all Sebastian says about your progressiveness and the Ambrose House traditionalism.'

Michael smiled.

'Oh yes,' he said, 'that's just one of Sebastian's little games. I have a few pet ideas of my own, of course, but I learnt all I know about being a schoolie here when I came out of the Navy and naturally the two places are pretty much alike in lots of ways.'

'Then what's worrying you?' Ned said.

Michael's firm set mouth, his blue eyes unflinching.

'The truth of the matter is,' he said, 'that my place hasn't done too well. The boys didn't come in as fast as I'd hoped. If Irene does pack up I'll be okay. Otherwise I'll probably have to abandon ship.'

'But, Michael,' Penny said, 'you don't want to let that worry you. Thank goodness something good has come out of all this.'

Michael smiled.

'All the same,' he said, 'I do worry. As soon as I realized what might happen I made up my mind to close my place straight away as a matter of fact. But then I thought of the point Ned here has just been making. If by staying on at it I can be of help to Irene, then I feel I ought to.'

The keen blue eyes. A cloud on the horizon.

He smiled.

'There's another complication, too,' he said. 'I've no doubt the police will realize I benefit pretty considerably by Humphrey's death, if Irene does close Ambrose House, as I suppose she almost certainly will. Of course, it doesn't actually matter being under suspicion, but I catch myself wondering how I ought to behave to convince them I'm innocent.'

He shrugged his shoulders. With reticence.

'Pretty tricky passage one way and another.'

'It was a pretty tricky passage,' said the man from *The Examiner*, 'but you should have heard how he played it. Superb. You'd think he was just running off a simple scale. And tomorrow night I shall be hearing him again. I can't pretend I shall be sorry. I've come to the conclusion I make a better critic than a reporter.'

'Good luck to you,' said the old hand. 'I must admit this "Gang warfare at Blandford Parva" story will be a bit more in my line. Sounds as if there'll be some good stuff from what the news editor was telling me on the blower just now. Anyone else on it?'

'You can keep it,' said the girl. 'I'm off to Italy. Big "Starlets in sex orgy" story. I'll get an extra ration of summer with any luck.'

The up-and-comer secretly hugged his drink.

'All right,' said the old hand, 'don't tell us *The Daily Post* is going to keep you stuck in this dead-and-alive hole.'

'No,' said the up-and-comer.

'Blandford Parva?'

'No.'

'You don't speaka da Italian?' said the girl.

'Stories like that are two a penny, chum.'

'Not when I write them up,' said the girl.

'Supposing you just whisper to me what it is,' *The Examiner* said. 'After all, I can't see us using a beat on whatever it is, even in the unlikely event of us getting one.'

'I'll tell you all as much as I can,' said the up-and-comer.

'You'll stand a round first,' said the old hand.

'Okay, four whiskies and one – what is it? – Guinness.'

'Thank you,' said *The South Sussex Trumpet and Messenger.*

'Well,' said the up-and-comer, 'it's a big story, it's a good story and it's a nasty story. That's the lot.'

'It'll be an exclusive then?' said the pale young man.'

'They don't send me on stories any fool can pick up from the P.A.,' the up-and-comer said. 'If my by-line's on something chum, it counts.'

'Such as the Croquet Lawn Murder,' said the girl.

'We all make mistakes,' said the up-and-comer.

'I wonder all the same who did do it,' *The Examiner* said.

'What's it matter, chum?' said the up-and-comer. 'The police will turn it in pretty soon, mark my words.'

'But – ' said the pale young man.

'My personal bet, for what it's worth,' said the girl, 'is that mad neurotic Mrs Ravell. She did it because she disagreed with him over the best method of long division or something. But she'll get away with it. No one will ever believe a murder could have been committed over a thing like that.'

'Oh, I do,' said *The Examiner*, 'I'm inclined to believe a good many murders are done for what wouldn't seem on the face of it to be adequate reasons. After all, you've got to be a little out of the ordinary to bump someone off.'

'You're right, of course,' the old hand said. 'I've come across some pretty paltry killings in my time, believe you me.'

'But if Mrs Ravell – ' said the pale young man.

The girl turned to him.

'No proof,' she said. 'There won't be any simple logical proof, and so they won't cotton on to it.'

She drained her glass.

'And yet, you know,' she said, 'I bet there's something. I bet there's some little point which no one has thought of. And it would prove it just like that.'

'Then you think it was – ' the pale young man said.

'No, I don't,' said the girl. 'That could apply to any one of them.'

She slipped off the bar stool.

'Must be off,' she said. 'If I'm going to sunny Italy I must look out some respectable clothes – respectable in a strictly limited sense, that is.'

The man from *The Examiner* put on his bowler and picked up his umbrella.

'Well, good-bye, old chap,' he said to the pale young man. 'Where are you off to now?'

'Here,' said the young man.

'Oh yes, of course, I forgot. And what's your next big assignment?'

'Well, there's always the county council.'

'Ah yes, the county council.'

'But I think I'll still keep an eye on Ambrose House. You never can tell. In fact I might just take a bus up there now.'

Ultimate

Ned strolled out into the afternooon sunshine on the veranda. The sun was warm on his face, but it felt as if it had taken a long time to get to the point of having any heat in it.

He looked at the deserted playing-field in front of him with the croquet lawn in the foreground still smooth although it had not been cut since the murder.

Stillness in the sunlight. Motion arrested. An air of peacefulness.

Ned frowned sharply.

He was standing just in front of the rack of croquet mallets. He picked one sharply from its place. The faint twang of the spring clip.

A sudden shouted scream.

And Leonard Driver standing up at the other end of the veranda, looking wildly around. His smooth black hair tousled, the heavy jaw dropping agape.

'Jeez,' said Ned, 'I'm awfully sorry. Did I startle you? I had no idea anyone was about.'

Leonard relaxed. Sudden colour flushing back to his cheeks.

He laughed. Two sharp grunts.

'I was having a bit of a doze as a matter of fact,' he said. 'Haven't been sleeping too well lately. I sat down here in the sun and I must have dropped off.'

'I'm terribly sorry,' said Ned.

'That's all right. Glad to wake up actually. Think I was having a nightmare of some sort. The noise you made came into it somehow. Can't quite think in what way. The details are fading. Good thing too.'

He shuddered elaborately.

Ned swung the mallet that was still in his hands.

'Care for a knock-up?' he said.

Leonard looked at the mallet as if it was something he had never seen before.

'Croquet?' he said.

Suspicion.

'Yes,' said Ned. 'Croquet. It's a very interesting game, you know. Combines the subtlety of chess and the skill of golf.'

'I know that,' said Leonard.

Tetchiness.

'I was talking to Michael about whether it was okay to play or not,' Ned said. 'He seemed to think Irene would have to get used to the idea sooner or later.'

'I hadn't thought of that,' said Leonard. 'I don't see that it's any reason not to play. You shouldn't let sentiment bog you down.'

'Come on then,' said Ned. 'I've a feeling I owe you a hiding. After all you beat us to the doubles prize.'

Leonard looked at him sharply.

'Well, we did,' he said. 'It's no use fuzzing over things. I've a notion one or two people looked askance at me because I happened to mention the prize the other day. Lot of silly nonsense. The tournament had been finished and there was no point in leaving loose ends.'

Ned took the four balls out of their box and bowled them one by one off the veranda and down on to the croquet lawn. The red, the yellow, the blue, the black.

'They're all right as people,' Leonard said, 'but they've no experience of real life. They've none of them a notion of how a business is run, and they've stuffed up their heads with a lot of silly nonsense about fine sensibilities and what-not.'

He stumped down the veranda steps.

'Fine sensibilities wouldn't have got this country where it is today,' he said. 'We'd have been under. Under years ago.'

He took a half-crown from his trouser pocket.

'You call,' he said.

The silver coin spinning in the sunlight.

'Heads,' said Ned.

Tails.

'You're lucky,' Ned said.

'Makes no difference,' said Leonard. 'You ought to know that

216

by now. It's one of the beauties of the game. It makes no difference who gets away first. The other fellow can always overtake him by better play. It's like life.'

'You don't go much on luck, then?'

'I don't. What gets you anywhere is doing the right thing and doing it a damned sight harder than the next man. Ever been in business?'

'I had a job as a clerk once. I may have mentioned it.'

'Well, if you ever go into business, just remember that one rule. It's all you need.'

'That why you prefer business to life?' said Ned.

He fished the blue and black balls towards him with his mallet.

Leonard looked up at him.

'I don't prefer business to life,' he said. 'You've been listening to Irene, I suppose. Let me tell you something, young man, business is life. Don't make any mistake about that.'

Ned shrugged.

Leonard set his red ball carefully on the baulk line.

'Still,' said Ned, 'it seems to me that luck comes into life quite a bit. Look at the way Humphrey was murdered for instance. Piece of luck for the murderer that no one saw them.'

'Nonsense,' said Leonard.

The smooth rhythmical swing of the mallet. The red ball travelling over the dark green grass and rolling to a gentle stop on the far side of the court.

'There was no luck about it,' Leonard said. 'Whoever killed Humphrey chose their time damned well. At that hour of the morning who was there possibly to see? No, murderer they may be, but in a way I admire them. They made a good job of it.'

Ned played his shot. With care. Aiming right across the court at the red ball.

They watched his ball, the blue, rolling quickly on.

'You shouldn't have gone for it,' said Leonard. 'It was a tice. Too far to be sure of – '

With a gentle click the blue hit the red.

'Luck?' said Ned.

Leonard looked at him.

'I don't think so,' he said. 'I mustn't make the mistake of underestimating you.'

Ned strolled across to gather up Leonard's ball for his next shot.

'What you were saying interests me,' he said. 'If you believe the murder was committed by someone who "made a good job of it" you must have ideas about who was likely to do that.'

Leonard grunted.

Ned took his stance. As his mallet struck the blue ball he said:

'Cicely, for instance, she seems a likely candidate. She has no doubts about how well she does what she sets out to do.'

The blue ball ran short.

'Don't be a damned fool,' said Leonard.

He came up to take his strike.

'Cicely hasn't the guts to commit a murder. If she had, she'd have polished off that appalling Peke Abou years ago. A woman who's under the thumb of a nasty little pekinese is not going to solve any problems, much less kill her way to a solution.'

His ball running truly across the dark green of the grass.

'No, I guess you're right,' said Ned. 'She works out her violence on poor old Abou – not that he seems to worry.'

'Works out her violence? Sounds like a lot of psychological poppycock. The truth of the matter is that she hasn't the strength of mind. And that's that.'

Ned watched him taking his next stroke.

'I suppose that would apply to any woman,' he said.

Leonard waited to answer until he had sent his ball on its accurate way.

'I'm surprised at you,' he said. 'I didn't think you would have fallen for all this sensibility nonsense Humphrey and Irene and all their family go in for. Women are every bit as ruthless as men if they're built that way.'

They played for a while in silence.

'So you'd say Irene's got too much sensibility to be a murderer?' Ned said.

'No,' said Leonard, 'curiously enough, I wouldn't. She prates a lot about it, but if you ask me she's about as sensitive as a steam-

218

roller herself. She couldn't get into such stupid situations unless she was.'

'Such as believing Humphrey was being unfaithful with the matron?'

Leonard played another shot. The rounded click as the face of his mallet hit the ball fair and square.

'All right,' he said, 'personally I think Irene may well have killed her husband.'

'I don't,' said Ned. 'Irene's incapable of deceiving anyone – except herself naturally. If she'd killed Humphrey she'd have told everybody. She'd have thought she was so right to do it that one and all would agree with her.'

Leonard's mallet stopped in its swing upwards.

'No,' he said, 'I think this is where I let you come in.'

He changed his position and sent the ball carefully across to the far corner of the court under the huge mulberry.

Ned looked round.

'You've left me in a tricky spot all right,' he said. 'This is where I could do with some of old Skuce's spoiling tactics.' He played a shot.

'All yours again,' he said.

Leonard went across to the red ball.

'If croquet's anything to go by,' Ned said, 'Sebastian is one of the blokes who knows how to get their own way.'

'Hm,' said Leonard.

'What does that mean?'

Leonard played his shot. The red ball ran on from striking the blue and lay neatly in front of Leonard's next hoop.

'It means that Sebastian concentrates on being top dog at croquet and on being nasty to other dons – I was talking to one of those newspaper chaps who'd been to his lectures: he said they were slander from start to finish – and when it comes to anything else Master Sebastian just opts out.'

'Very good,' said Ned. 'You seem to go in for understanding people every bit as much as these sensitive types you're always on about.'

Leonard ran the hoop.

'You've got to be able to sum people up in business,' he said. 'It's just ordinary shrewdness, no damned sensibility about it.'

'So Sebastian would have made a fool of Humphrey on the croquet court rather than killing him?' said Ned. 'Could be. Especially as I don't think he had any motive.'

Leonard rested on his mallet.

'You can't always know what motives anybody might have,' he said. 'Look at you, for instance, you're meant to be an innocent Australian with no possible connexion with Humphrey, but how do we know?'

'Good on you,' said Ned. 'You don't know. Better not let me get behind you when you're playing a shot.'

Leonard walked forward two or three paces, and bent his head over the yellow ball. The rhythmical swing of his mallet. A perfect stroke.

'Tell me,' said Ned, 'have you ever wondered if your kid might have decided to help her old man out of a tight spot?'

Leonard straightened up. Abruptly.

He turned towards Ned.

His suffused face.

'What the hell do you mean?' he said. 'Are you telling me that Penny's a murderer?'

His hand clamped tight on the grip of the mallet.

'Easy, easy,' said Ned. 'If you haven't thought of it, she has. She was worried about it all right a day or two ago. Then she decided no one would suspect her after all, because of her appealing innocence, I guess.'

He grinned.

'I think she's right really,' he said. 'Only I kidded her a bit that I had my doubts on her. Keep her on the hop, you know.'

'What precise motive was she supposed to have?' said Leonard.

The mallet pushed into the turf.

'This shares business,' Ned said. 'You believed Humphrey was stopping your ex from selling them to you and you needed them pretty badly – devoted daughter removes obstinate Uncle Humphrey.'

'What filthy rubbish. And I thought I'd told you once that I didn't particularly need those shares.'

'You did,' said Ned. 'Only Penny explained to me just how badly you did need them.'

Leonard stood stock still. Statue of the croquet player.

'You're in play, you know,' said Ned.

Leonard relaxed his grip on the mallet but made no attempt to go over to his ball.

'All right,' he said, 'perhaps I did think it would be wiser if I didn't underline the importance of those shares. Of course I do need them. I must have them to push through the new policy. But you don't think that makes me a murderer, do you?'

'Why not?' said Ned.

The sun went behind a cloud. The chilliness in the air.

'Because if I thought the only way to get those shares was to put Humphrey out of the way I wouldn't have gone about it in such a way as to make it look as if he'd been murdered,' said Leonard. 'And besides how could I be sure that Humphrey's death would lead to me getting the shares?'

Ned smiled.

'Exactly,' he said. 'The shares business is no motive for murder.'

Leonard walked across to his ball. He sent it neatly across to hit Ned's black.

'We have been going through the list,' he said. 'Who's been missed out?'

'Michael.'

Leonard ran another hoop.

'Michael,' he said.

'Yes,' said Ned, 'you know what the case against him is? His new school's on the rocks; if this place folded up he'd get a lot of the boys.'

'Michael's a pretty determined fellow,' said Leonard. 'You've heard about his war record?'

'Yes ' said Ned. 'I hear he had the habit of going straight in at the enemy. I wouldn't call killing Humphrey so that some of his boys might possibly change schools going straight to the enemy, would you?'

Leonard hit the blue ball with the red, leaving himself with a difficult shot at his next hoop.

'So what then?' he said. 'You've run through all the so-called suspects to your own satisfaction and got nowhere. Perhaps it's time you left this sort of thing to the police.'

He played his shot. The ball hung for a moment on the wire of the hoop and then trickled through.

'We certainly cleared the ground,' said Ned. 'But we've been going on a wrong assumption, you know. We've been talking as if it was necessary to have a good motive to kill someone.'

Leonard paused over his stroke.

'Of course it is,' he said.

'It isn't, you know,' said Ned. 'Does a kid need a good motive for punching someone in the eye? No, he doesn't. He just feels he's got to poke someone or bust.'

Leonard played. His ball shaved Ned's blue.

Ned stood looking at him, his feet a little apart, knees flexed.

'You know what first put me on to you?' he said.

Leonard stopped dead for a moment. A darted look at Ned. Then he set off across the court to make his next stroke.

'Just a tiny thing, really,' Ned said. 'You let the super understand that you hadn't been up early on the morning of the murder, but when I came down to breakfast that day you told me you'd heard the early bulletin on that little transistor radio of yours. You made a mistake.'

Leonard looked at his next hoop.

'I've left myself with not much of a rush on this one,' he said.

'Of course, that's no proof,' Ned said. 'And it tells us nothing about motive. But as I was saying it's an error to look for a hundred per cent rational motive. We ought to look for the kid who feels he's got to take a poke at someone.'

Leonard took his stance.

'So who've we got?' said Ned. 'We've got the bloke whose business is in a hell of a jam, who's being badgered about marriage when his only try at it was a failure, and who's got such a success fixation that he must win the Ambrose House croquet tournament even if he has to kill someone to do it.'

Leonard played. The ball struck the wire of the hoop and bounced back. Leonard caught up his mallet in both hands, brought his knee up with a sudden access of blottingly furious violence and snapped the shaft clean in two.

He dropped the two pieces and turned to face Ned.

'But there's no proof,' he said. 'No proof at all. You admitted as much yourself just now.'

'You'd deny it if the police questioned you?'

'Of course. I'd deny it absolutely. And there's nothing anyone could do about it. I killed Humphrey and I'm going to get away with it.'

'Look,' said Rosy, 'there's young Sid Martin who's on *The Trumpet* now just coming in at the gate.'

Bert glanced down through the gaping window frame.

'Snap,' said Rosy.

She gathered up the last of the cards into her pile.